unexpected SURRENDER

J.M. WALKER

Cover Design and Formatting: Just write. Creations
Editing: Joanne Thompson

ISBN: 978-0-9938369-7-8

DEDICATION

To my Jems:
I wrote this book for you.

PROLOGUE

WITH HIS COCK DEEP inside me and his mouth firmly on mine, I submitted. The soft silky rope dug into my wrists, stopping me from touching the dark stranger who had full control of every inch of me. Whether I liked it or not, I was giving over my all to someone I didn't know. All because I had no choice. All because I had to save my brother.

The man grunted, his mouth brushing along the length of my throat, but he didn't say anything. No. How could he? We weren't allowed to speak. It was against the rules.

And I couldn't see him. Again, rules. The silk sash wrapped around my head shielded him from me, but I could feel him. Every inch. Every throbbing vein as he moved slowly in and out of me.

He had gone in completely bare. Another rule. We had to go through rigorous testing before we were even considered for the job. *Job.* Fucking please.

The stranger grunted again. "Relax." His voice had been so soft, I wasn't sure if I heard him correctly. No. He couldn't have. Could he? If he was caught speaking to me, the session would end, and I would be leaving without what I came here for in the first place.

Even if I was dreaming it, I willed myself to relax.

He groaned, sliding back inside me.

Arching beneath him, I took him even deeper. His rough, calloused hands slid over my hips before cupping my ass.

I shivered, spreading my legs even wider for him.

The stranger groaned again, pumping into me slowly and deeply. It wasn't fast. It wasn't hard. But it was perfect. It made me wonder why he was at this place?

The Club.

I was sure he probably wondered the same thing about me. Or he didn't care. Probably the latter.

God, stop thinking so much, Lex.

Taking a deep breath, I squeezed my eyes shut even though I was blindfolded, and just felt. His hands on my body. His breath on my skin. His thick length deep inside of me.

The more he thrust, the higher I climbed.

Spots danced in my vision. My hands tugged on the ropes.

Another thrust and I broke.

I whimpered, chewing my bottom lip to keep from crying out. Another rule.

His hot breath scorched the side of my neck, his release following soon after. It coated me, heating me from within.

I moaned, tilting my hips up and then up even higher still. God, I was greedy for him.

A dark chuckle escaped him. Placing a gentle peck just beneath my ear, his lips roamed over the soft skin.

Just when I thought he was done, he pushed into me even harder.

I gasped, my back bowing off the bed I laid on.

The stranger waited, kissing me softly on the mouth before slipping free from my body. A door sounded a moment later and I was left to my own thoughts.

Whoever just left my body, made an impression. On my skin. On my damn soul. I wanted more, and I didn't know why. I had never wanted more. Not until him. Not until the stranger. Not until I was forced to fuck a man I didn't know just to save my brother.

ONE

Lexi

3 months ago

I WAS GOING TO kill my brother. No, better yet, I was going to torture him first and *then* kill him. It was his turn to take care of the bills. Both of us worked, split our paychecks, and paid the bills. It was now my month to pay but as it turned out, he hadn't been paying at all. Not for at least three months. I flipped through each bill. Big bold letters in red, screamed back at me.

Overdue. Bill due immediately. Notice. Pay now.

How the hell had I missed this? Oh right. My brother had hidden the bills until I found them stashed away in his laundry basket beneath some dirty clothes. God I was so stupid. I loved him. I loved him sometimes more than he deserved. Especially right now. I was going to kick his ass.

I had an hour before I had to open up the deli. One hour to sort through this shit and hope for the best we had just enough money to satisfy these companies or else we would lose our place of work and our home.

This sucked. This sucked a whole fucking lot.

The front door opened, the bell at the top dinging when my brother entered.

Ma's Deli.

God, if only our mother could see this place now. She was probably rolling over in her grave.

"Hey sis." Charlie came toward me, a bright smile on his face. He sat in the booth across from me and placed an envelope on the table between us. "I have some good news."

"Well I don't." I sat back, crossing my arms under my chest. "You haven't been paying the bills. We're on the verge of losing this place, Charlie. How do you think Mama would feel if she were still alive?"

The smile fell from his face, his jade eyes turning even darker. "Well she's not alive, now is she?" And just like that, his mood switched. While I got our mother's small physique, he got his temper from our father. Thankfully, besides his large built, that was the only other trait my brother got from that bastard.

"Charlie, we can't keep doing this. We could lose this place." I sighed, trying to calm the anger rushing through me.

"We're not going to lose this place." He pushed the envelope toward me.

"What's that?" I asked, raising an eyebrow.

"Open it." He grinned.

I grabbed the envelope and opened it. "What the hell?" My mouth fell open. "Where did you get this?" My gaze snapped to his, back down to the envelope in my hand, back to his. My thumb grazed over the wad of cash. One-hundred-dollar bills. And a lot of them. "How much is here?"

"Two-fifty," he said, like it was no big deal and I didn't have two-hundred and fifty thousand dollars in my hand. I had never seen so much money in my life, let alone had it in my hands.

"Charlie." My stomach twisted, my heart racing. "What did you do to get this?"

His jaw clenched, his green eyes that mirrored my own, took on a faraway look like he was remembering. Something big. Something bad. Something so damn desperate, he didn't give a shit what he had to do to get it.

"Charlie," I whispered, placing the envelope back on the table in front of me. "I can't take this. This isn't right."

"This is for us," he said gently, covering my shaking hands with his. "This is to make this place better. To fix up the things that need fixing up. To make our apartment in the back more livable. To get rid of the damn rats that like to live rent free."

A laugh escaped me. "We can't keep this money."

"Too late." Charlie squeezed my hands. "It's already ours."

"Who did you get this from? What did you have to do?" There was no way someone would hand over this kind of cash without needing something in return.

"I haven't done anything." *Yet.*

"Charlie," I whispered.

"Look." He smiled, grabbed the envelope, and stuffed it into the inside pocket of his leather jacket. "You've been working so damn hard. This will give us the boost we need. It'll help us be able to afford to hire some staff so we're not killing ourselves by working twenty-four-seven."

It would be nice to have a cook, so I didn't have to do it all myself.

"Trust me, Lexi. This is for you. For us."

"Tell me who you got this money from." I needed to know. I needed to know who we owed.

"Don't worry about it." Charlie ran his fingers through his shaggy brown hair, giving me a wink. "Now, let's get some of these bills paid." He grabbed the stack of papers spread out in front of me and slid from the booth.

As much as we needed the money, why did I feel dirty? Why did I feel like I was suddenly owned by someone?

Charlie may have had good intentions, but he was young, foolish and so damn desperate to make ends meet.

I appreciated him trying to help but why did I feel like he had sold his soul to the Devil? And knowing how ruthless some of these people were in our city, it would only be a matter of time before the Devil came to collect.

TWO

Lexi

IT HAD BEEN A month since Charlie brought home the money and I still hadn't touched it. He used some to pay the bills but that was it. It sat in a kitchen cupboard on the top shelf. A part of me was scared to touch it, let alone spend it. I kept thinking that as soon as that first dollar was spent, a black SUV would show up with guys in suits and they would take us away and throw us in jail. Or worse.

But what I wouldn't give to use it to fix up the deli.

It was our mother's life before she died. When she left it to us, it was her only insurance that we would have some sort of future that was at least a little better than hers.

It wasn't much but it was home.

The deli stood on a corner in an older neighborhood with an upstairs apartment we could access from a stairway in the hall on the first floor.

We served simple, hearty food that the local working class had come to love and count on, but we were mostly known for our sandwiches.

It kept us busy, but being busy didn't always amount to huge profits and it was nothing we could count on. That was why that envelope of money was so damn tempting.

No, I couldn't. I didn't know where Charlie had gotten it from. Not that he would tell me anyway.

"Are you still stewing?"

I jumped, spun on my heel, and found Charlie leaning against the doorframe.

"It's not going to bite you," he teased, lighting up a smoke.

"I know." I chewed my bottom lip.

"This came in the mail." He handed me an envelope. "Maybe it'll change your mind."

I frowned. "You opened it already?"

"Yeah because I want to know which part of you I'm going to have to deal with for the rest of the night."

"Great." I pulled out the letter. It was another past due notice. "Oh, God." I slid down the wall, landing hard on my ass.

"I bet that money looks really good now, doesn't it?" Charlie sat beside me, hooking an arm around my shoulders.

"We're going to lose everything." My vision blurred.

"No, we aren't." Charlie released me, went to the cupboard, and came back a moment later, kneeling in front of me. "I love you, Lexi, but I hate seeing you kill yourself. You work way too damn much." He placed the envelope in my hand. "Take this and get whatever's needed to help fix up the shop."

"How much is left?" I sniffed. As far as I knew, Charlie hadn't used it since he paid some of the bills last month.

"Just enough to get the utility companies off our asses." He shrugged. "There's plenty here to fix up the shop, pay the bills for the next few months if we wanted, and you can even get yourself a new purse. Or whatever you girls like these days."

I laughed, wiping under my eyes. "I have a bag. And the purse I want, we can't afford."

"Why not? What is it? A couple grand?" Charlie pulled out a wad of cash stuffed into the envelope and handed it to me. "It's Hermes isn't it?"

"You remembered?" I asked in awe.

"Of course. Here. This should be enough."

"No." I shook my head. "I couldn't. It's like five grand, Charlie. That's way too much money to spend on a bag. We have more important things to buy."

"Lexi." He tried giving me the money again but I pushed him back and rose to my full height.

"I can't." I took the bill and went to the kitchen table. Turning on my laptop, I went through the money we had saved to see what we could afford to pay. The *legal* way.

"I'm going to see if I can get some friends to help us. Fix up whatever needs done to the deli and all that shit. Maybe give it a new paint job." He shrugged.

"But then we'll owe them." I shook my head. "We can't afford to pay them."

"You let me worry about that." He knuckle-rapped the table. "I'm heading out. You going to be good here by yourself?"

"I'm a big girl." I smiled, giving him the reassurance that I would in fact be fine when really, I was beginning to feel desperate. And that money started tempting me.

"Okay." Charlie kissed the top of my head. "I'll bring you home a bottle of wine."

"Thank you." My head snapped up. "Wait."

"It won't be an expensive one. Shit, Lex. Live a little." He left the apartment, closing the door behind him.

I sighed, rubbing the back of my neck and cracking my knuckles. "Alright, Lexi. Let's do this. Let's pay some bills. Such a fun fucking Friday night." And I was talking to myself. "Great."

A few hours later, when a kink was settling on my shoulders, I pulled away from the table and shut the lid to the laptop. I managed to pay some of the most important bills. At least enough where the companies would leave us alone for another month. And it was all done with legal money too. I had to dip into my savings. Not that I had a lot in there, but it was almost enough to pay for a new stove.

My chest tightened that I would have to wait a little longer to get the stove and oven I had been looking at. It would help me cook at the normal speed and not take twenty minutes to make scrambled eggs.

But that could wait. Bills were more important.

Stretching my arms up and over my head, my gaze landed on the clock mounted on the wall above the TV. It was almost midnight. Where was Charlie? He was usually out late but when he promised to bring home wine, it meant he would be back within an hour or two. But that had been almost six hours ago.

My heart jumped. Thoughts of him lying dead on a curb somewhere forced their way into my head. No. I would not think that. He was fine. He was perfectly fine.

Suddenly, a heavy bang landed against the door.

I jumped, a shriek escaping my lips. Clutching my chest, I took a deep breath.

"Lex."

I frowned at the muffled voice coming from the other side of the door.

"Lex." It was louder that time.

"Charlie?" I rushed to the door, unlocked it, and swung it open just as he fell to my feet.

I gasped, letting out a sharp scream and dropping to my knees. "Charlie!"

He groaned. Dark purple bruises marked his face. One eye was swollen shut and a split was in his lip. The white shirt he wore when he left the apartment hours ago, was now covered in blood.

"What the hell happened?" I hooked my arms under his and pulled him into the apartment.

Charlie mumbled some words that I couldn't make out.

"You need the hospital." I sat him on the floor just inside the apartment.

"No," he croaked. "No hospital." He hugged his arm to his side. "I can't."

"Charlie," I said gently. "Then tell me what happened?"

A large shadow filled the doorway. "*I* happened."

THREE

Lexi

I FELL BACK ON my ass at the deep voice sliding into my ears. It slithered over my skin like a cobra ready to strike its victim. I swallowed hard, staring up into the cold, dark eyes peering down at me.

The large man towered over us. He was dressed in a suit that probably cost more than our apartment and deli combined. He reeked of power and strength, and he scared the utter shit out of me.

My heart jumped behind the walls of my rib cage.

The man pulled out a white cloth from the inside of his jacket and started wiping blood off his knuckles. Tattoos lined his skin that hadn't been covered up by the expensive suit. The black intricate designs were on the backs of his hands and sides of his thick neck, stopping just below his ears.

His hair was dark, almost as black as night. Bangs fell into his eyes every so often and with a swipe of his finger, he would push them out of the way.

I swallowed hard, the small movement sending a shiver down my spine.

"What do you want?" I asked, my voice shaky and not as strong as I would have liked.

"Money," he said, his brow furrowing in the middle like I was dumb for even asking such a question.

"We don't have any money." What the hell had Charlie gotten himself into?

"Well you see, little girl—" The man took a step farther into our apartment and shut the door behind him. "—I happen to know that you *do* have money. And quite a bit of it in fact."

"No." I shook my head. "We don't. I swear we don't." And then I remembered the cash Charlie had brought home a month ago. "In the kitchen. In one of the cupboards. There's an envelope with money in it. Take that."

The man's jaw clenched. Stuffing the cloth back inside the pocket of his suit jacket, he crouched in front of us. "This is your sister," he said to Charlie.

Charlie only groaned, muttering under his breath.

"Who *are* you?" I asked, not liking how the farther he got into our apartment, the smaller I suddenly felt.

This man seemed to take up so much space around him without physically doing so. He was large. Even in a crouched position. His piercing dark eyes bore into me. "Your brother here, owes me money. A lot of it. I gave him a down payment to do a job and he hasn't done it yet."

"What kind of job?" I asked, my voice weak under the intense scrutiny of this man staring back at me.

"Doesn't matter. What *does* matter is that he hasn't completed the job yet. I have quite a few clients depending on me and if the job isn't done, they're not happy which makes *me* not happy." His lips pulled up into a wicked grin. "And we don't want that to happen, now do we?"

"How much does he owe you?" I nudged Charlie. "How much do you owe him, Charlie?"

Charlie's good eye fluttered open but he wouldn't meet my gaze.

"Charlie." I shoved him again.

He grunted.

"Tell me," I demanded.

"Half a mil. And that's not including the money I already gave him."

My gaze snapped up, landing on the dark stranger in front of us. "Excuse me? You're kidding right?"

The man raised a black eyebrow. "I don't kid about money." He stood.

I jumped to my feet. "You can't expect us to come up with that sort of cash. It's just not possible."

"Well I guess you're going to have to figure it out, now aren't you?" The man stalked toward me, forcing me back a step. "I could just collect you. Use you as down payment until he can get the rest of the money for me but I'm not into paid pussy."

"Excuse—" I tripped over my feet, landing hard on my ass. A slice of pain shot up my tailbone. "You can't just buy me, asshole," I bit out through clenched teeth, breathing through the agony sliding over my skin.

The man chuckled and knelt in front of me. In a quick move, he grabbed my ankles and pulled me beneath him.

I gasped, slapping my hands against his chest. A chest that was hard and clearly spent hours in the gym. My fingers tingled.

He cocked his head to the side, a slow grin spreading on his face. "You see, little girl, or Lexi is it?"

My stomach twisted that he knew my name.

The man gripped my inner thighs, spreading me open. "I didn't just earn my money and reputation by not giving a shit who I do business with. Your brother has been working for me for quite some time now. I trusted that he would get the job done. And now that he hasn't, I'm going to have to deal with a lot of unhappy people. It makes me look bad as a businessman. If my rep gets ruined because of some fucking kid, I will make him disappear. You got me, Lexi?"

"Please," I pleaded. "Just take the envelope and go. I'll…I'll find a way to pay you."

"Oh, I know you will." He leaned over me, brushing his mouth along the shell of my ear.

I shivered, pushing against him. "Please…please don't hurt me."

"Trust me, Lexi." His hot breath scorched the side of my neck. "When we fuck, it'll be because you beg for it."

"I don't think so." I struggled beneath him. As beautiful as he was, he beat the shit out of my brother and threatened him. There would be no way I would ever sleep with this bastard.

"I like that fire in your eyes." The man chuckled. "And I can't wait to get fucking burned."

FOUR

Lexi

"W-WHAT DO YOU WANT?" I stammered, unable to take my gaze away from the man staring down at me.

In a quick move, he wrapped a large hand around my throat and squeezed. Leaning down, his nose was mere inches from mine. He was so close, I could smell the mint on his breath. I could see the gold specks in the chocolate brown of his eyes. A smattering of gray showcased through the dark scruff on his strong jaw.

"P-Please let me go," I pleaded, digging my fingers into his thick biceps.

The man turned my head toward Charlie. "He loves you and would do anything to see you happy. And you would do anything to make sure he's safe. Isn't that right, Lexi?"

My heart pounded in my ears. "Yes."

"Tell me exactly what you would do for him." The man brushed his mouth along the length of my jaw. "Would you steal for him? Commit murder? Sell your soul?"

I stared at my brother leaning against the wall. His breathing was ragged but he was alive. Thank God he was alive. Even though he looked like hell.

"Would you sell your body to keep him alive?"

Blood pounded in my ears at what he was asking. "I…"

The man chuckled, the sound cold and vile. Like the Devil himself was between my legs. No, this was worse. Much worse.

"Why?" I shoved my head out of his grip and glared up at him. "Are you wanting to buy me?"

He smirked. "Careful, little girl. I wouldn't need to buy you when you'd be offering me this pussy for free." Suddenly, he reached between us and cupped me.

I gasped. Struggling against him, I tried to move, I tried to push him away, but his hand remained firm on my lower body.

"I'm going to tell you this once and only once." He fisted my hair with his free hand, forcing me to look up at him. "You will get me my money. I don't give a shit how you do it. I want that cash but now…" He licked his lips, his gaze trailing down the length of me. "I think I'm going to add interest."

"Stop." I shoved against him, kicking my legs out. Hair ripped free from my head, but the burn only made me struggle harder.

The man flipped me onto my stomach and straddled my ass. "Get me my money, Lexi." He kissed my cheek and pushed off of me.

"When? I can't come up with that kind of cash in a day. I'm not you who probably owns the whole damn city."

"I don't own the city." He popped the collar of his jacket.

Rising to my feet, I hugged my arms around myself. "I've seen movies. You came in here like you own the damn place. I'm not stupid."

"No." He peered down at me. "You aren't stupid, are you? But your brother sure is. He took money from me, guaranteed me that he would get a job done and hasn't yet. Get me my money, Lexi." He reached into his pocket, pulled out a small card and placed it on the end table. "This might help." He tapped it once and headed toward the door. "You owe your sister, Charlie. You owe her a whole fucking lot. Because if she weren't here, you'd be dead." He gave me one final glance before he left the apartment, taking all of the air in my lungs along with him.

As soon as the door closed behind him, I rushed to Charlie. "What did you do? What the hell did you do?"

"I'm sorry," he grumbled. "I'm so fucking sorry."

"Who was that?"

Charlie sat up, wincing with the movement. "Luther Knight."

A laugh fell from my lips. "Yeah. Okay." The guy was powerful and clearly an asshole but there was no way he could be Luther Knight.

"Why are you laughing?" Charlie frowned.

"Because Luther is old and that guy…" Although he had gray in his beard, he didn't look that old and he was…God, he was beautiful. I shook my head, ridding myself of those thoughts. He was a dick and wanted my brother dead. I couldn't think he was hot.

"You're thinking of his father. Luther Senior. Luther Junior is definitely not old." Charlie pushed to his feet.

He swayed a bit before I caught him under his arm and stopped him from falling.

"What job didn't you do?" I asked, helping him walk to the couch.

"It doesn't matter, Lex." He dropped onto the cushions, letting out a groan. "The less you know, the better."

"Something isn't right."

Would you sell your body to save your brother's life?

"I'll get this figured out." Charlie laid back on the couch, breathing slow and even.

"Right." I scoffed. "And how are you going to do that, Charlie?" I spun on my heel with every intention of going to the kitchen when my gaze landed on the black business card Luther had placed on the table. Picking it up, my thumb grazed over the shiny embossed red lettering.

The Club.

It had been a week since Luther kicked Charlie's ass and showed up at our apartment. It had also been a week that the little black business card sat on my nightstand. It was taunting me, daring me to call the number on the back of it.

Luther said it might help our situation. I wasn't sure what he meant by that. Could they help me make enough money to pay him?

A soft knock on the door to my bedroom pulled me from my thoughts.

"Yeah?" I called out, staring at the stupid card.

"I'm heading out," Charlie said, peeking his head into the room. "You still stewing over that card?"

"I am." I huffed, crossing my arms under my chest. "He said it could help. What does that mean? And why haven't we heard from him? If he wants his money that badly, he'd be checking in all the damn time but he's not." And it was clearly driving me crazy.

"Why does Luther do anything?" Charlie shrugged. "It's not like I can ask him. That bastard scares the shit out of me. And his fists hurt."

I sighed, looking up at my brother. His bruises had faded some, but he still walked with a limp. I had tried getting him to go to the hospital, but he refused.

"Call the number, Lex. I don't think he was suggesting you to. I think he actually wants you to call it."

"Maybe." I picked up the business card and my phone. Taking a breath, I dialed the number.

"Greetings. You were randomly selected to attend The Club. If you've received our business card in error, please destroy it now."

I frowned at the automated voice on the other end of the phone.

"Your first session will begin this coming Friday night at 8pm Eastern Standard Time. Please show up half an hour early. The location will be sent via text." And with that, the call ended.

My phone buzzed.

I checked the small screen and saw a text from an unknown number with an address. Odd. Very odd.

"What did they say?"

I jumped, forgetting that Charlie was still standing there. "I have to go on Friday night." My gaze flicked to his. "What all do you know about Luther?" Something was off about this whole thing, but I couldn't figure out what it was.

"He's powerful. Took over his father's business after he died." Charlie shrugged. "That's about it."

He was lying. He had to be. There was no way that was all of it.

"Don't worry so much, Lexi." Charlie came toward me and pulled me in for a hug. "We got this."

"Says the guy who had his ass kicked a week ago by the very man we owe money to," I mumbled, my voice muffled by his shirt.

Charlie grunted and released me. "*I* owe him money. Not you."

"You don't seem worried." I stared up at him. "Why not?"

"I'm heading out," Charlie said without answering my question. "I'll be back later."

I followed him out into the hall, watching him walk away from me. How the hell he could be so calm about this shit was beyond me. Something was eating at me. Something that didn't make sense. This whole situation seemed off. And why the hell hadn't Luther been by?

My body heated as memories of him touching me slid into my mind. I shivered. I did not need to think naughty thoughts about the man who wanted my brother dead. God, what the hell was wrong with me?

Giving myself a shake, I headed to the kitchen and poured myself a glass of wine. I leaned against the counter, staring down at the card still in my hand. Friday night couldn't come quick enough.

FIVE

Lexi

I STOOD IN FRONT of the steel door, stared up at it, and frowned. I double-checked the address on my phone. The location was right but there was no indication that I was actually in the right spot. There was no sign. Nothing.

It was finally Friday night and I had no idea what the hell I was doing. Maybe this was a bad idea. I could figure out how to pay Luther back a different way.

"You owe your sister, Charlie. You owe her a whole fucking lot. Because if she wasn't here, you'd be dead."

Blowing out a slow breath, I hiked the strap of my bag higher on my shoulder and knocked on the door.

A lock clicked free, the door opening slightly but when it didn't open more, the little voice inside of my head screamed for me to run away. But I didn't listen for fear that Luther would know and come after my brother.

Pulling open the door, I paused, glancing back down the alley that I had come from. No one was around. I was down a side street that normally didn't get a lot of traffic. Especially on a Friday night when everyone would be making their way downtown to hit the bars.

Taking a deep breath, I stepped into the building. I closed the door behind me and waited. The hallway was dark, but no one was around. Not even the person who unlocked the door. This was strange. Very very strange.

Suddenly, a light flicked on at the end of the long hall, revealing another door. My feet moved of their own accord, knowing I had to do this for my brother. To keep him safe. To stop Luther from kicking his ass again or worse. But this still didn't make sense. It made me wonder if he was playing games with us. Or with me at the very least.

Mustering up whatever courage I had left, I trudged down the hall until I reached the blood red door. Giving it a gentle knock, I waited. Again.

Another lock clicked free and the door opened slightly. "Lexi Adams?" came a soft feminine voice.

I nodded. "Y-Yes."

The door opened even more, revealing a tall woman. She had raven black hair that was pulled back into a tight ponytail that fell down her back. Her eyes were lined with black liner, her lashes long and thick. The bright green orbs burned into me, roaming down to my feet and back up to my head. She nodded once. "You'll do." She stood to the side, indicating for me to enter the room.

"What are you talking about?" I asked, walking over the threshold.

The woman shut the door behind me and grabbed my bag from my hands. "You won't be needing this." She walked around a large black desk and knocked on a door behind it. It opened, and she handed my bag to whoever stood on the other side, all the while staring at me.

I suddenly felt exposed, like as soon as she took my bag from me, I became naked.

"How old are you?" She grabbed a clipboard off the desk and flipped through the papers.

"Twenty-five," I murmured, ringing my hands in front of me.

"Stop that." She nodded toward me. "No one here is going to hurt you. Not unless that's what you agree to. Come with me." She walked out from behind the desk and to another door to my right. Using a small card, she swiped it through the keylock. She opened the door and paused. "This is your last chance, Lexi. If you don't want to continue, you can leave now."

"Right." I laughed, rubbing the back of my neck. "So you all can come find me and kill me?"

Something flashed behind the woman's eyes.

I cleared my throat and took a step toward her. "I was told this could help me make some money. I wouldn't be here if I wasn't desperate."

She nodded, opened the door all the way, and stepped through.

I followed her, the door banging shut behind me.

"You will go through extensive training and there are rules that you must follow. If you don't, you won't get the money that you're so desperately seeking to find."

"I…" I snapped my mouth shut when she shot me a look over her shoulder.

"You can deny it, but you wouldn't be here if you didn't need the money. There's nothing wrong with that. Everything that goes on here is completely consensual. Anything goes as long as all adult parties sign our waiver and release form." She grinned. "We don't need any lawsuits."

A shiver raced down my spine.

"You're a little on the bigger side so we'll have a certain selection of men for you. Not that you'll see them of course but they'll see you. Each of these men have a type. Even women actually. But I imagine you're straight?"

I frowned, looking down at myself. I was hardly a hundred and thirty pounds. "Uh…yes, I am. I'm straight." I appreciated the same sex, but I was never into women. I just wasn't sure how she would know that.

"I have that way," the woman said, as if she could read my thoughts. We continued walking down a long hall that felt like it led to nowhere. The carpet was red. The walls were painted a chocolate brown. Circular lights hung from the ceiling every few feet.

"Am I allowed to ask questions?"

"You can but you won't get many answers. I'm the only one you'll ever see here. Everyone else is completely hidden to protect their identities. Why is that you ask? We have celebrities, politicians, even royalty that attend our establishment. We have to protect them as much as we have to protect you."

I nodded like I had any idea what she was talking about. I really had no idea what I was signing myself up for. All I knew was that if it helped me save my brother, I would do it and shove all morality aside.

"Are you a virgin?" the woman asked, stopping once we finally reached another door.

"No." My cheeks burned.

"But you're not experienced," the woman added.

"Not overly." I had been with a few guys, but they were nothing to write home about.

"Everything you think you know about sex, forget it. We'll teach you things about yourself you never even knew were possible." The woman slid her card through another key slot.

"We?" I asked, my heart racing at what she was even suggesting.

"Yes." The woman opened the door. "The first rule once we enter this room is to be quiet. You'll be given a questionnaire that you must complete in its entirety. Do you understand?"

"Yes, ma'am," I murmured.

The woman gave me a soft smile. "Good girl." She moved behind me, placing her hand on the small of my back. "After you, pet."

I shivered at the term of endearment, clutching my sweater closed.

Once we entered the next room, I was not expecting what laid before me.

White. Everything was white. The walls. The furniture. The floor. So much white it made my eyes hurt. I was almost expecting to see some sort of sex dungeon. Or people off to the side fucking. Like some big orgy. But when I didn't see any of that, disappointment fluttered through me. I thought maybe seeing a sex dungeon would explain exactly what I was setting myself up for. But I still had no idea. At all.

"You were expecting something different, weren't you?" the woman asked with her hand still at the small of my back as she led me to a desk at the far right corner of the room.

I opened my mouth to answer but remembered the first rule and nodded instead.

"This is the first part." She stepped out from behind me, her hand grazing my rear.

My heart jumped. I had never been attracted to a woman before, but this wasn't your average woman. Although it was probably just a game to her and she hit on everyone who came into this place.

"You will answer this questionnaire." The woman pulled a file from a drawer and placed it on top of the desk. "You will answer all of it, Lexi. Even the questions I'm sure you'll find far-fetched. We need to know it all. While everything that goes on here is strictly consensual, it's still a business. Do you understand?"

Not really. I nodded again.

The woman gave me a small smile. "Take your time in answering the questions, pet." She stood from the chair. "I'll come back in an hour." She went through a door that I hadn't seen until now. It silently closed behind her, leaving me alone to my own thoughts.

The room, although white and clean, still made me uneasy. A floor to ceiling curtain sat in the corner behind me. It looked like it had come out of a hospital room.

Glancing back at the desk, I grabbed the file and opened it.

1. When was the last time you had sexual intercourse?

Oh God, this was going to be interesting.

SIX

Him

"I WANT HER," I said, as the door shutting sounded throughout the room.

"She still has several months of training." My sister, Vanessa, came toward me. She pulled out the elastic holding up her dark hair that mirrored my own and ran her fingers through it.

"I don't give a shit." I sat back in my chair, tenting my fingers under my chin and stared at the security camera. "Let me train her."

"Right." Vanessa snorted. "Remember what happened the one and only time you trained someone? They ran off screaming that you gave them a booboo."

"I gave them more than a booboo." I let out a hard sigh at the memory. It was not my fault that the woman had checked off that she was into everything. From anal play to fisting, she wanted to try it all. I got three fingers deep and she used her safe word. "It wasn't meant to be." I frowned, staring harder at the monitor. Lexi was beautiful in a natural sort of way. Her dark auburn hair was a mess of curls around her face. She kept pushing them off her forehead and tapping the pen on her chin. She sat at the desk, working diligently on the questionnaire she was given.

I had argued with my sister to just bring her to me, but she was having none of that.

"She has to go through the training just like everyone else."

"You won't be selling her to anyone else," I said.

Vanessa pulled her hair back into a tight ponytail and sat on the edge of my desk. "I wouldn't do such a thing." Her gaze flicked to the screen. "But I won't be giving her to you until I know she's ready. Until I know she can handle you."

I grunted. "She won't even see me."

"Doesn't matter. She could still freak out that a stranger is touching her and eventually fucking her. But something tells me she won't. She's desperate. Poor girl. She is a pretty little thing though. She has some meat on her bones too. So she won't break when you finally do fuck her."

No, she wouldn't. Would she? I stared a little longer at Lexi.

"I'm actually surprised she showed up." Vanessa pulled a tube of lipstick out of the pocket in her leather pants and used her phone as a mirror.

"Why?"

"Because." She caught my gaze, letting out a huff. "Come on, big brother. She's an innocent. Probably into vanilla sex and shit." She pursed her lips, applying the blood red lipstick. "She's too damn innocent for you. I know she's desperate for money. All of them who come here are but there's something more to her. I just can't figure it out quite yet." She jumped off the desk, stuffing the tube of lipstick back in her pocket. "But I'll make her perfect. Just for you."

She was already perfect in my mind. I didn't give a shit about her being an innocent as my sister said. I wanted Lexi and I would have her too. She would also be screaming for more by the time I was done with her.

(Lexi)

After I finished answering all two-hundred questions, there was a kink in my neck and my wrist hurt. Although I just had to put a checkmark beside whichever answer fit best, it still sucked. A lot. Questions were asked that I had never even heard of before. Most of them having to do with all kinds of sexual kink that I didn't know existed. Some even had to do with bodily functions and if you would do it for your partner or if you would allow them to do it for you. That was putting it politely too. I didn't mind a little kink or even a lot of it, as long as it was consensual, but pissing or shitting on someone? Not my thing.

The door behind me suddenly opened, revealing the woman from before. I realized then that I still didn't know her name.

"Did you answer the questions?" she asked, coming toward me. The door closed behind her with a soft whoosh.

I nodded, handing her the file.

She leaned her hip against the desk, flipping through each page. "Interesting." She slapped the file closed. "I have the perfect man for you."

I opened my mouth to speak when I remembered the rule. Ah, screw it. "I need to know more."

She raised an eyebrow. "Rules, Lexi."

"I'm selling my body. Fuck the rules."

Her lips twitched but she didn't smile. "Come with me." She pushed away from the desk and headed to the door she came from.

Like a good little girl, I followed. Not that I had a choice or anything. Oh God. Maybe I screwed myself out of getting the money I needed. *Rules, Lexi.*

I should have listened. I knew that. But I needed answers and I was tired from answering the stupid questionnaire.

Once we left the white room, we ended up in another hall. But this one wasn't like before. It was brighter, with the same red carpet and brown walls, but this one had photos on them. You couldn't see anyone's faces as the heads were all cropped out, but the images were stunning. Some were in color, but most were in black and white.

"Wow." I stopped in front of one with a man's hand wrapped around a woman's throat. My heart jumped, my body flushing unexpectedly.

"These photos were donated to us," the woman said, standing beside me.

"Will you ever tell me your name?" I asked her.

"You can call me Miss Vee." She turned on her heel and snapped her fingers. "Come, Lexi. You're lucky I don't bend you over my knee and spank that ass of yours for speaking out of turn. First rule, be quiet, and you already broke it. Second rule?"

I swallowed hard, rushing to her side. "Ma'am?" I didn't know how she wanted to be called besides using Miss Vee, but I thought I'd be as polite as I could.

"Second rule, don't call me *ma'am*."

"Sorry, I just have so many questions."

Miss Vee stopped and stepped in front of me. Pinching my chin, she tilted my head back. "You're a defiant one but you're also loyal and a desperate little thing, aren't you?"

"I…I don't know what you mean." I stared up at her, wondering how she could get caught up in a place like this. Not that I knew exactly what this place consisted of.

"I get it," she murmured and released me.

When I was about to ask what exactly it was that she got, we stopped at another door.

Miss Vee knocked twice. It opened a second later, revealing someone dressed in a white robe that covered them from head to toe. Their eyes were the only thing that weren't covered. There was a red patch of cloth covering their mouth but other than that, there was no color at all. Again with the white.

"Like I said, I'm the only person you will see. We have to protect everyone here. Do you understand?" Miss Vee asked me.

I nodded this time.

"Thank you, pet," she told the person who opened the door for us.

They nodded, backing away so we could enter the room.

This one wasn't white but dark instead. It held a table that looked like the uncomfortable one you sat on at the doctor's office.

A heavy feeling sat in the pit of my stomach. There was something off about this room. Like it would lead to a life that I would never be able to get away from.

"We make sure all of you are tested for every disease possible," Miss Vee explained as we walked farther into the room. "Even the clients are tested as we don't allow the use of condoms."

No condoms. Holy shit.

"You won't get your first client for at least a few more weeks, but you will be given a down deposit. So, you will be paid during your training." Miss Vee walked over to the table and patted the top of it. "Come here. I'll have the doctor check you out and we'll draw some blood. You'll get the results in about a week and then you'll get a text with what day and time to come back here. Understood?"

I closed the distance between us and clutched the sides to my sweater, wrapping them tightly to my body.

"Don't be nervous." Miss Vee opened a cabinet and pulled out what I could only assume was a hospital gown off the top shelf. "Get undressed."

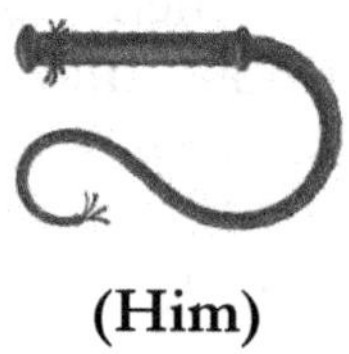

(Him)

When Vanessa had left my office to check on Lexi, I told her to give me some kind of hint when she would be undressing for the physical. I had never felt like a creeper by watching the videos before but with Lexi, I wanted her consent. Even though she wouldn't see my face, I wanted to go in knowing that she was giving her all to me. That she was giving me her undying submission.

I knew there was a submissive woman inside of her by the way my sister interacted with her. It almost made me jealous, knowing Vanessa went for both sexes, but I knew that Lexi would be mine. Even if Vanessa made her question her sexuality, I would own that pussy between her legs.

"Lay back on the table," I heard Vanessa say and I glanced back at the monitor.

Lexi did as she was told which stirred every dominant cell in my body. When she had said 'fuck the rules,' I almost shot my load. This girl would be a challenge and I couldn't wait to break her.

"When was the last time you had a physical?" Vanessa asked, standing at the head of the table.

"A year ago," Lexi murmured, her voice sliding over every inch of me.

"Any complications?"

"Not at all."

The doctor took that moment to appear. She didn't say anything as she went to work on Lexi and made sure she was in perfect health. It didn't matter to me, but it did to my sister. She wanted it to look as real as possible. Anyone else and it would have been, but Lexi was strictly mine.

Once the doctor was done, she pulled the gown Lexi was wearing back down and snapped off her gloves before putting on a new pair.

"Sit up," Vanessa said gently.

Lexi complied, running her hands down her thighs.

While the doctor drew some blood, Lexi glanced my way.

My back stiffened before I remembered that she couldn't see me and only the camera in the corner of the room. I shook my head at my stupidity. This woman had me all over of the place.

When the doctor finished, she nodded once, pulled back the curtain, and left Lexi alone with my sister.

"Get dressed and then I'll walk you out." Vanessa glanced at the same camera Lexi had been looking at.

I knew my sister thought I was insane. Before Lexi, I would have had my choice of women. They would get paid and be on their merry way. But not this time. This time I wanted Lexi. I wanted her before, during, and after. I just had to figure out a way to convince her that she wanted me back.

SEVEN

Lexi

A week later

I REALLY HAD NO idea what the hell I was doing anymore. I loved the deli, but I was getting sick of making turkey sandwiches for ungrateful customers. They had no respect for the deliciousness my mother had created before she died.

I huffed, scrubbing my hands down my face. I was losing it.

It was ten minutes before closing time and we were usually slow at this point in the evening. Although I never wanted to close the deli early because we needed the money, but by law, we had to stay open until the advertised time.

Sitting on the floor, I started cleaning the bottom shelves when the chime on the door dinged. Of course someone would come in when I was about to close up.

"We're closing…" My voice trailed off when a large shadow loomed over me. Looking up, I stared into the dark eyes that had invaded my nightmares from the moment I met him just over a week ago. "Luther."

The corners of his full mouth twitched. "What are you doing on the floor?"

"I'm cleaning." I pushed to my feet, placing the cloth on the counter. "Although I'm sure you don't know what that means. You probably have people who do that for you, don't you?"

"If you're implying I've never cleaned in my life, pet, you're very wrong," he said, a hint of amusement coating his voice.

Pet.

A shiver trembled through me at remembering Miss Vee calling me that last Friday. "What are you doing here? Did you come by to kick my brother's ass again?"

"No, Lexi." Luther's gaze roamed down the length of me, his nostrils flaring. "He knows that next time, it'll be more than me just kicking his ass."

My stomach twisted. "What do you want?"

"To talk." His shoulders tensed.

I snorted, ignoring the flutter that raced through my lower stomach at seeing the way his muscles bunched beneath the fabric of his shirt. "Right, Luther. A man like you doesn't talk." I walked out from behind the counter and locked the door to the deli. I wished he would leave but at the same time, happy that I wasn't alone. Charlie hadn't been home much over the past few days. Ever since I had visited The Club. He never asked questions about it, although I wished he had. Not that I knew what to tell him, but I still wanted to talk to someone about it just the same.

"Did you call The Club like I suggested?" Luther asked, sitting on a bench at the counter.

He looked out of place at our deli. His expensive suit could probably pay our bills for the next six months. Although his exterior looked put together, something told me that internally, he was a mess.

"I did." I swallowed hard, my palms becoming sweaty.

"And?" Luther picked up a stack of napkins and started putting them away in the napkin dispenser.

"Uh…" My cheeks burned. "I went there and answered some questions. I don't know what happens next." Which was a lie seeing as I was heading back there tomorrow night. Miss Vee had said that Saturday nights are their busiest nights of the week and she wanted me to see more of what went on. Not that I had any idea what she meant by that.

"You're lying," he said but he didn't look at me.

I rolled my eyes. "How could you know that?"

"By the tone of your voice. It shook. And I told you that they could help you, implying that they could help you pay me back. Even though it shouldn't be your responsibility."

"It *is* my responsibility. He's my brother." Not that my brother deserved it at the moment, I still had to help him. He was family and our mother wouldn't want it any other way.

Luther shrugged which was odd in a way for him. Such a big guy making that small of a movement. It almost seemed too casual for him. Like he should pay someone else to shrug for him instead.

I laughed, shaking my head at myself.

"What's so funny?" he asked, raising a dark eyebrow.

"Nothing." I walked back around the counter and grabbed the napkin dispenser from him. "Thank you."

He nodded. "Tell me what's funny."

"Well…" The back of my neck heated. "I was thinking how when you shrugged, that it almost seemed too casual for you. Like you should be paying someone else to shrug for you."

His face broke out into a grin. "I'll have to budget for that."

I laughed harder, put the napkins away, and continued wiping down the counter when I realized that I was suddenly alone with Luther Knight. And I locked the door. But when I waited for the expected fear to take over and it didn't, a sense of peace washed over me. Could the man who wanted my brother dead, still be a good guy just the same? I mentally smacked myself.

I nodded to the door. "You should go."

"I won't hurt you, Lexi." He searched my face. "Although some women deserve it, I would never lay a finger on the opposite sex. Not like that anyway." He winked.

My skin flushed.

"Lexi." His brows narrowed.

"You hurt my brother. You should leave. You should really leave." I backed up until I hit the counter.

Luther rose from his spot on the stool and came around the counter.

Before he could close the distance between us, I hightailed it to the back of the deli.

But of course, Luther followed. He stalked toward me, rubbing his jaw.

"I can't say I've ever had a woman run away from me before." He smirked. "It's kind of exhilarating."

"You shouldn't be back here." I backed up. "You shouldn't be here at all."

"Why not, Lexi?" Luther shoved his hands inside his pants pockets, his dark eyes peering into mine.

"Because you kicked my brother's ass. We owe you money. This…" I waved between us. "Isn't right."

"I'm not doing anything wrong. You aren't doing anything wrong." Luther closed the distance between us in three long strides. Grabbing my hips, he jerked me towards him.

"Stop." My hands landed on his chest. "My brother—"

"Is a bastard who would do anything to make some extra cash." Luther leaned down to my ear, his hot breath scorching the side of my face. "I want you, Lexi, and one way or another, I will have you."

"You can't if I say no," I panted, my chest rising and falling at the feel of him so close to me. I could sense the heat radiating off of him just from his fingers digging into my hips.

"You won't say no, pet." Luther's mouth moved closer to my ear. "I promise you that."

"How can you be so sure? Whatever you think of my brother, it doesn't matter. He's my family. He's…"

"You smell like heaven," Luther murmured, ignoring me. "You smell like the fucking light I've never seen before." Cupping my jaw, he turned my head toward him at the same time he crushed his mouth to mine.

A hot tongue invaded me, separating my lips and pulling a moan from the back of my throat. Rough hands gripped my hips, pulling me against a hard pelvis and backed me up until I hit the wall behind me.

My hands moved of their own accord, wrapping around a thick, tattooed neck.

Luther tasted of mint mixed with a hint of liquor. It reminded me of mint chocolate chip ice cream. The two sensations messed with my head, sending an icy cold chill racing down my spine.

"Luther," I whispered against his mouth.

He broke the kiss, brushing his thumb along my bottom lip, but didn't let me go. He only stared. His eyes became even darker as time went on. "So fucking beautiful." He pushed his thumb between my lips.

I closed my lips around his thumb before I could even stop myself.

His nostrils flared.

I released his thumb with a pop and shook my head, clearing it of all the dirty thoughts racing through it. I knew this man was dangerous but there was something more to him that I couldn't quite figure out. "You should leave."

"Why? I happen to be enjoying myself." He gave me a small smirk.

"Luther," I breathed, inhaling the spicy scent of his cologne. "This isn't right."

"And you think your brother is a fucking angel?" Luther stepped back, putting some distance between us and cupping himself.

My body heated, knowing I had caused that reaction in him.

"I'm not a patient man, Lexi." Luther adjusted his pants and leaned against the table opposite me.

"Doesn't matter if you are or not. This can't happen." But God, that kiss. My lips still tingled from the dark scruff on his jaw.

"But you want it to," he added. "Don't you?"

Of course I did. "No."

"Liar." He waved a hand between us. "This will happen."

"One way or another. Yeah, yeah. I know. You said that already." I started pacing. "But why me? There are a million other women in this damn city who would drop their panties just to have you look at them."

His brows narrowed. "What are you saying?"

I stopped suddenly. "You really don't know?"

He shrugged. Again with the shrugging.

I stared at him. "You really need to look in the mirror. Suits. Tattoos. Scruff. And you're built like a…"

"Like a what, Lexi?" Luther pushed off the table and came toward me.

"Don't." I held up my hand, stopping him. "I can't think straight with you so close to me. You're gorgeous, Luther. You have to know that."

"I don't give a shit what I look like. I keep myself healthy and I work out constantly but not because I want to look good for women. I do it to stay safe. The stronger I am, the better."

I frowned. "What does that even mean?"

"It means that I have bad people who are always after me." He took a final step toward me, brushing his knuckles down my cheek. "But it doesn't matter. They'll never catch me."

"How can you be so sure?" I asked, a hot shiver skating down my spine.

"My men are always with me." He turned his head, nodding toward the front of the shop.

"They're here right—" Obviously, they would be. A man of Luther's stature didn't travel alone.

"They are, pet." Luther pinched my chin, tilting my head back. "I meant what I said. I will have you. Wet. Ripe. So fucking drenched, one thrust of my cock and you'll be screaming my name."

My breath caught at the delicious images he was creating in my mind. "It can't happen." But my voice didn't come out as strong or sure as I would have liked.

"Maybe not now." He kissed my cheek. "But it will. Eventually. When neither of us can no longer fight it. We'll both lose that control together. And I can't fucking wait." He placed a soft peck on my mouth, released me, and headed back out to the front of the deli. A moment later, I heard the familiar ding to the bell as the door closed.

Letting out a slow breath, I slid down the wall to the floor.

What the hell just happened?

EIGHT

IT WAS FINALLY SATURDAY night, and I still hadn't seen my brother. I was also a damn mess. I couldn't sleep last night. And when I did actually fall asleep, my thoughts were invaded by a dark, dangerous, but so damn delicious, man that it only made the ache between my legs that much worse. But I wouldn't sleep with him. No matter what he said. I wasn't experienced, but I wasn't that desperate either. I had toys and two hands. At least they didn't want to murder my brother.

Scrubbing a hand down my face, I took a deep breath and knocked on the steel door leading to The Club. I was actually thankful for the distraction that this place would hopefully offer me this evening. Fingers crossed anyway.

The door opened, revealing Miss Vee. A deep frown sat between her brows. Her eyes glanced down the length of me, giving me a once over.

I shifted from foot to foot. "Everything okay?"

Her brows arched a bit before she scowled. "Yes. Of course. Why?"

"I don't know. You just look…stressed." My cheeks heated. Although she was a woman and I had never been attracted to the same sex before, there was something about her that I liked. She wasn't the warmest person I had ever met but I liked the dominant air about her. Maybe that was why I latched onto Luther so quickly. I had been taking care of my brother for as long as I could remember, I needed someone to take care of me. Oh God, now I had a daddy complex. My cheeks burned even more.

"Don't worry about me." Miss Vee cocked her head to the side. "But what are you thinking about that's putting that beautiful blush in your skin?"

"I…" My voice cracked.

"Tell me now because as soon as we get into the production room, there will be no speaking." She smirked. "Not from you anyway."

I swallowed hard; my tongue suddenly thick. "I was thinking how I like y-your d-dominance." I looked down at my feet, wringing my hands in front of me.

A firm finger pushed beneath my chin, tilting my head back. "I know." Her dark eyes twinkled. "That's why you're perfect."

I laughed nervously. "I am far from that."

"Maybe." Miss Vee released me and stepped back into the building. "Come, pet. We have lots to discuss tonight."

I followed her into the building, jumping when the heavy door closed behind me.

"As you know, we have prestigious people who attend our club. They pay to get off basically. To not have to deal with the press or worry about their partners finding out or even catching them with their pants down around their ankles kind of thing," Miss Vee explained, heading down the hall to the door that led into the white room.

"They pay to cheat?" I asked her.

"We don't get paid to care about their morals, pet," she said, staring down at me. "As long as they give us money, we keep our mouths shut."

"So, don't judge them basically."

She tapped her nose. "You're a fast learner."

I rolled my eyes, my lips pulling up into a smile.

"You know…" Something flashed behind her eyes. "If you were mine, I'd spank that ass of yours for rolling your eyes at me. But you're not, so I won't. I do suggest not doing that again though or I *will* spank your ass and then I'd have to deal with your Master." She rolled her own eyes that time. "And I prefer to not have to deal with him when he gets that way."

"Excuse me? My Master?" What the hell had I signed myself up for?

"Ah, little pet." Miss Vee winked. "You really are naïve, aren't you?"

"I…" My cheeks heated. "I'm new to this, yes, but I like to think that I'm not naïve exactly. Just cautious."

She laughed, shaking her head. "Same thing in this case." Once we reached the end of the hall, she swiped her key card into the lock. "Are you ready for what I'm about to show you?"

"Not really but let's get this done and over with so I can get home and curl up with a bottle of wine."

"Oh." She grinned. "He's going to enjoy you."

I opened my mouth to ask what she meant by that but was cut off short by the whoosh of the door when she opened it.

Miss Vee stepped into the white room and much like before, I kept my mouth shut. I had never been a huge talker to begin with but not being able to ask questions was driving me crazy.

My Master.

Had I been picked already? How was that even possible? There were security cameras. Was he watching me? Were they recording me? Had she shown him videos? I had only been here once so far. How could I have a Master so soon?

So many more questions bounced through my mind but like a good little girl, I followed Miss Vee across the white room. We stepped into the second hall and continued walking in silence. I had never been this far before. It was exciting and scary all at the same time.

"I know you have a lot of questions burning through that beautiful brain of yours," Miss Vee said once we reached the end of the second hall. "They will get answered in time." Swiping her card through another key slot, she opened the door and I was hit with a scent of spice. It smelled like a hint of…

My body heated.

Luther.

My lips tingled remembering the way he had kissed me. The things he had said to me. The way he touched me.

"I will have you. Wet. Ripe. So fucking drenched, one thrust of my cock and you'll be screaming my name."

A part of me was begging for it but the rational part, screamed to keep him at a safe distance. But somehow, I knew that even if we were across the country from each other, he would always find me.

Miss Vee caught my gaze. "Everything good, pet?"

"Yes." I didn't give a shit what Luther said or how my body responded to him, I would not sleep with him.

(Him)

Watching my sister give Lexi the grand tour of The Club stirred something inside of me. It was almost like she was in my home, taking in everything around her. And she was even more beautiful now than the last time I saw her. My body buzzed. My dick throbbed. My balls fucking ached. My hand wasn't cutting it anymore. I needed her. But I knew I had to be patient just the same.

As if my sister could hear my thoughts, she glanced at the camera, raising an eyebrow.

I sat back in the leather chair behind my desk, tenting my fingers under my chin.

When she was satisfied that I wouldn't come barging through the doors and carry Lexi away like a caveman, she continued.

"This hall leads to the rooms that you'll be playing in with your Master," Vanessa explained, taking Lexi down a hall that held windows on either side. They were tinted with the curtains closed unless the patrons decided to have an audience. It all depended on what the submissive agreed to. Everyone had their own special kink and our job was to make sure they were completely and utterly satisfied.

"Everyone who comes here, has their own kink," Vanessa continued, taking the thoughts right out of my head. "It's our job to comply and give them what they're looking for. The only thing we won't allow is anything to do with a minor or animals."

Lexi nodded.

Clicking the mouse, I zoomed the camera in on her beautiful face. Her dark eyes held so many questions that I couldn't wait to give her the answers to. But for now my sister would have to do that for me.

I zoomed the camera back out, waiting for the right moment to strike. This was the part I hated. I wanted to play. That beast inside of me needed sustenance and if I didn't satisfy him and soon, I was afraid Lexi would be ripped apart before I even had a chance to enjoy her.

(Lexi)

"You will spend most of your time in one of these rooms. Whatever you checked off in the questionnaire will dictate what rooms your Master puts you in." Miss Vee stopped at the end of the hall and slapped her hand on a button on the wall. The curtains in the rooms opened, revealing all different types of, what I could only assume, were scenes. "Do you know anything about the BDSM lifestyle?"

"I've read some books and seen dominance play out in movies, but I've never been to a club or anything." My cheeks burned even more.

"That's fine. You're not expected to know everything. These rooms are scenes that you will do with your Master. I noticed in the questionnaire that you'll try anything at least once. Except for threesomes. Why is that?"

My body heated. I had forgotten that others would be looking at the answers I had checked off. I was lost in the moment and answered honestly. I wasn't supposed to speak, so I waited instead.

"If you're asked a direct question, you can talk." Miss Vee gave me a small smile.

"Because I don't like sharing," I whispered.

"Fair enough and there's nothing wrong with that, pet. You're a gift. Most people already know what they won't do or aren't into. The fact that you are new to this, will be exciting for both you and your Master. You can learn together what you like."

I opened my mouth to speak again but remembered the rule. Letting out a soft sigh, I waited until I was given permission.

"I know you have questions, but this rule is to prepare you for what's to come. You won't be talking to your Master. He will be doing all the speaking and will be doing that through touch and touch alone." Miss Vee walked past me, stopping in front of one of the large windows. "This room is my favorite. It's our Sensory Deprivation room. Take away one sense to heighten another." She sighed, her hand fluttering to her throat. "It can be quite intoxicating for both the sub and the master. Or mistress in my case." She winked.

I stepped up beside her, my gaze roaming around the room. It didn't look like much. The walls were dark and there was a large bed sitting against one of them much like the others. But this one had a table stocked with feathers and other items that I couldn't quite make out from where I was standing.

"Have you ever been tickled into an orgasm?"

I coughed and shook my head quickly.

Miss Vee grinned. "This way." She walked past me, to another door. "Remember, whatever your kink is, your Master will not judge you. Do you understand, Lexi?"

I nodded. *My kink.* I bit back a scoff. I was so in way over my head.

"Where the hell have you been?"

I looked up from behind the computer screen and frowned. "Me?" I asked Charlie as he strode into the apartment. "I haven't seen you in a week." I glanced at the time at the corner of the screen. "It's almost three in the morning. Where the hell have *you* been?"

Charlie shrugged, headed into the kitchen, and came back a moment later with a bottle of beer in each hand. Handing me one, he sat down beside me.

"So…" I waited.

"So…" He raised an eyebrow.

I huffed. The men in my life were frustrating as hell. "Where have you been, Charlie? You could have been dead, and I wouldn't have known."

He only shrugged and took a swig of his beer. "Did you go to that club?"

"Yeah," I mumbled. That was why I couldn't sleep. After Miss Vee showed me the rest of the scene rooms, that was it for my lesson tonight. It didn't make sense. I felt like I wasn't learning much but at the same time, a part of me knew not to question her motives.

"Did you get paid yet?"

My stomach twisted. "Yeah." Fifty-grand had been wired into my bank account after I gave Miss Vee a blank check. I suddenly felt dirty at the reminder.

"And?"

"And what?" I shook my head. "I'm not giving you the money. It's going to bills and to Luther. You know that. That's why we're in this mess in the first place."

"Your brother's a bastard. He'll do anything for some extra cash."

Luther's words bounced around in my head, but I ignored them and shut the lid to my laptop. "I'm heading to bed. Are you going to actually be around tomorrow to help me at the deli?"

"Yeah," came Charlie's mumbled reply.

"Good." Rising from the chair, I stretched my arms up and over my head.

"I have some of the guys coming over to help fix up the place." Charlie pulled back the rest of his beer before grabbing the bottle he had placed in front of me.

"We can't afford to pay them." I was trying to save us money. Not spend more of it than we had.

"They won't need money as payment." Charlie crossed an ankle over the opposite knee.

"What does that even mean?" I loved him but sometimes his desperation for more made me leery of him.

"Don't worry about it, sis." He stood, bringing his empty beer bottles into the kitchen. "I'm heading back out."

"Charlie, tell me. What the hell kind of payment are you giving them? We don't have any money." I let out a frustrated cry when he continued walking to the door, ignoring me. "Charlie. Answer me."

He spun on me. "I said, don't fucking worry about it."

"I need to worry about it because right now my brother is being shady as hell. Are you giving them money that I don't know about? Doing a job for them? Something else? Tell me. Please."

"They'll get paid," he bit out through clenched teeth. "And how I'm paying them is none of your concern because I can't have you knowing that shit."

"What?" I was taken aback by his confession. "What do you mean?"

"It's not safe." He turned toward the door. "I'm going out."

"At this hour?" I whispered.

"Yeah." He came toward me and pulled me into his arms. "We got this. Whatever is going on through that head of yours, don't worry so damn much."

That was easier said than done when he wasn't the one currently in training to sell his damn body.

NINE

Lexi

"YOU WILL LEARN TO please your Master without actually having to touch him. You will remain bound until he decides otherwise." Miss Vee paced back and forth in front of me. "Do you understand?"

I nodded, glancing around the room I had been in for the past hour. We were now two months into my training. If you could even call it that. The last few times I had been at The Club have consisted of paperwork, more blood tests, and several tours of the building. The tests came back negative for whatever diseases they were looking for, thank God. At least I didn't have to get a physical for a while.

It was Saturday night at the end of August and I was hot. Although the air conditioning was turned on in The

Club, I couldn't get cool. I wasn't sure why. I was feeling alright. Just anxious. I hadn't seen Charlie much in the past few weeks. Something was going on with him, but he refused to talk to me. His friends, if that was what you even wanted to call them, helped fix up the deli. I appreciated it, but I was still cautious when they said they didn't want money. Their lingering stares suggested they wanted something else.

I also hadn't heard from Luther since he showed up at the deli and kissed the hell out of me.

"Everything okay, Lexi?" Miss Vee stopped in front of me. "You look a little flushed. Are you feeling alright?"

"It's hot out and I can't seem to cool off," I told her, keeping my hands on my thighs like I had been taught rather quickly. I was kneeling on top of a king-sized bed. The black satin sheets were soft to the touch. I shouldn't have been so damn hot when I only had on a thin white robe and nothing else.

"There's a shower through that door. The bathroom is stocked with every toiletry item you could ever need. Once you're done for the evening, you can take some time to cool off."

I nodded. "Thank you."

"We wouldn't want you getting sick on us." Miss Vee headed over to the thermostat on the wall by the door leading into the room and pressed a button on it. It beeped several times before she turned back to me. "Better?"

Cool air washed over me once the fan kicked in. "Yes. Thank you."

"You're welcome." She came back toward me. "Your Master is here."

My skin suddenly became flushed. "W-What?"

Her lips twitched. Pulling a red silk scarf out of the back pocket of her leather pants, she held it up to my face. "You won't be having sex with him tonight if that's what you're worried about."

"I…" Was I worried about that? I didn't even know anymore. But I was anxious to meet him. Even though I wouldn't be able to see him, I just wanted this to start so I could get it done and over with.

"Did you eat today?" Miss Vee placed the back of her hand against my forehead.

"I had toast this morning with peanut butter." It was an unusually humid day which was probably why I wasn't feeling myself.

"Could be nerves." She walked over to a black leather chair that sat in the corner of the room and pulled a small silver flask out of her red bag. "Here." She came back toward me. "Take a swig of this. It'll help relax you."

I took the flask from her, opened the lid and took a swig without even asking what it was. The liquid burned down my esophagus, heating every inch of me.

"Better?" Miss Vee asked, taking it from my hand and closing the lid.

I took a deep breath. "Yes."

"Good." She gave me a small smile and handed me the red silk scarf. "Tie this around your head, pet. And remember the rules. He won't talk to you and you can't talk to him."

"Will he ever talk to me?"

"Maybe." She placed a soft peck on my forehead. "Don't worry so much. He won't hurt you. There are cameras everywhere and the security in this place is top notch. You're safe."

"Okay." I took another deep breath and slid the scarf around my head, tying it tightly at the back.

The sound of a door closing a moment later made my heart jump.

I could probably take off the blindfold so I could see my Master but the part of me that wanted to play by the rules thought better of it. What if I took it off and all of this ended? I would be out the money we owed Luther. But I had a feeling that no matter what I did, it wouldn't be good enough for my brother.

A sudden scent of spice wafted into my nose. I lifted my head, inhaling deep. The scent was laced with something sweet. I couldn't quite figure out what it was, but it reminded me of…sex.

A soft noise sounded close by. Like someone had dropped something on top of a table or in this case, a dresser. My stomach tumbled when I realized that I was no longer alone.

The hairs on my body tingled, my lips parted. Although I couldn't see anything, I could feel him. Hot breath scorched the side of my face. It was mint mixed with a hint of a spicy liquor and it reminded me of Luther.

My heart jumped. Shaking my head, I forced thoughts of him to the back of my mind. I did not need to get mixed up with that right at the moment.

A firm hand pressed against the middle of my chest, pushing me back onto the bed. Though I wasn't bound yet, I knew I had to keep my hands to myself. Although I wanted to reach out to him, I couldn't. Maybe in time? If he let me. God, I hoped he let me. I frowned, not quite sure why I was thinking this way. He was a stranger, but I found that I still wanted to touch him.

Rough hands grabbed my wrists, pinning my arms up and over my head. Something soft wrapped around them, restraining me and holding me in place.

A shaky breath left me.

The bed dipped beside me. A warm body pressed up against me. It was so close but felt so far away at the same time. Miss Vee said I wouldn't be having sex tonight. I was fine with that at first but now, I wasn't so sure.

(Him)

She was absolutely perfect.

I had asked my sister to leave Lexi in the white robe because I wanted to strip her myself but now I wished she was completely naked. She would be. Soon.

When I entered the room and found her kneeling and still covered, the dominant inside of me roared and came to life.

With Lexi lying beside me, her eyes blindfolded by the red silk scarf and her arms bound above her head, she was damn near flawless. The red tinge to her cheeks shot right to the tip of my dick.

It took every ounce of control I had not to rip the robe free from her body and dive into her hot cunt. But I wouldn't. Not yet. This was all about true domination. On my part and Lexi's.

Untying the belt at the middle of her waist, I opened the robe, revealing her creamy skin. Her chest rose and fell, her skin erupting into tiny goosebumps.

Pulling the fabric open even more, the material fell at her sides and revealed every inch of her. Her rosy nipples hardened in the cool air washing around us. Freckles adorned her skin. And her pussy had a light smattering of hair on it that made my mouth water.

Brushing my thumb along the line of her jaw, I watched her lips part. Her wet tongue peeked out, licking along her bottom lip. Her nostrils flared, her head tilted back.

With just my thumb on her skin, I trailed it along the lines of her body.

(Lexi)

My skin came alive at the mere touch of what I could only assume was his thumb. It trailed over every inch of me. Along my jaw. Down to my collarbone. To my throat. It pressed lightly against my jugular, sending a rush of fear mixed with heat racing throughout every nerve ending. With a snap of his hand, he could break my neck but somehow, I knew it wouldn't happen. But the possibility that it could, was exciting and dangerous all at the same time.

A mixture of feelings rushed through me. Shame. Anxiety. Guilt. What the hell was I doing offering myself this way to a stranger?

The hand suddenly wrapped around my throat, squeezing it lightly but firmly. I gasped, tugging on the ropes binding my wrists.

Warm lips kissed the corner of my mouth. The fingers around my neck squeezed harder as if he were giving me a warning. What it was, I wasn't sure, but I took a deep breath and willed myself to relax.

The hand released me, brushing down the length of my torso.

My nipples pebbled, my hips arching of their own accord.

The hand tapped my inner thigh.

Spreading my legs, I waited.

TEN

Lexi

THE HAND ON MY thigh was rough and calloused, with years of hard work embedded into the flesh. I almost felt owned by the firm grip he had on me. When the hand moved, my heart started racing. I had no experience when it came to sex. Losing my virginity in high school was awful, and I hadn't looked back since. Other than a few other times I experienced the act, I had no desire for it. I knew sex could be good with the right partner, but I never sought it out. Until now.

Before I knew what was happening, the hand between my thighs cupped me. I gasped, chewing my bottom lip. Even though he hadn't done anything yet, it ignited a burn inside of me I had never felt before.

Spreading my legs even more, I hinted with everything in me for him to take it further. How far I wanted him to go, I wasn't sure, but I knew that I needed something. Something else. Something to take me so far out of my head, I needed his help finding my way back.

A finger brushed over my clit, sending a jolt of pleasure shooting through every nerve in my body. It moved slowly back and forth over the bundle of nerves. The pressure wasn't enough to make me come but it was still just as sweet. So damn sweet.

The man leaned down to my ear, his hot breath fanning over my face. The scruff of his cheek scraped over mine, his tongue licking along the soft skin just beneath my ear. In a rough move, his finger thrust inside of me.

My back bowed off the bed, a gasp silent on my tongue.

The finger was soon followed by another and another. Filling me, stretching me, owning the part of me I had kept to myself for the past several years. It burned. It hurt. But it mixed with pleasure and fucked with my head. The fingers were thick, almost like he was thrusting his cock inside of me instead.

All too soon, the hand left my lower body. A drop of liquid landed on my bottom lip, an acidic scent wafting into my nose.

Licking along my lip, I swallowed the taste of my own desire.

A growl left the man. It was so soft and faint, but it still shot right to the core of my very being.

The hand moved back down to my center. Fingers slid into me. Gentle at first. But when the thumb came into contact with my clit, I swallowed a cry. The fingers sped up then. Thrusting hard. Thrusting deep. All the while rubbing my clit at the same time.

Pleasure coursed through me. It consumed every waking thought. It was intense. It was raw. It was powerful.

"Oh—" A heavy hand covered my mouth while the other pleased my lower body. Squeezing my eyes shut, my cheeks burned at my mistake. Miss Vee had said we weren't allowed to talk but I didn't know I couldn't express how good this man was making me feel.

The man, my Master, pushed his fingers into me as deep as they would go.

I whimpered, which earned me another dark delicious chuckle.

Begging was on the tip of my tongue. *Pleading* was on the verge of falling from my lips as he shoved me into a pool of utter ecstasy. A scream lodged in my throat.

Once my trembling body simmered some, the man removed his hand from between my legs. A sense of loss washed over me.

With a gentle touch, a thumb ran over my sensitive clit.

I jumped, trying to get away but he only continued until another release hit me.

(Him)

She was beautiful in the way she came for me. The way she arched her back like a cat. The soft mewls and whimpers from her lips were enough to push me over the edge. I had no intention of giving her an orgasm. Not after only our first session. But she needed it just as much as I needed to give it to her.

Placing a soft peck on Lexi's cheek, I brought my hand up to her mouth and slid my fingers, soaked with her cum, onto her tongue.

She moaned, lapping and sucking. She swallowed everything I had to give her.

Leaning down to her ear, I gave it a gentle nip. "I'm going to untie you. You're going to wait two minutes and then take a shower. No matter what Miss Vee says, come back here next Friday night." I kissed her cheek and rose from the bed. Sticking my fingers in my mouth, I sucked the taste of her sweet saliva off of them.

Lexi would be mine. Every inch of her. Her mind. Body. Soul. Her fucking life. *Mine.*

(Lexi)

"No matter what Miss Vee says, come back here next Friday night."

I had been toying with the idea of not actually listening to him. Why would I? If I did, I could be out the money that I actually owed Luther. Another man who did funny things to my belly. But something struck me as odd about the man's voice. It sounded familiar, but it had been so low and soft that I couldn't quite make it out. I swore I'd heard it before.

After the man, my Master, whatever he was, left the room, I counted down the two minutes before pulling off the blindfold. Laying there, I stared up at the ceiling. This man, this dark stranger, had given me the best orgasms of my life. Could it happen that after two orgasms, you became an addict? I wanted more. No, I *needed* it.

But how the hell could I go see him on Friday when I didn't even know what he looked like and Miss Vee ran the show here? The guy was delusional if you asked me. Maybe it was a test to see if I would listen to him or not.

Rising from the bed, I rubbed my wrists and headed to the bathroom.. The room was larger than my own bedroom. It held a white claw bathtub along with a shower stall. A vanity made of a dark cherry oak wood sat in one corner. A long counter stocked with toiletries sat to my right. Not wanting to spend more time here than necessary, I quickly cleaned myself up and got dressed. I was just hiking the strap of my bag higher onto my shoulder when the door opened, revealing Miss Vee.

"Oh, you're dressed."

"Yes." I was half tempted to curtsy.

"I'll walk you out." She turned abruptly and headed back out into the hall.

Frowning, I followed her but stopped at the doorway. Glancing back at the bed, my body heated. The sheets were crumpled. The ties that had bound my wrists were red like the scarf that had cut off my vision.

Shifting my sights between the bed and out into the hall, I quickly went to the bed and snatched the scarf. Stuffing it into my bag, I left the room.

(Him)

"What the hell did you do?" Vanessa demanded, slamming the door shut behind her.

"I didn't do anything." I rose from my spot behind my desk and walked to the minibar. "You know I want her. You made it so I would have her." My gaze flicked to my sister over my shoulder. "Thank you for that by the way."

She scowled.

"And I will continue to have her."

"This isn't right. You are too close to this shit. I gave her to you because I thought you could handle it. You weren't supposed to actually give her an orgasm tonight. And you sure as hell weren't supposed to tell her to come see you. *'No matter what Miss Vee says, come back here next Friday night.'* What the hell—"

"Watch your tone, sister dearest. Remember who Father put in charge of this…*business.*" I growled the final word.

"Do I look like I give a shit? He's dead and gone, leaving me with you but no, you can't think about anything but getting your dick wet. These are *my* girls. Mine. I have to protect them and keep them safe from vipers like you."

"She won't come see me anyway," I threw at her. "And you weren't supposed to hear that." I poured myself a drink, shot it back and poured another before taking it back to my desk. The liquid burned in the pit of my stomach, but it did nothing to curb the craving I had for my little pet. Her coming around my fingers had been the sweetest thing I had ever experienced.

"Listen," Vanessa said gently, sitting in the chair across from me. "I know you like her. Even though you don't even know her."

Oh I knew her. I knew her more than she thought I did. We were one in the same, her and I.

"I don't get it but whatever," my sister continued. "But what I *do* get is that this is a business. She's not here because she wants to be. Have you ever thought of that?"

Placing the tumbler on top of my desk, I sat back in the leather chair. "I'll make her want to be here."

"There are cameras every—"

"Doesn't matter. I'll take her to a different club where no one knows us. Where she can actually see my face and find out my name." I wanted her screaming it.

"It doesn't work that way." Vanessa scrubbed her face. "Listen to me. Do you think she would be with you if she knew who you really were?"

"Yes." And I would make damn sure of it.

ELEVEN

Lexi

HUMMING TO MYSELF, I cut up the veggies and cheese that I would be using for the sandwiches I was making for customers who ordered them. Slipping a piece of the fresh turkey into my mouth, I sighed as I ate the delicious meat.

"I don't think you're supposed to actually eat the food while you're making it."

I jumped, spun around, and found Luther leaning against the fridge door. He was wearing black dress pants and a white buttoned up shirt. The sleeves were rolled up to his elbows, making the tattoos on his forearms pop. My stomach tumbled.

"Didn't you know that a cook always tastes what they make? Why would I serve this if I didn't eat it myself?" I held a piece of turkey out for him. "What are you doing back here anyway?"

He took it from me and brought the meat up to his mouth. "Your brother told me where you were. So here I am." He ate the slice of meat I gave him, letting out a low groan. "Fuck me, that's good."

My cheeks heated. "It's fresh. Got it from the butcher yesterday and cooked it overnight." I glanced over his shoulder at the door leading to the front of the deli. "Why would my brother let you back here?"

"Because he knows he can't do shit about it." Luther shrugged, stepped beside me, and picked up a cutting knife. "What am I chopping up?"

"Uh…all the veggies." I swiped a hand out, indicating the bowls of lettuce, carrots, cucumbers, and more.

Luther started chopping the veggies. I didn't even have to tell him how to chop them. It was like he knew. He cut the tomatoes in even slices. I was in awe because even I couldn't keep them perfect and I had been cutting them up for years.

"I feel like you've done this before," I said an hour later when I was putting a pie in the oven. Turning it on, I ignored the ache in my chest that it would take longer to bake the pie than usual because the stupid machine was on the verge of dying on me.

"My grandmother taught me to cook when I was a kid," Luther explained, handing me a bowl of salad. "She said that it would help me keep a wife."

"Well, the ladies do love a man who knows how to cook." I shrugged, taking the bowl from him and placing it in the fridge.

"Do you love a man who knows how to cook, Lexi?" he asked, stepping behind me.

"Um…" I swallowed hard, the warmth from his body enveloping me in a blanket of need. My mind traveled back to the man at The Club. My stomach twisted. Shutting the fridge door, I stepped away from Luther, putting some much needed distance between us.

He chuckled.

"What?" I glared at him.

"Nothing." He rubbed his mouth. "Nothing at all."

A shiver rippled down my spine.

His tattooed fingers ran along his lips. His dark eyes locked with mine. His beautiful stupid face morphed into a grin. Stupid stupid face.

I scowled, turned away from him, and grabbed a pie that had been cooling for the past hour off the table. "I'm going to put this in the display out front. You're going to come with me because you are not supposed to be back here." Although him helping me chop up vegetables did let me get things done faster. I just wouldn't tell him that.

"Yes, ma'am." He saluted me.

I paused, watching him.

"What?" Luther raised an eyebrow.

"Why are you really here? Why are you helping me?" He had an ulterior motive. I just knew it.

"Can't a guy help out a girl who clearly needs it?" Luther swiped a hand out in front of him. "You have no staff."

"I have two girls working out front while I make the food." We weren't busy today, so I had sent my third girl home early.

"Lexi, you need to hire a cook or more waitresses." Luther nodded once. "Who helped fix this place up? Last time I was here, the paint was chipping, and this kitchen wasn't as clean as it is now."

My jaw clenched. I cleaned constantly but most times, I couldn't keep up. "You noticed that?"

"I notice everything, pet." Luther crossed his thick arms under his chest, the veins in his forearms popping at the movement.

My tongue tingled. What I would give to lick along those—

"Lexi?" Luther's eyes darkened.

I shook my head. "Charlie had some friends help fix up this place."

Luther's back stiffened. "Friends? What did you give them as payment?"

"Fuck you," I snapped, pissed that he was implying I didn't have money to pay them. I didn't but I also didn't need that thrown in my face.

"Tell me," he demanded.

"Why?" I frowned. "That's none of your damn business."

"It *is* my business when your brother owes me a shit ton of money and you're brought into the middle of it." Luther took a step toward me. "So tell me. What did your brother offer up as payment?"

My heart raced. "What are you asking me?"

"I know how your brother works and what men like him, and his so-called friends, want. If it wasn't money, what was it?"

"I don't know," I murmured. "Charlie wouldn't tell me. He told me not to worry about it."

"Of course." Luther rubbed the back of his neck. "Be careful. For the love of God, please be fucking careful."

"Why do you care what happens to me, Luther?" I went to walk past him when he grabbed my arm.

"I don't know why I care but I do." His jaw clenched. "If something happens to you at the hands of your brother's desperation, I will skin him alive and leave him to die in his own piss as he begs for me to kill him."

I stared up at Luther, his words resonated with something inside of me. Something dark. Something feral. Something…dangerous. "He's family."

"He is, pet." Luther cupped my cheek, brushing his thumb along my bottom lip. "But sometimes family doesn't mean shit when it comes to things we need or think we need in your brother's case."

"We *do* need money and…"

"What, Lexi?"

"I'm standing here with the man who keeps threatening my brother's life." I wasn't sure how that made me feel. I was confused. But Charlie wasn't an easy person to love. I knew he loved me. I knew he wouldn't hurt me. Not directly anyway. Could Luther's words be true?

"I wouldn't threaten him if he did his job and paid me back the money he owes me." Luther released me and started pacing. "This…" He waved a hand between us. "Is fucking with my head."

"And you think it's not fucking with mine?" I scoffed. "Come on, Luther. You're…well…you're you and I'm me. I'm a nobody and you're like the most powerful man I have ever met. But I…"

"What?" He stopped, his dark eyes flicking to mine. "Tell me."

"I like the way you look at me. I don't know why but I feel comfortable with you and it isn't right." And that fact alone is what kept me from begging him to touch me again. To kiss me again. Hell, to just say my name. Again.

"Come back here Friday night."

My stomach twisted. I shouldn't have been thinking about my Master while I was talking to Luther. Not like this. Although, my Master was only my Master while I was at The Club. It wasn't like he actually owned me. But if that were the case, why the hell did I feel so damn guilty whenever Luther touched me?

"What's wrong, Lexi?" Luther asked, his deep voice lowering.

"N-Nothing. Nothing at all." I headed back out to the main part of the deli and slid the fresh baked cherry pie into the display case.

"Lexi."

I jumped at the barked demand of my name and spun on Luther. Stomping up to him, I pushed him back into the kitchen. I didn't need my staff or customers seeing him or overhearing our conversation.

"Go." I pointed to the door leading to the office.

He smirked and much to my surprise, did as he was told.

I followed him, rubbing the back of my neck to ease the tension. As soon as I joined him in the office, I shut the door behind me. "Listen, I don't—"

Rough hands grabbed my face, a hot mouth silencing me.

I pushed him back, breaking the kiss before it turned into something more. "This…this can't happen."

He only grinned. "Are you sure?"

"Of course I'm sure. This is dangerous. I can't…we can't do this. You can't keep touching me."

Luther grabbed my upper arm, spun me around, and pushed me up against the door. "I've never had a woman tell me what to do before," he said, ignoring me. "I have to admit that it's hot as hell. But…" His hands gripped my hips before sliding around to the front of my waist. "As hot as it is…" He popped the button on my jeans. "I'd much rather be in control."

My breath caught. I didn't know what to do. Push him away or demand that he took it further?

His fingers danced along the soft skin just below my belly button. The touch was so gentle, my skin erupted into tiny goosebumps. His other hand on my hip, slid up my side before cupping my jaw. Tilting my head back, he pushed his other hand lower into my jeans. "Tell me to stop, Lexi. Tell me you don't want this. That you don't want me. Push me away."

"I…"

"Say it, pet." He nipped my ear. "Say you don't want more. That this pussy doesn't crave the pleasure you know that I can give it. Tell me you can't feel it every time we kiss."

"We've only kissed twice," I breathed, covering his hand that was in my jeans.

Luther tilted my head back even more. "Look at me."

I met his gaze.

"Say it, Lexi. Tell me how you feel." His fingers didn't move to the spot I wanted him most. They teased and tickled. "Tell me."

"Confused," I blurted. "I feel confused."

"Why?" His hand moved lower, cupping me. His finger brushed back and forth over my slit. "Lexi," he growled.

"I don't know." I pushed back against him. "Luther. God. Just…"

"What, Lexi?" His hold on my jaw tightened. "Tell me what the fuck you want."

"I don't know what I want." I was so damn confused. Thoughts of the man, my Master, invaded my mind but the way Luther was touching me quickly replaced him.

"Yes, you do." Luther pulled his hand from my pants before ripping the fly open completely. Grabbing the waist of my jeans, he shoved them lower. "Tell me." His hand landed against the seat of my ass. "Fucking say it."

"I don't know what I want." My body burned. It buzzed with pleasure and fear. Fear of the unknown. Of him. Of what he could do to me and how he could make me feel.

"Lexi, damnit." His palm connected with my rear again.

A low moan escaped me.

"Fuck." Luther pulled my hips back. "What the hell do you want?"

"You," I whispered, squeezing my eyes shut. Shame tore through me. I wasn't this girl. I was never this girl.

"Louder." The sound of a belt buckle followed by a zipper lowering, sent a shiver down my spine. "Lexi." A tinfoil wrapper crinkled, igniting this inferno blazing inside of me.

"You," I repeated, louder that time. "You. Just you."

Before I knew what was happening, Luther thrust all of his inches inside of me.

Pain turned into a thrum of pleasure. With my hips back and my face pressed against the door, I received the brutal thrusts of Luther's cock. I had never experienced someone like him. Even before he fucked me. Even before he kissed me. He was intense on another level I had never witnessed. From the first look to the first touch, he had consumed my dreams. My thoughts. My *life*.

Luther gripped my ass, digging his fingers into the cheeks and spreading me open. His thumbs ran over the edges of the part he was currently fucking.

"So fucking good," he groaned, pushing into me as far as he could go.

I swallowed a gasp, a ripple of pleasure erupting through me.

Luther shoved me up against the door, holding his arm against the back of my neck. "This pussy is tight. Have you been saving it for someone special or has it been a while?"

My cheeks burned. "It's been a while."

"How long?" His thrusts slowed.

"A few years," I confessed.

"Hmm…this pussy now belongs to me."

My stomach sunk. It didn't. It couldn't. No matter how much he demanded of it, I would never belong to just him.

"Say it, Lexi," Luther growled, sinking his teeth into the side of my neck.

"No." I pushed back against him, taking from him what I wanted. He wanted to play this game, I could play it right back. I may not have been experienced like him, but he could go to hell. "Just fuck me. That's all you're getting from me."

He chuckled.

A soft knock on the door jarred through me. "Lexi? Are you in there?"

My eyes widened. *Charlie*.

Luther's hips picked up speed, pounding into me, fucking his heavy cock deep inside my body.

"Tell him you're busy getting stuffed with cock," Luther murmured against the side of my throat.

"Lex?" The knock came again.

"I-I'll be out in a second," I called out.

"I think it's going to be more than a second, pet." Covering my mouth with his hand, he pulled me back against him at the same time he sat in the chair by my small desk. "Whoever else you're fucking, this pussy will always be mine, Lexi." He cupped my inner thigh, spreading me open further for him. His hand connected with my pussy.

I yelped, a sharp pain spreading through me.

"Say it," he growled, releasing my mouth. "Say this pussy is mine no matter who's inside it." He smacked my center again.

A flush of heat washed over me. "Luther," I whispered.

"Say it," he demanded. "Lexi." The next time his hand smacked my clit, I broke. Before the scream left my lips, his hand covered my mouth. The release tore through me which only heightened his need to fuck me harder and faster.

My cries were muffled by his hand.

"That's my girl." Wrapping his arm around my waist, he lifted me, his cock falling free from my body. Ripping off the condom, he tossed it in the garbage can and curled his fingers around his thick length. He pumped once, twice, before coating my pussy with his cum.

He groaned, sinking his teeth into my arm.

I sighed, falling back against him.

Luther gently pushed me off his lap and righted his pants before helping me with my own. He kissed the cheek of my ass and slid my jeans and panties up to my waist.

"What now?" I asked, doing up the zipper and button. My stomach tumbled knowing his scent was now on my skin.

Heavy arms wrapped around me, pulling me back onto his lap. "Go out to dinner with me."

"Right, Luther." I laughed. "We're just going to go on a date like a normal couple." I patted his arm and rose from his lap. "Sure. Okay."

"Don't mock me." He stood, straightened his shirt, and tucked it back into his pants. "I'm being serious. I have a restaurant we can attend where we won't be disturbed."

"You are serious, aren't you?" I asked, raising an eyebrow.

"I wouldn't ask you if I wasn't serious." He pinched my chin. "Say yes."

"If I don't?" I grazed my hands down his chest to his hard abs. What I wouldn't give to see him completely naked. Completely stripped with no barriers between us.

"You won't keep me away, pet." He placed a soft peck on my mouth, sliding his lips down the length of my jaw to my ear. "And remember whose cum is currently coating your pussy when you fuck whoever it is you're fucking." He smacked another hard kiss on my lips before leaving the office.

Blowing out a slow breath, I slumped into the chair. My cell vibrated, indicating an incoming text.

Miss Vee: Your next session has been moved up to tonight.

My stomach tumbled. No. There was no way.

Miss Vee: Correction, it's been moved up to 3pm. I suggest you not keep your Master waiting.

I checked the time. That was twenty minutes from now. *Shit.*

TWELVE

Lexi

"YOU'RE LATE."

I winced, following Miss Vee down the long hallway.

"I got caught up at work." And with a man who drove me crazy. I couldn't believe I had sex with Luther. Of all people, it just had to be him. If my brother found out, he was going to kill me.

"Well your Master is waiting and he's not happy that you're late." Miss Vee's steps sped up.

"I wasn't expecting to come here today and it's not my fault I had to work. Some of us actually have to do that for a living."

Miss Vee stopped suddenly, spinning on me.

I jumped, taking a step back. My cheeks burned at my outburst.

"You're lucky you don't belong to me, pet," she snapped.

"I don't belong to anyone," I corrected her. "I wouldn't even be here if it wasn't for my brother forcing my hand."

Miss Vee grinned. "Oh, I like to think that you would be here no matter what. There's a natural submissive in you. You've been in control for your whole life. It's about time you give that control to someone else."

"How can you know that?" I asked her, crossing my arms under my chest and lifting my chin defiantly.

She laughed. "You're fun, Lexi. So damn fun." She spun on her heel. "Let's go."

I swallowed a sigh and did as I was told. Again.

Once we made it to the hallway between the scene rooms, I realized that the curtains were closed. "Are they being used?"

"They are. It seems like everyone wanted to up their appointments today." Miss Vee shook her head. "I don't even know what's going on anymore."

That made two of us.

"Alright, pet. Your Master wanted you in a different room tonight. But I've been instructed to put the blindfold on you before you enter the room." She caught my gaze. "You good with that?"

My heart jumped. "Is something wrong?"

"No." Her face softened. "Not with you." Her dark eyes moved back and forth over my face. "I think…listen, I can't say too much. Which I know has never stopped me before, but I will tell you that your Master has had a rough day. That's all I know. That's all I can say."

A sense of pride washed over me that he needed my help to make him feel better. Should I be proud of that? Should I *want* to help him?

Miss Vee continued walking toward the end of the hall, stopping in front of a door. She handed me a red scarf. "Put this on," she instructed. "I'm assuming you don't have the other one you took with you?"

"Uh…no." I didn't realize she knew I did that.

Miss Vee smiled. "It's not a big deal that you took the scarf. I'm sure your Master would be honored that you took something that reminded you of him."

All I could do was nod as I took the scarf from her. I wrapped the cool soft material around my head, the world disappearing in front of me.

"Breathe, pet," she whispered in my ear. "You'll enjoy this just as much as he will."

Somehow, I had a feeling that I would enjoy this a whole lot more than him.

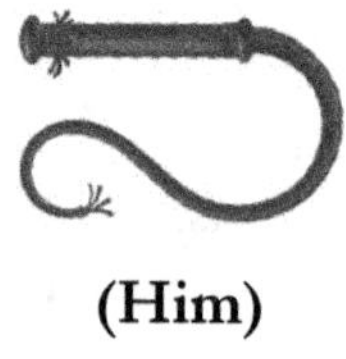

(Him)

Pacing back and forth, I waited for my sister to bring Lexi to me. The rage inside of me grew the longer time went on where she wasn't kneeling before me. It shouldn't be this way. After the morning I had, I needed her to make me feel better. To make me feel like a man and not like the monster I had come to be.

Footsteps sounded from the other side of the closed door.

I stopped pacing and waited.

The door opened slowly, revealing Vanessa and Lexi. My sister caught my gaze, her brows narrowing in the center, but she didn't say anything and gently pushed Lexi farther into the room before exiting and shutting the door.

Lexi and I were alone.

Finally.

It had felt like years since I traced her body with my fingers. Since I had her coming apart in my hands. I needed more. I needed everything this woman had to offer me. And I would take it. Every inch. And I would use her to make us both feel good.

My dick throbbed, twitching against the fly of my pants. A hot tremor traveled through me, the lust thick in the air between us.

Lexi's cheeks reddened, the red scarf tied around her head making the flush more crimson.

Taking a step toward her, I scented the air. Something sweet wafted into my nose. Flowers maybe. It was so faint, I couldn't be sure exactly what the scent was but either way, it only made my dick harden even more.

Closing the distance between us, I leaned down toward her, careful not to touch but tease instead.

Her lips parted, her pink tongue licking along her bottom lip. With my mouth mere inches from hers, I watched her chest rise and fall. The red in her cheeks became even more pronounced. Her hands clenched into fists at her sides. This sweet girl had been in control for so long. Of her life. Her job. Her brother. It was time I helped her out of her head and showed her how powerful true submission could be.

(Lexi)

Something was off with him. My Master. I could feel the tension rippling off him. Even though I couldn't see him, I bet his brows were furrowed. His jaw clenched. His piercing eyes burning through me. I imagined they were dark. Or maybe crystal blue. I knew he was strong and powerful but gentle at the same time. He had touched me with the lightest of touches and made me fall apart beneath him. It only heightened the desire I had for this man which in turn made my cheeks heat even more. Was it natural to become addicted to someone you'd never even talked to, let alone seen? I wasn't a shallow person. I didn't care what he looked like because I sure as hell was attracted to him.

An image of Luther flashed into my mind, but I forced it back. I couldn't worry about him. It wasn't like I was the only woman he was sleeping with anyway.

With nimble fingers, my Master started undressing me. I had come from work, so I probably smelled like the deli. As soon as I stood naked before him, a soft growl left him.

My body heated. Clearly, he didn't care if I smelled like sandwich meat and salad.

He brushed the back of his knuckles down the center of my torso.

The scent of musk and spice wafted into my nose, like he had just taken a shower moments before coming to see me.

My nipples peaked, the tiny hairs on my body tingling under his soft touch.

With a firm hand, he pushed me back until my calves hit the edge of what I assumed was a chair. My Master spun me around and bent me over the edge of something hard. Running his fingers down my spine, he landed a palm against my ass.

I gasped, my body burning for him.

Wrapping his fingers around my wrist, he bound it at the base of whatever it was that I was bent over. He did the same with my other wrist and both of my ankles. I had no idea what I was bound to. I mentally smacked myself for not doing more research when it came to BDSM.

With a firm grip, he fisted my hair and placed a soft peck just beneath my ear. "I know you fucked someone else today," he whispered. "I can smell him on you."

No. That wasn't possible. Was it?

"Are you a little slut, pet?" he asked, his voice so low, I almost couldn't hear him. "One cock isn't good enough for you?"

My heart started racing. No, he couldn't be mad. He had no reason to be. I opened my mouth to speak but remembered the rules.

The man chuckled. The sound was dark and depraved. It sent a shiver of fear trembling through me and there wasn't a damn thing I could do about it.

Releasing my hair, he kissed my cheek. "Your safeword is *Charlie*."

Lexi

MY STOMACH TUMBLED. HOW the hell could he know my brother's name?

"Hold up two fingers if this gets to be too much for you." Brushing his hand down my cheek, my Master placed a soft peck on my lips. "Open."

Before I could ask what he meant, an item was shoved against my lips, forcing me to open my mouth. My teeth sunk into the rubber while he locked the item in place behind my head. I was bound and helpless to this man I didn't know but craved. I had never seen him or touched him but wanted him just the same. God, did I ever want him. To take me out of my head. To control me in ways I never thought were possible. None of this made sense but I was at the point where I just didn't care anymore.

"I won't hurt you," he murmured in my ear, "but I will cause you pain."

My heart picked up speed, my body heating at the dark promise hidden beneath his words.

He moved behind me, grazing his hand down the length of my spine. Suddenly, his palm connected with the cheek of my ass.

I jumped, the sting of his touch caressing me in a hard embrace.

Swat. Swat. Swat.

I moaned, squeezed my eyes shut, and further sunk my teeth into the ball between my lips.

Swat. Swat. Swat.

My breath came out in short bursts of air. My skin flushed with a sheen of sweat.

Swat. Swat. Swat.

Spots danced in my vision, my body becoming numb. I vaguely heard a zipper lowering somewhere in the distance.

Swat. Swat. Swat.

My Master suddenly thrust into me.

I cried out, my voice muffled by the gag between my lips.

He grunted, dug his fingers into my hips, and sped up his hips. It wasn't slow. It wasn't gentle. It was violent and brutal, each thrust of his cock going faster and harder.

My body tingled, my core stretching to meet his size. My Master was punishing me. I didn't know how I knew that, but I could feel it down to the marrow of my bones. He knew I had sex today. How he could smell Luther on me was next to impossible, but he said it and it fucked with my head. I shouldn't have felt guilty, but I did. It also wasn't my fault. I had no intention of coming to The Club today.

Another swat landed on my ass, forcing me back to the situation at hand.

My cries became louder the longer he fucked me.

Swat. Swat. Swat.

My body shook, a hard release shattering through me. My pussy clenched around him, sucking him in deeper than before.

He groaned, digging his fingers into the cheeks of my ass to the point my eyes burned with unshed tears. But the pain, as brutal as it was, only seemed to heighten the release I just had as it rolled right into another one.

My legs shook, my hands tugging at the restraints.

More. Please give me more.

I had no idea I would be into this kind of sex, but it felt good. It felt so damn good. I was addicted. I moaned, attempting to arch my hips even though I couldn't go very far.

He chuckled, landing another swat on my ass before rubbing his thumb over the tight rim that had never been touched by another person before.

My heart picked up speed. I was restrained with nowhere to go. If I wanted him to stop, all I had to do was hold up two fingers. But the sick part of me was curious to see just how far he would take it.

My Master pushed his thumb into me, breaching past the tight barrier.

I cried out, my body burning at the foreign feeling rushing through me.

He removed his thumb and replaced it with a finger, followed by another and another. Stretching me. Making sure I would fit whatever else he had to give me.

More.

God, what the hell was wrong with me?

The man released me, pulled his cock free from my body and lined the tip up with my ass.

I took a breath at the same time he thrust into me in one smooth move. Inhaling a sharp gasp, my vision faded in and out.

The brutal thrusts of his cock in a place no man had ever been, sent me over the edge. It felt as though he was splitting me in two and while the pain turned into pleasure, I couldn't help but feel like he was fucking me with every intent to hurt me.

My clit swelled, aching to be touched. My pussy leaked, dripping down his balls that slapped against me with every thrust of his cock.

"Come," he demanded, landing a hard swat against the cheek of my ass.

My body shook. I was so far gone, deep within my head, that I didn't know what was going on anymore. A shiver raced through me. That one command unleashed pleasure coursing through every single vein beneath my skin.

He grunted, leaning over me. His hot breath scorched the side of my face. Pulling most of the way out, he slammed back into me.

A release rocked through me, hitting me in a spot no one had ever been able to reach before.

After a few more thrusts, he grunted, his dick swelling inside of me. A warmth coated me from within, enveloping me in a blanket of bliss.

My Master pulled out of me, placing a soft kiss on my tailbone and unshackling me from whatever it was I was bent over.

Lifting me into his arms, he cradled me like a child against his chest.

I latched onto him, shivering as the cool air washed over me. I was placed on something soft. A bed?

With his arms wrapped around me, he grazed his hand up and down my spine, placing soft pecks on my face. "You did well, pet," he whispered. "I'm so proud of you."

I whimpered, grabbing his shirt and pulling myself against him. I couldn't explain it, but I needed more. To touch him. To taste him. To feel his skin against mine. For him to kiss me. "Let me see you," I blurted.

The man stiffened and released me.

A cold draft washed over me. "No." I reached out but couldn't find him anywhere. "Please."

A door closed in the distance.

Ripping off the blindfold, I found that I was alone. "*Shit.*"

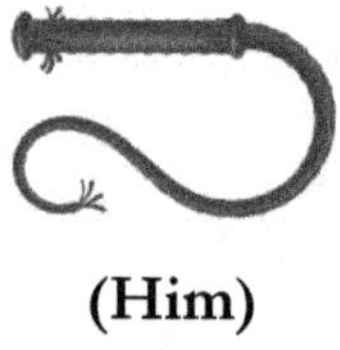

(Him)

Loosening the tie around my neck, I started pacing back and forth. I shouldn't have done that. I shouldn't have been so damn rough with her but there was something inside of Lexi that called out to me. Her submissive to my Dominant. Her innocence to my depravity. Her fucking purity to my evil.

Blowing out a slow breath, I rubbed the back of my neck and flexed my fingers into fists. I was antsy and when I was antsy, someone usually paid for it. Tonight, it had been her.

The door to my office opened, revealing Vanessa.

"You good?" she asked, leaning against the doorframe. Under normal circumstances, she would have given me shit for how I left Lexi, but this wasn't normal.

Not in the least. I left her that way before I truly destroyed what little innocence she had left. She asked to see me. I *wanted* her to see me, but I chickened out and pulled away from her, leaving her alone. When she was in that fragile state of mind. I fucked up. I should have administered aftercare after she hit subspace. But I was a pussy.

"I can't keep doing this. I have to reveal who I am." The desperation in my voice pissed me off. Stomping to the minibar, I poured myself a glass of whiskey. Drinking it back in one gulp, I let the amber liquid burn its way down into the pit of my gut. Although it calmed the racing of my heart, it didn't stop me from wanting to punch the shit out of someone.

"I had someone give Lexi some chocolate. She's resting now." Vanessa held up her hand, checking out her fingernails. "I won't ask why you didn't wait for her to get out of subspace. You know what can happen—"

"Of course I fucking know," I yelled, slamming the shot glass onto the top of the bar. Lexi could have gone into subdrop. Depression could hit her hard and I was an asshole who didn't see her through it to make sure that she was okay.

Moving to my desk, I wiggled the mouse until the screen came to life. Opening up the security system, I clicked on the camera to the room Lexi was in. She was lying on the large bed I left her in, the red sheets now wrapped around her naked body.

I blew out a slow breath of relief and sat back in my chair.

"You can't do that again." Vanessa came around the desk and rested her hip against the edge of it. Her gaze landed on Lexi's sleeping form. "There's something about her."

"I know." *Fuck.* "I know," I repeated.

"What are you going to do about her brother?"

My gaze popped to my sister's then. "Nothing at the moment." I would do something. Eventually. But first, I needed to explain to Lexi exactly how I knew who her brother was. And once she found out, I just hoped she would give me a chance to make things right.

FOURTEEN

Lexi

IT HAD BEEN A few days since I visited The Club and my Master unleashed his wrath on my body. But something told me that it wasn't the full extent of what he was capable of. It had also been that long since I'd seen Luther. Something was strange about this whole thing and it nagged at me, but I couldn't figure out exactly what *it* was.

Placing the cloth on the counter, I glanced around the deli before me. It was pushing nine at night and there hadn't been a customer in the past hour. Some nights were slow, but this was unreal. There was no other deli or restaurant on this street, no new eating places nearby. Something was up, and I had no idea what it was. Did people see Luther here? Could that be it? Were people so damn terrified of him, that they refused to eat at places he frequented?

The chime dinged as the door opened. Charlie strolled into the diner, pausing in his steps and glancing around him. "Slow night?"

"Yeah." I sighed. "I have no idea why." When I finished wiping down the counters, I locked up. My chest tightened. Maybe this was it. Maybe I would have to close the deli. If business was going to remain this slow, I would have no choice but to close up shop.

"We have to promote this place more," Charlie said, pulling me from my thoughts.

I grimaced. Knowing where he was going with this, I turned toward him. "I hate social media. You know that."

He shrugged, sitting on the stool at the counter. The same stool Luther sat on in what felt like weeks ago.

"What's wrong?" Charlie asked, pulling his phone out of the inner pocket of his jacket.

"Nothing." The hairs on the back of my neck tingled. Glancing out the window, I frowned. Nothing seemed out of the ordinary on our street. Other businesses were closed this time of night. Especially with it being a Sunday. A few cars sat at the curb. A large black SUV drove down the street, almost as if it appeared out of nowhere. Maybe I was being paranoid but it felt like they had been watching me the whole time.

"Have you talked to Luther?"

My body heated at the mention of his name. I headed behind the counter and grabbed the cloth before making my way to the back. "No, I haven't," I told Charlie.

He followed me. "Is he paid off yet?"

My back stiffened. I frowned, glancing at him over my shoulder. "Why do you ask?"

"I was just wondering if maybe that's why he hasn't been by." Charlie met my stare head on. "Why? Does it bother you that he hasn't been by?"

Yes. "No."

"I heard that he's been spending a lot of time at ToKnight."

"ToKnight?" I repeated. "What's that?"

"His restaurant." Charlie pulled a pie off the cooling rack.

"Where is this restaurant?" I needed to talk to him anyway, but I wasn't sure how he would feel about me showing up unannounced.

"I'll text you the address." Charlie nodded once. "Just be careful. His restaurant stays open after hours but only for him and his people."

"I don't even know what that means," I confessed. *His people.* God, who the hell had I let inside my body?

"Be careful. That's all I ask." Charlie left the kitchen, taking the pie with him.

Miss Vee had given me another check after my Master left the room abruptly the other night, after my damn slip up. I knew the rules, but I had still begged to see him. Although I was being paid, we still owed Luther money. Even if we didn't, something held me back from telling Charlie that information.

I stared after my brother, wondering what had gotten into him and why suddenly he was forthcoming with information about Luther.

ToKnight.

Looked like I was making a trip.

I stood outside ToKnight and stared up at the large building, not really sure why I was here in the first place. Luther had messed up my life and while I wanted to be pissed at him for it, I couldn't. It was exciting and dangerous. And why my brother actually gave me the location of Luther's restaurant, was beyond me.

There was no open or closed sign in the large bay window of the restaurant, so I wasn't actually sure if it *was* open or not.

Crossing the street, I was just about to try the door when it opened suddenly. A large man peered down at me, his brows furrowing in the middle.

"We're closed," came his gruff reply.

"Oh." My heart sunk. "Okay." I was about to turn away when a deep voice stopped me.

"Let her in."

My body heated at the rough demand.

The man stepped out of the way, revealing Luther.

"Hello, Lexi," he greeted me.

I swallowed hard. "Hey.

"Are you hungry?" Luther asked, his dark eyes roaming down the length of me.

"I can eat." What could I say? I loved food and there was no way I was turning down food from this place.

"Good." He turned to the large man standing off to the side who watched the exchange between Luther and me. "Tell the cook not to shut down yet."

The man nodded. "Yes, Sir."

"Do you drink wine, pet?" Luther held his hand out.

"I do." I placed my hand in his.

"Grab us a bottle of the pinotage that was just shipped from South Africa." Luther led me to the back of the restaurant.

"Yes, Sir," the larger man called out.

"So what brings you by, Lexi?" Luther asked me, releasing my hand and cupping my nape.

"We need to talk." But now that I was here, I wasn't sure how to say what was on my mind.

He searched my face. "Everything okay?"

"I think so." Hell, I wasn't sure anymore.

We headed to the back of the restaurant in silence. The place was big, much larger than what it looked like from the outside. The furniture was black with raindrop chandeliers hanging from the ceiling over each table. It was classy and modern with a vintage vibe.

"Did you design this place yourself?" I asked, once we stopped in front of a booth. I slid onto the black leather bench.

"I did. When I'm not controlling the city, I'm an interior designer."

I gaped at him. "Seriously?"

He chuckled, sliding into the booth after me. "No, pet. While I designed this place, I'm not an interior designer. I can't ruin my rep and all that shit."

I laughed, shaking my head. "I actually believed you," I said, gently punching his shoulder.

"I know." He grabbed my hand, kissing my knuckles. His tattooed hands were dark in comparison to my pale skin. "What?" he asked, raising an eyebrow.

"You're..." I pulled my hand out of his grasp. "We need to talk. Or I need to talk rather, and you need to listen." I took a breath, playing with the napkin folded on the table. "I...I slept with someone else. Well, it wasn't really sleeping. We had sex. The same day you and I had sex. And I know how that sounds. But I'm sorry. I also know that we haven't made anything official and it was obviously just a one-time thing, but I still feel guilty because I'm not that girl. So yeah..." A leaden weight sat in the pit of my stomach. "That's all."

"You feel guilty for fucking another man after I fucked you?"

My chest tightened. "Yeah. I do."

Luther cupped my jaw, forcing me to look at him. "Why?"

Something flashed in his eyes, but it happened so quickly I wasn't sure if I actually saw it or not. "B-Because it wasn't right of me." Not that my Master cared in the least. It seemed to only make him fuck me harder. My core clenched. I squirmed in my seat.

Luther's jaw clenched. "We never made anything official. You said so yourself."

I swallowed hard. "Yeah but I'm not this person. Hell, I hadn't had sex in years and then you…"

"And then I fucked you. In your office. Like a damn slut. And you enjoyed it."

I looked away, the back of my neck heating. "I did." What the hell does that say about me?

Luther cupped my nape, giving it a light squeeze.

My stomach tumbled at the hold he had on me. It wasn't rough, but it was firm, and it let me know that he was in control. Something hit me as familiar about his touch.

Master.

Before I could dwell on that thought, my face was pressed against the table top. I gasped, struggling beneath Luther's hold on me but he was too strong. "Luther."

He leaned down toward me, placing a soft peck on the corner of my mouth.

"There's something you should know, Lexi. I don't actually give a shit who you fuck." His other hand cupped my knee, sliding beneath my dress and up my inner thigh. "I know you will always crave my cock. We may have only fucked once but I will make it so my dick is the only one you come for. So go back to whoever it is you're letting inside this tight little body. Let him do whatever he wants to you but know that it will always be me you truly want."

FIFTEEN

Lexi

"YOU THINK JUST BECAUSE you make me feel good, you can be an asshole and treat me like this?" I struggled beneath Luther, but he still didn't move.

He only raised an eyebrow.

I continued. "I came here to tell you what happened because I felt guilty. I shouldn't feel guilty knowing what you've done to my brother."

"Your brother is a shithead, Lexi." Luther's hold on my nape loosened but he didn't remove his other hand from my thigh.

"I don't care about that. I don't care what he's taken from you or what he owes. I sold my fucking body to pay you back. A man I like. And I have no idea why." I pushed against him.

He released me, rubbing the dark scruff on his jaw. "This is interesting to me."

"What?" I frowned, sitting up.

"I usually get women submitting to me with no issues but you are something else."

I rolled my eyes. "I—"

A sharp pinch landed on my inner thigh.

I yelped, glaring at him.

He cupped my nape again, leaning toward me. "I like that you challenge me, Lexi, but that only goes so far. Your Master may take this shit, but I sure as hell won't."

"I have no idea what you're talking about." It wasn't like I could actually talk to my Master anyway. I hadn't seen him since my slip up.

"No?" Luther's mouth brushed along my ear. "I'm the one who gave you The Club's business card, remember? I know what goes on there. I know what they do. What those rooms are used for." His hand on my inner thigh grazed even higher. His fingers brushed over the crease at my thigh and pussy.

My heart started racing. I wrapped my fingers around his wrist. I should have pushed him away. I should have done a lot of things but instead, I encouraged him to go higher.

"I'm the one who introduced you to that life," he murmured, pushing his finger beneath the crotch of my thong.

"Maybe I already knew about that life," I grumbled.

He chuckled, brushing his thumb up and down the length of my neck. "You're so damn beautiful but you're also a shitty liar."

I pulled the hem of my dress out where it had bunched at my pelvis and covered his hand. "Maybe." Lifting my right knee onto the bench, I leaned my head against the back of the booth. "But you seem to like it. Me. This. All of it."

His dark eyes searched my face. "I do like it. All of it and I can't figure out why." He turned his big body toward me and brushed the back of his hand down my cheek.

My eyes fluttered closed. The touch was so gentle. Nothing like the man with his other hand between my legs. Although he never took it further, he didn't release me either. He teased. The touch was too soft for it to do anything but it still reminded me that he was, in fact, very much in control like he said.

"Lexi." Luther kissed my forehead. "Spend the night with me."

My eyes popped open, finding his face mere inches from mine. "Really?"

"Yes."

"Why?"

His jaw clenched. "Because I didn't want to fuck you in your office, but I did. I don't want to finger you in my restaurant but I am." He thrust his fingers into me.

I whimpered, chewing my bottom lip to keep from crying out.

Wrapping his arm around my shoulders, he leaned toward me and watched me. "I don't want you to come in a public place but you're going to." He kissed the sensitive spot beneath my ear, the spot that had a direct connection with my clit, and continued pumping his hand between my legs. "You want to know why?"

"Why?" I whispered.

"Because I'm losing control. When it comes to you, Lexi, I have no idea what the fuck I'm doing. You challenge me. You opened up something inside of me. And I want more. I want you. I want this."

"I…" I took a breath as pleasure threatened to consume me. "I don't know what you mean."

"I want to play with you. I want to show you what true pleasure feels like. I want you to submit to me."

Oh God. No. No. That was too much like what I was doing at The Club. Why? Why the hell would Luther even mention this?

"I…" A fast release shattered through me. "I can't," I moaned.

"You will." Luther kept his fingers inside of me. "You want to know why? I'll tell you. Because this body is mine. It was mine from the first moment I saw you. The first moment I touched you. I watched your eyes dilate. I had kicked your brother's ass and yet, you still responded to me. It took everything in me that night not to carry you out of there."

"What?" I laughed. "Are you fucking kidding me right now?"

Luther pulled his hand free from my body and cupped my jaw in a rough move.

I gasped, the scent of my desire wafting into my nose, the liquid of my release coating my cheeks.

"I suggest watching your mouth, little girl. I don't like being second-guessed. I know what I saw. You wanted me. Whether you want to admit it or not."

"Why are you nice and sweet one moment and then a complete douche the next?" I threw at him. "Do you have it out for me or something? You want to treat me like a slut and be done with me? Is that it? Are you having a mid-life crisis?" The sass that left my lips was not what I expected. The words just tumbled from my mouth and I couldn't stop them at all.

Luther released me and sat back.

Much to my surprise, he sucked his fingers into his mouth. "Hmm…" He glanced at my lap before meeting my gaze. "Want a taste?"

I shivered, looking away just as a young man neared our table.

"Sir, your wine." He poured the red liquid into two glasses and placed the bottle on the table.

"Thank you," I grumbled and wiped my cheek before grabbing the glass. Taking a large gulp, I let out a sigh as it sent a flush of heat washing over me. It was sweet with a hint of bitterness, but it eased the nerves racing through me.

"Good?" Luther asked, watching me.

I nodded, my cheeks heating.

"Perfect." He turned to the young man. "Have the cook make the usual for me. And have him do the same for my date. I think she'll like it."

"Yes, Sir." The young man hurried off.

"Are you allergic to anything?" Luther asked me, cupping my knee and grabbing his own glass of wine.

"No." I crossed my leg over the other and placed my hand on top of his. As much as he pissed me off, I actually liked this. His arm on my leg, his thumb brushing back and forth over my knee. And me, snuggled into his side. A yawn escaped me.

"Tired, pet?" Luther asked, reaching into his jacket and pulling out his phone.

"Yeah. A little." I nodded at the phone. "Why do you do it?"

"Do what?" He glanced down at me.

"This job. You don't seem to like it too much."

The corners of his full mouth twitched. "I do like it but if I went around with a smile on my face all the damn time, these fuckers would think they could take advantage of me. While they still try to, it doesn't last. It didn't take your brother long to figure that out either."

"What did he do? Or not do?"

"He had one job." Luther scrubbed a hand down his face. "Listen, no matter what happens, you can't trust him. I'm not just saying that to try and get you to spend the night with me. That's going to happen regardless."

I scoffed. "You're full of yourself, aren't you?"

"Baby, you're fucking wrapped around me right now."

I went to pull away when his hold on my knee tightened.

"Don't. I…" He shook his head. "Listen, just be careful. I'm an asshole. I get that. Do I want you? Yes. I meant every word I said. I don't lie. I have no reason for it. Spend the night with me and I'll show you me. Not the Luther that you see in public. But me. The real me. And if you still don't like what you see, I'll leave you alone."

My eyes flicked back and forth over his face. "Really?"

He nodded. "Yes, Lexi. No woman has ever affected me like this."

I chewed my bottom lip. "You terrify me."

He smirked. "Good."

I rolled my eyes.

"Lexi," he growled.

I smiled.

He huffed, shaking his head. "You drive me fucking crazy."

"Well, baby. Looks like that makes two of us," I said, taking another sip of my wine.

Luther went back to texting on his phone and doing who the hell knew what else. Answering emails maybe? Playing a game?

I swallowed a laugh at the thought of watching him play *Toon Blast* and getting frustrated over it.

"What's that smile for, pet?"

My cheeks heated. "Uh…I was just wondering what you were doing and if you were maybe playing a game."

"I don't play games." His brows narrowed. "But if I did, I would always win."

"Why? Because you cheat?"

He laughed. "No, because I'd pay others to lose."

"That's not really losing then if they're getting paid for it."

He shrugged. "Semantics."

I shook my head. "That doesn't make sense at all."

"Doesn't have to." Luther kissed my cheek. "Just know that the man you're letting spend time between your legs is fucking powerful."

My body heated at that thought. "How powerful?"

He tilted his head, almost like he was thinking about what he should say next. But I never got an answer because the food was brought out. It smelled delicious, but I couldn't help but wonder what his answer would have been. I also wondered how he could show me another part to him that I hadn't seen yet. There were clearly different sides to Luther Knight and spending the night with him was either going to end badly or worse.

I could fall for him.

SIXTEEN

Lexi

THE FOOD WAS DELICIOUS. The man sitting beside me, even more so. Luther kept his hand on my inner thigh, his thumb brushing back and forth. I ran my fingers over his tattooed knuckles. Symbols I had never seen before, covered his tanned skin.

"What do these mean?" I asked him, turning his hand over and noticing a scar sitting in the middle of his palm.

"Peace. Love. War," he answered while typing on his phone. "And other shit."

"Luther?" I ran my thumb over the soft pink skin. It was in the shape of a star. "What happened?"

His back stiffened. Pulling his hand away, he cupped my thigh, hiding the scar from me. "Don't worry about it."

"Tell me," I pressed. If he wanted me to spend the night with him, he had to give me something. Anything.

"Lexi," he said, his voice filled with warning.

"You want me to spend the night with you."

He looked my way. "I do."

"Then tell me something about yourself. I don't know you, Luther. I know this." I waved a hand between us. "But I don't know anything else."

"There are ears, pet. Ears that would fucking kill me if they found out anything about me that they don't see on the exterior." He pinched my chin. "I can't ruin my rep."

I frowned. "What you do in public is so they, whoever *they* are, fear you?"

"Yes." He leaned toward me, placing a soft peck on my forehead. "It's also to keep you safe."

"Me?" I pulled back. "Why?"

"Your brother is lethal, Lexi. Not because he's smart. But because he's fucking desperate. That makes him dangerous. And I worry that you'll be brought into the middle of it when the time comes. That's another reason I want you to spend the night with me. Then I can keep you safe."

"My brother won't hurt me," I murmured, not liking the worry written all over Luther's face.

"Maybe not but it doesn't mean others won't." Luther pulled away. "If you're done, I need an answer. I'm not a patient man, pet, but I need you to tell me if you're coming home with me or not."

"Why?" I circled my fingers in his.

"I already told you why. I want to get to know you. And I can't do that in public." He released me, signalling the young waiter over. "Tell the cook we're done here, and he can close up. Have Georgio contact me tomorrow."

"Yes, Sir." He backed away, heading to the large man who greeted me at the entrance just over an hour before.

"Lexi," Luther barked, his voice rough. "Give me an answer. *Now.*"

"Ask me nicely."

His jaw clenched. "Will you come home with me? Pretty please."

A laugh escaped me.

His lips twitched. "I'm waiting."

I pushed him, indicating for him to move out of the booth. I stood, staring up at him. "Take me to your home, Luther."

Grabbing my hand, he led me out of the restaurant just as a sleek black car pulled up. A giant of a man stepped out of the vehicle and handed Luther a set of keys.

"Thank you." Luther clapped him on the shoulder. "After you, pet."

I took a breath and headed to the car.

Once we reached it, Luther stepped around me and opened the passenger door for me.

My heart warmed at the moment of chivalry coming from him. "Thank you," I murmured then slid into the vehicle.

Before closing the door, Luther leaned inside. "I promise I won't hurt you," he said, cupping my cheek. "You have nothing to be nervous about."

I nodded, covering his hand with mine. "Take me to your home, Luther. Show me you."

He nodded once. Closing the door, he headed around to the driver's side.

My phone rang. It vibrated with incoming texts, but I ignored it. I turned off the sound, my heart jumping behind the walls of my rib cage when I realized it was

Miss Vee trying to get a hold of me. I wasn't supposed to head to The Club until the following Saturday night. I still had a week.

Miss Vee: Your Master wants to see you. Tonight.

That was the last text I read before I put my phone away.

I needed this. Whatever Luther had to give me. Although this was probably going to come back to bite me in the ass, my Master would have to wait.

We drove across the city in silence. With Luther's hand on my inner thigh, I couldn't help but wonder what he was thinking about. Or how this night would go. Or what he wanted from me. Would he actually show me parts of himself he had never revealed to anyone else like he said? Or did he just say that to get me to spend the night with him? I wasn't sure anymore but as we drove down a dark street with houses bigger than I had ever seen before in my life, I knew that I was in way over my head.

"You live here?" I asked him, leaning forward and staring out the window in awe. The house was larger than anything I had ever seen before. I was never in this part of the city, so it was like driving into a whole other world. The house was a provincial type home with a grand water fountain sitting in the middle of the circular driveway.

"I do. I inherited my father's estate after he passed away. If I could sell the place though, I would."

I turned to him. "How come?"

"It's too big. My sister used to live here but moved out a year ago. So now it's just me but it's usually filled with people. Men who worked for my father. Business associates. Maids. Cooks."

"Why can't you sell it?"

"My father wrote it into his will that it can't be sold. Not that I ever would but sometimes, the house is a little much. It can be overwhelming at times when you're here by yourself. The house is old."

"So when it's quiet at night and so on, it can be a little unsettling?"

He nodded. "It wouldn't be so bad if I had someone to share this space with."

"Why don't you?" Not that I complained seeing as he was taking me to his home, but I also wondered why he was still single.

"I'm not an easy man to get along with, pet." He pulled us down a long gravel driveway. "The women I've been with didn't stick around very long."

"I'm sorry." My heart ached for him.

He shrugged, pulling the car into the garage. It held three other vehicles: a black SUV, a red sports car, and a black sedan. The garage was huge and could probably fit my whole deli inside it *plus* the vehicles.

"I've never been in a house this big and this is only the garage." My eyes were wide as I took in everything around me.

Luther put the car into park and killed the engine. "Where did you grow up?"

"Here but we had nothing. My dad was an alcoholic and died when we were young after his liver gave up on him. Our mother changed after that. She was happy. I think it was one of those situations where she felt like she had to stay with him for us. But we were too little. We couldn't tell her to leave for herself and that she deserved to be happy." I shrugged. "As much as I miss my mom, I like to think that she died happy. Finally."

Luther nodded. "I get that."

"It's been my brother and I ever since, and even though he drives me crazy...I never would have met you…" My words trailed off, my cheeks heating at the intense scrutiny coming from Luther.

He left the car and came around to my side. Opening the door, he held his hand out.

I placed my hand in his, letting him pull me out of the car and into his arms.

He gripped my hips, backing me up and closing the door at the same time. Leaning down to my ear, his mouth brushed over the shell of it. "I like to think we would have met no matter what. Just maybe not the way we did."

"You mean we could have met like normal people?" I asked, brushing my fingers inside his suit jacket. "Not after you kicked my brother's ass?"

Luther chuckled, the deep sound vibrating through me. "You make me laugh, Lexi. I like that."

"You don't laugh a lot." I leaned back. "Do you?"

"No." His mouth brushed over mine. The touch was soft, sweet, nothing like the man holding me.

Circling my arms around his thick tattooed neck, I deepened the kiss.

He groaned, pushing me up against the car with his pelvis. His tongue slid into my mouth, controlling every waking fiber of my being.

"Luther." I released him, taking a deep breath. "Take me inside."

His lips twitched. "This is a big house, pet. I could spend the night fucking you in every inch of it."

I swallowed hard at the delicious promise and pushed out of his hold. "Where would you start?"

Cupping himself, he stalked toward me. "Here. I'd bend you over the hood of my car and impale that sweet body with my cock so your pussy leaks all over it."

Holy hell.

I shook my head, patting his chest. "Take me inside, Luther." I gave him a small smile.

"Yes." He kissed my temple. "Ma'am."

I laughed.

Luther's phone rang. "Shit." He pulled his cell out of his pocket. "I have to take this. Make yourself at home, pet. It's just you and I here this evening. The staff went home already." He kissed my cheek. "I'll come find you."

Before I could protest, he disappeared down a long hallway, leaving me on my own. The house was so damn big, I was nervous being in it with just him. I didn't know that we would be alone. I was definitely in way over my head.

(Him)

"You're not pissed but you should be." Vanessa's brows narrowed. "What gives?"

"She'll show up at the next meeting. I can't expect her to drop everything for me."

"Then why did you have me text her?" Vanessa asked.

"Because I wanted to see what she would do." I moved my phone, leaned it against the screen of my laptop, and sat back in my leather chair. "She's not like anyone I've ever been with."

"Of course she isn't." Vanessa scrubbed a hand down her face, peering at me from the small video screen on my phone. "You like her. You like her a lot."

"We've already established this," I murmured, tenting my fingers under my chin.

"Does she know about your sessions?"

My chest tightened. "It hasn't come to that yet." And I wasn't sure if it ever would. There was something about Lexi that curbed the dark side of my personality.

"But it will. It always does. What are you going to do if she can't give you what you need?"

"She will." I rubbed my jaw. "She might not like it. Hell, I don't even like it, but she will help me. I know she will." Because it was how she was wired.

"When are you going to reveal yourself to her?"

"Next Saturday. I'll have you place her in the room with the mirrors. She won't be able to get away from me then." A soft knock sounded on the door to my office. I grabbed the phone. "I have to go." I disconnected the video just as the door opened.

SEVENTEEN

Lexi

THE ESTATE WAS GINORMOUS. You could probably fit five of the delis in it. And the backyard, from what I could see, was even bigger. I imagined what it would be like growing up in a place this size. Although with the house being this big, I could imagine that it would get quite lonely at times. It would be hard to run into anyone.

"You have a good night too."

I turned at the sound of Luther's voice. He stood with a man in the foyer. Yeah, because this place had one of those.

Luther shook the man's hand. The man glanced my way and gave me a small smile. He turned on his heel, heading toward the front door while Luther approached me.

The sound of the front door closing made my heart skip a beat. I didn't know that we hadn't been alone. Must have been one of the crew who worked on the estate.

"Everything okay?" I asked Luther when he closed the distance between us.

He gripped my hips, pulled me flush against him, and kissed the side of my neck. "Now it is."

My heart stuttered at the deep growl of his voice. "Luther." I turned my face toward him at the same time he lifted his head. Taking a breath, I placed a hard kiss on his lips.

He groaned, tightened his hold on my lower body, and backed me up until I hit a wall. His large hands roamed up my sides and cupped my breasts. "Tell me what you want, pet."

"Luther," I breathed, my chest rising and falling.

"Tell me." He pushed my breasts together, covering a nipple with his mouth.

Although I was still wearing clothes, I could feel the pressure of his lips right down to my toes.

His teeth grazed over the hard nub, sending a jolt of pleasure straight to my clit. "Tell me."

"I need more," I whispered.

Luther hooked an arm around my middle, throwing me over his shoulder.

I gasped, grabbing onto the waist of his pants. "Luther, what are you doing?"

He didn't answer and carried me through the house to what I had assumed would be his bedroom. But when he dropped me on my feet, he spun me around and pushed me forward. Opening the door in front of me, he gently nudged me. "Light's on the wall on the right. Turn it on."

I grazed my hand over the wall, came into contact with the switch, and flicked on the light. I winced, blinking a few times to clear the spots dancing in my vision. When the room came into view, my eyes widened.

Luther cupped my shoulder. "Everything in this room is used for pleasure. Or pain. Depends on what you're into. We can figure that out together. I told you I wanted to play with you, Lexi. I want you to feel things you've never even dreamed about." He pushed me into the room, shutting the door behind us. "But what I want most, is to control you."

Unable to take my gaze away from the room spread before me, I listened. Luther's words washed over me, promising me hours of pleasure. Maybe even longer. He wanted to play. I already had someone to play with. Something about this situation was familiar. Although I couldn't see my Master, I could see Luther and yet they still reminded me so much of each other.

"Tell me what you see, pet." Luther nudged me forward a couple of steps.

"B-Black carpet. Black walls. Black everything." I took a breath. "So much black."

"What else do you see?" he asked, brushing the scruff of his thin beard against my cheek.

"Items." Most of them looked like benches and a cross sat against the far wall. Miss Vee had taught me what these items were. St. Andrews Cross. Sawhorse. And more.

Luther guided me to a large unit with two doors. "Open it."

I did as I was told, revealing whips, floggers, butt plugs and handcuffs. I reached out to touch them but pulled my hand back.

"You can touch them, pet," Luther murmured in my ear.

I ran my fingers along the soft ends of the floggers. They were leather and all different colors. A shiver trembled through me at what they would feel like running over my skin. Or slapping against my ass.

Luther ran his hand down my spine, brushing his fingers over the cheek of my rear. "Do you know what they are?"

"Floggers," I answered breathlessly.

"They are. And they're all handmade by an artist in Italy. These also haven't been used on anyone, but I would like to use them on you."

I swallowed hard.

"I would like to use everything in this room on you, Lexi." Luther kissed the spot beneath my ear. "I know there's a submissive inside of you. You've always been in control of everything around you. You need someone to take you out of your head, pet."

"You're going to be that someone?" I asked him, my throat going dry.

"If you let me." Luther released me and grabbed my hand. "Any questions you have, just ask."

"Why this? Why not have sex the normal way?"

He tilted his head to the side. "Because I'm not a normal man. I have needs. Unconventional needs. Not many people can satisfy those needs, but I think you can. It'll be a challenge, but I know you're willing to do whatever it takes to make those you care about, happy."

"You think I care about you?" I asked, raising an eyebrow.

"If you didn't, you wouldn't have felt so damn guilty about letting another man fuck you."

My back stiffened. Pulling my hand from his, I walked past him and moved around the room. "I don't know anything about this lifestyle. But I've seen movies." I ran my hand over a blood red bench. Miss Vee hadn't told me what this type of item was. I had a feeling that it was custom-made and not something you would normally see at The Club. Unless it was in a special room and I just hadn't been introduced to it yet. It had two wooden posts on either side of it. The posts had a large hole in the top of them.

"Give me your wrist." Luther held out his hand.

I placed my hand in his.

His fingers wrapped around it and he pulled me toward the post. "Your hand goes in here. And this—" He pushed the top of the post until the hole closed, leaving my wrist locked in the wood. "—closes so you can't get out. You would be completely restrained with your ass in the air for me to do whatever the fuck I want to do."

"I wouldn't be able to move," I whispered, unsure how I felt about that.

"That's the idea." He smirked. "It's a mind fuck but it also builds trust." He lifted the top of the post until the hole became bigger.

I removed my hand, rubbing my wrist. It reminded me of being restrained by my Master. It was the same idea anyway. But this would be different. I would be able to see Luther. I wasn't sure what was worse. Looking into a man's eyes as he controlled me completely or not being able to see him at all.

"Did it hurt?" Luther asked, his brows furrowing.

"No. Not at all." I looked up at him then. "Luther?" I brushed my hand down his chest. "Hey."

His eyes popped to mine. They were dark, stormy, and so damn intense, they took my breath away. Something flashed behind them, but I couldn't figure out what it was. A memory maybe?

"Are you okay?" I asked him.

"I don't want you going to The Club." He grabbed my hand, pulling me against him. "I need...I need you here."

"I am here, Luther." I leaned back. "I'm not going to The Club. Not tonight."

He nodded, that muscle in his jaw ticking.

"What's going on?" I ran my hand up and down his arm.

Luther cupped my cheek, placing a soft peck on my forehead. "So sweet," he murmured. "Forgive me."

Just when I was about to ask what he meant by that, he turned me around and bent me over a nearby bench.

"No." I struggled against him when it reminded me too much of my Master. If Luther wanted me to know him, he would have to show me other parts. I didn't want to know him like this. Not yet.

"Lexi." He pushed against my upper back, keeping me still. "I have to show you this side of me."

"Not right now." Not until I was done at The Club. It was too much. Too soon. Too damn familiar. It fucked with my head.

"Lexi," he snapped, cracking his hand against my ass.

I yelped but it only made me struggle harder.

"Stop fucking moving," he yelled, fisting my hair and pulling my head back. "Stop."

"Please, Luther. I can't...I need you. Just you. Not this."

"Tell me why," he said gently. "Say it."

"Because it's too weird," I confessed.

"Why is it weird?" His hands brushed down the sides of my body, reached the hem of my dress, and lifted the fabric to my hips.

"It reminds me too much of The Club," I blurted.

Luther pulled the dress up and over my head, leaving me in a black lace bra and panty set. "Come with me." He turned, heading to the door and throwing the dress on a nearby red leather chair. "*Now*, pet." He glanced at me over his shoulder. His dark eyes roamed down the length of me before meeting my gaze. "Leave the heels on."

Like a good little girl, I followed him.

The hall we walked down was long and narrow. The carpet was a deep red and the walls were a dark brown. Maybe even black. It looked like Luther had a thing for the color red. Or it had been like this all along and he never changed the design.

Once we reached a set of double doors, still on the main floor of the large house, Luther placed his hands on the doorknobs and glanced at me over his shoulder. "This area is where I spend most of my time if I'm not in my office. Make yourself at home here, Lexi. I'd prefer if you didn't roam the grounds when I'm not with you."

"Why not?"

"Because it isn't safe. The men who come and go from this place are vile human beings." He pushed open the doors. "They make me look like an innocent kitten."

I scoffed, shaking my head. "Right."

"Welcome to my home, pet."

I stepped around him, my eyes widening. "This is all yours?"

He nodded. "Obviously the estate is mine, but I spend most of my time in this area. No one else is allowed in here except for you."

My heart jumped. I took a step forward. The doors led into a sitting area. Again, with dark furniture, blood red carpet, and black walls. The wall to the left was lined with bookshelves. They were filled with leather-bound books. From what I could tell, they looked like original copies. My fingers itched to dance along the spines.

Walking through the sitting area, I stopped in front of another set of doors.

"Open them, Lexi."

I took a breath and did as I was told. Once I stepped into the second room, my gaze landed on a large four-poster bed.

"Get on the bed." Luther brushed his fingers down the length of my spine. "Now, pet."

I turned to him. "Tell me what we're going to do."

He raised an eyebrow. "I suggest listening to me."

"Tit for tat, Luther," I said, ignoring him. "Tell me something. You wanted me to get to know you. I'm standing here in my bra and panties because I listen to you. You seem to know me so well. Let me know you."

"Ask me," he demanded, his voice firm.

I grabbed his hand, brushing my thumb along the star-shaped scar in the middle of his palm. "What happened?"

"I was burnt with a cigarette until I could withstand the pain without screaming. Tell me about your Master."

"Wait." I shook my head. "What? You were burnt? Why?"

"That's not what you asked, Lexi." Luther pulled from my grip and started unbuttoning his black dress shirt. "Tell me about your Master."

"I don't know him," I said, not pressing anymore about his scar. I would ask again but later. Much later.

"How many times has he fucked you?" Luther asked, pulling off his shirt.

My mouth fell open. His torso was lined with tattoos of all intricate designs. I had seen guys covered in ink before, but Luther's skin looked like he was trying to cover the flesh completely.

"Lexi?" Luther tossed his shirt on the bed. "Answer my question."

My gaze popped back to his. "I only had sex with him once."

"Did you enjoy it?" He unbuckled his belt and pulled it out of the loops of his pants with a snap.

"I did," I breathed, my chest rising and falling as I watched Luther strip for me.

"Why?" He unzipped his pants, popping open the button of the fly.

My mouth watered. Dark hair led from his belly button to the treasure beneath his pants. A part of him I had felt. A part of him that had given me so much pleasure in such a short amount of time.

"Tell me, Lexi." Pressing a palm against the center of my chest, he pushed me back against the bed. "Tell me why you enjoyed it."

"B-Because he took my control," I whispered, sitting on the edge of the bed.

Luther smirked. "I told you I would take your control and yet you gave it to him." As quickly as the small smile spread on his face, it disappeared even faster. His voice came out rough, his stance stiff. In a quick move, he pushed me until I was lying back on the mattress.

"Luther." I grabbed his hand.

"What did you enjoy most about giving up your control, Lexi?" He hooked a finger in the side of my panties and pulled. The thin material snapped right off my body.

"I-It was freeing. But I didn't have a choice."

"Are you saying that he fucked you against your will?" he bit out, kneeling between my legs and reached into his pants.

"No. Never. I had to sign a contract. I had to answer questions about what I was willing to try and wouldn't try. I—" My gaze fell to his waist.

Luther pulled out his thick cock, stroking from base to tip. "What are you willing to try, pet?"

I swallowed hard, my throat going dry. "A-Anything."

"Really?" He lined the tip of his cock to my soaked entrance but didn't take it any further. "Have you done anything yet that you didn't like?"

"No."

Luther brushed his thumb along my bottom lip. "You're willing to try anything at least once?"

"Yes." I cried out when he thrust forward, filling me to the brim. "God. Luther."

"So if I wanted to tie you up, whip this beautiful ass and pour wax all over your body, you would let me?" He kissed the corner of my mouth. "At least once?"

I ran my hands down his back, my fingers brushing over bumpy ridges on his skin. "Yes," I whispered, my stomach twisting at the possibility I was feeling scars on his back.

"What about threesomes, pet?" He turned my head until I was staring directly into his dark eyes. "You want to be shared?"

"No." I slid my hands into the back of his pants and cupped his ass, pulling him forward.

He shivered.

"That was the only thing I said no to."

"Hmm…" His hips remained slow, pumping hard and deep. "I've never felt a tighter pussy. You're my drug, pet." He bit my ear lobe. "I'm going to get so fucking high off of you." Luther sat back on his heels, falling free from my body.

My breath caught at the sight before me. His cock glistened with my cum.

"So beautiful." His dark eyes snapped to mine. "Take off your bra."

I sat up, reached behind, and unhooked the back. "Did you want me to leave my heels on?" I asked, throwing the bra to the side.

His lips twitched but he didn't say anything. Instead, he stood, pulled off his pants and knelt back between my spread legs.

"Luther?" I cupped his face.

His eyes fluttered closed. Covering my hand, he pushed his cheek into my palm. "I've never had something as calming as you."

My breath caught. "What do you mean?"

When he opened his eyes, they were dark. Filled with so much lust, my core throbbed for him. Pushing his hips between my legs, he sank into me. "I need...*fuck*..."

Before I could ask anymore questions, his mouth covered mine.

I moaned, snaking my arms around his thick shoulders and running my fingers through his hair. His hips picked up speed, owning me with each soul-shattering thrust.

Pleasure seeped through me. A warmth spread from my toes, heating every inch of my skin. Our breathing became ragged.

"Harder," I begged against his mouth. "Please."

He growled, releasing my lips with a smack and flipped me onto my stomach. "On all fours. *Now.*"

I pushed to all fours when he thrust violently inside of me. A scream fell from my lips.

"Did your Master fuck you like this, pet?" Luther asked, fisting my hair in his hand and pulling my head back. "Or was it gentle and sweet?"

"It was rough." I gripped the blankets in my hands, letting this man own every inch of me.

"How many times did he make you come?" Luther sunk his teeth into my shoulder.

"I can't remember."

"Was it three times? Less? More?" He pulled my head back even more. "Tell me, Lexi."

"Twice maybe. I can't...I don't know. Please, Luther. I don't want to talk about it."

"We're going to talk about it, pet. You're going to tell me every detail." He shoved me forward, pressing his hand into the back of my neck and pushing my face against the mattress.

"And if I don't?" I threw back at him.

He chuckled, the sound dark and evil. "Try me, pet."

It didn't matter that we weren't in Luther's play room. No. Because he had everything in his bedroom. After I challenged him, he flipped me onto my back and wrapped both hands around my throat.

"Beg, pet. Beg and I'll let you fucking breathe." Luther's pupils dilated, his hips pushing between my spread legs. He thrust into me hard and deep, taking all of the control from my very being. Even though I wasn't bound, and he didn't use any toys, he didn't need to. Not when he used his body and his words to control and take from me what he craved.

I grabbed his wrists, my eyes rolling into the back of my head at how good he was making me feel. I lifted my hips, meeting him thrust for every delicious thrust.

"You crave it." He leaned down to my ear, his hot breath scorching the side of my face. "You like it dark, Lexi."

"I don't know what I like," I whispered through clenched teeth, a low moan escaping me.

"Right." He chuckled. "My hands are wrapped around your throat and your cunt is fucking soaked for me."

"I…" Damnit. He was right. I didn't know if that meant something was wrong with me, but I didn't have a chance to think about it when Luther released my throat and reached between our joined bodies. His finger came into contact with my clit.

I jumped, a jolt of electricity shooting through me.

"I won't tie you up now, pet, but I will. I will show you what I like. What I need." Luther placed a soft peck on my forehead. "And I'll make sure you crave it just as much as I do."

EIGHTEEN

Lexi

"YOUR MASTER IS PISSED."

I bit back an eyeroll and followed Miss Vee down the long hall. It had been several days since I'd spent the night with Luther at his estate. After he fucked me, he left me alone for the rest of the night. I wasn't sure why and I wanted to question him on it, but something happened in that short amount of time. It threw me off. His mood had changed rather quickly. When I showered, he went off and did something that caused him to become even grumpier than usual.

"You okay?" I asked him, running the towel through my hair.

Luther pulled the sheets back and slid into the bed.

I joined him.

He wrapped his arm around my waist.

I snuggled into him.

His tense body relaxed but something was still very wrong.

"Lexi."

I jumped.

"You're distracted." Miss Vee frowned. "You're seeing someone. Aren't you?"

"No." My cheeks burned.

"Right. Well come on then." Miss Vee stopped at a set of double doors. "He asked me to put you in here. Put on your blindfold, Lexi."

Taking a breath, I did as I was told. My heart started racing.

A warm body came up behind me. A rough calloused hand cupped my shoulder and slid softly down my arm. The scent of spice wafted into my nose.

Master.

It was a sweet scent, almost like it was mixed with a type of fruit. Still manly but not something I had ever come across before.

My breathing picked up. My hands twitched, aching to touch him but I didn't. I wouldn't for fear that he would pull away.

He pushed me forward, the sound of the doors shutting behind me sent a flush of heat washing over every inch of me.

My Master released me, brushing his hand over my hip and moving to my front. Suddenly, a hot mouth captured mine in a hard, bruising kiss. The blindfold was ripped off of my head.

I moaned, taking his tongue deeper into my mouth. My stomach flipped. Something struck me as odd about the kiss. It was rough and needy, but proved a point just the same.

He cupped my ass, lifted me in his arms, and lowered me to the ground. He released me, gripping my jaw and turning my head.

"Open your eyes," he demanded in a low voice as he reached between us.

My eyes fluttered open at the same time he reached beneath my dress and pulled my panties down my legs. I blinked once. Twice. I was staring at a mirror that lined the wall. A man towered over me, my Master, the one who had invaded my dreams as much as Luther. This man…he was actually…*Luther.*

"No," I whispered. I was in shock. Maybe I was dreaming.

Luther pulled me further under him and was inside me in one smooth thrust.

That seemed to snap me out of it. I struggled beneath him. "Get off of me. Get off. Stop this. Stop."

But instead of listening to me, Luther fisted my hair, holding my head in place, and stared at our reflection in the mirror. "That's not your safeword, pet. You do remember what your safeword is, don't you?"

"Charlie," I whispered, my heart pounding in my ears.

"That's correct." He kissed my cheek, his hips pumping slow and deep. "Tell me who you see, Lexi." His hand gripped my hair while his other held my jaw. "Tell me."

My blood burned through me. I tried shoving him off of me, but I couldn't move.

"Say my name, pet," he growled, pulling my head back even more. "Say it."

"Fuck you," I bit out through clenched teeth.

Luther kept his eyes locked with mine in the reflection of us. "Say my fucking name. Say who's deep inside you right now. Say who's been fucking you all along. Say it, Lexi." He cracked a hand against the cheek of my ass. "*Say it.*"

Keeping my mouth closed, I shook my head. This wasn't happening. This couldn't be happening. All this time I thought I was selling my body to a stranger to keep my brother safe when really, I had been selling it to the man who wanted him dead in the first place.

"I hate you," I murmured, shoving my head out of his grip and turning around. "You're a bastard. Is this the only way you can get a woman, Luther? You trick them into fucking you?"

His brows narrowed, his cheeks turning a mottled pink. "Careful, little girl. You are in no position to be insulting me right now."

"No?" I slapped him but that only made him fuck me harder and faster. I slapped him again.

A wicked grin spread on his face. He pulled out of me, flipped me onto my stomach, and slammed back inside me.

I cried out, trying to shove away from him but his hold on me was too tight.

"You want me to stop, you know what to say. That is what you agreed to when you signed that contract." Luther cupped my jaw, his dark eyes meeting mine in the mirror. "Or did you not read it?"

I read it. I read every inch of that damn contract, but I never thought my Master would end up being Luther. Or that I would need to use my safeword.

"You're mine, pet. You've always been mine. This pretty little cunt craves my cock. Doesn't it?"

Much to my dismay, my core clenched around him at his dirty words.

His grin grew.

With his fingers wrapped around my throat and his cock deep in my body, I was lost to him. As pissed as I was, I pushed back against him, taking him even deeper. A groan passed between us but I wasn't sure who made the sound.

"That's it, Lexi. Take my cock deep. You're a little slut, aren't you? Selling your body for sex. So damn desperate to keep your bastard brother alive."

I dropped my head, unable to take his burning stare any longer.

Agony ripped through my skull when Luther tugged my head back.

I screamed, the strands of hair ripping free.

"You will look at me when I'm fucking you, Lexi. You're going to hear what I have to say."

"Fuck you," I ground out.

"Oh, I am, little girl. I'm fucking you good and hard. It's what you like, isn't it? How does it feel knowing that all this time, you've been surrendering your control to me? The man who wants your brother dead?"

"Please stop this," I whispered, the pleasure he was forcing out of me, rippling down my spine.

Luther sat back on his heels, wrapping his tattooed arms around my body. "Even though it's me you've been fucking this whole time, it pisses me off that you developed feelings for your *Master*."

"I didn't want to." I turned in his arms, surprised that he released me enough that I could straddle him. "I wanted you. This whole time. But I'm not getting anything from you. With my Master, with that part of you, you showed me more."

Luther frowned.

Brushing my fingers over his cheek, I stood.

His cock was an angry shade of red, the skin glistening with the juices from my body.

I stepped between his legs, not overly sure what I was doing anymore. I was pissed that he kept this kind of secret from me, but I was curious even more as to why.

"Tell me why you kept this from me," I demanded.

Luther wrapped his hand around my calf, placing a soft peck on my knee. "It was the only way I could have you, but I wasn't expecting this to turn into something more." He ran both hands up the back of my legs, cupped my ass and pulled me toward him. "I wasn't expecting to need you in ways I've never needed someone before."

"Luther," I breathed, running my fingers through his dark hair.

"And I sure as hell wasn't expecting you to control me the way you do." He swiped his tongue over my clit.

I shivered, latching onto his head. "I-I don't control you."

He chuckled, blowing a hot stream of air over my mound. "Yeah. You do, Lexi. In more ways than I care to admit." Before I had a chance to respond, his mouth was on me.

I swallowed a gasp.

His tongue slid inside me, controlling the very sounds leaving my lips. Closing his lips around my throbbing clit, he sucked and pulled until his name left my lips on a shattered scream.

"That's right, Lexi. Scream my name. Let me hear who's controlling you. Who's your fucking Master?"

I groaned, undulating my hips against his face.

Luther released my lower body and shoved me to the ground. "I don't give a shit how pissed you are." He slammed back into me. "You're mine. You've always been mine."

"Get off me," I demanded, struggling beneath him.

"Lexi." Luther's voice washed over me, his hands running down my sides. "Use your damn safeword."

"Stop." I pushed away from him and grabbed my panties. Rising to my feet, I slipped them back on and smoothed down my dress.

"Lexi," Luther said gently. "I didn't want it to be this way."

"Then why didn't you tell me who you were?" I yelled, glaring at him. "You said after spending the night with you, I would want more. You were right. I did want more. Why didn't you tell me then that you were pretending to be my Master?"

"I wasn't pretending." Luther stood from the floor and righted his pants. "All of this was real. My feelings for you."

"Your feelings for me." I scoffed. "Right. You wanted sex. That was it. You beat my brother within an inch of his life and yet I still let you fuck me. You convinced me that The Club could help me pay you back." I shook my head. "God, I'm so stupid."

"No. You're not. The Club has helped you."

"How, Luther?" I snapped. "How has The Club helped me?"

His jaw clenched, his dark brows narrowing in the center. He tucked his dress shirt back into his pants. "I tried stopping myself from fucking you. I didn't want it to happen in your office."

"So, it's my fault?" I raised an eyebrow.

"What?" His eyes widened. "Fuck. No. It's my fault. I can't control myself around you." He took a step toward me.

"Don't." I held my hand up, stopping him. "Stay there. I can't deal with this right now. I'm done. This?" I waved a finger between us. "Is not happening. Ever again."

Much to my surprise, he laughed. The smug asshole actually fucking laughed.

"Alright, pet." Luther did up his pants and fixed the collar of his shirt. "I stopped even though you didn't use your safeword like you were taught. But you go ahead and keep telling yourself that this is done."

"I'm serious." Although I said the words, I wasn't so sure I believed them myself.

"Sure. I believe you." He came toward me.

I backed up until I hit the wall. "Luther."

"You keep telling yourself that there's nothing between us. That you can resist me. That you don't want me. That this will never happen again." He placed a hand on either side of my head. "You keep telling yourself that one look from me and you don't want to fall to your knees and beg me to do whatever I want to you."

I glared up at him.

He caged me in, leaning down to my ear. "You keep telling yourself that one command from me and your body doesn't become wet. Deny it all you want, Lexi. You want me. You will always want me. Because it's exciting. Dangerous. You've lived by the rules your whole entire life."

"I have no idea what you're talking about." But he was right. I had always played it safe. Maybe that was why I was so damn attracted to him.

"Sure, pet." He kissed my cheek. "Deny it all you want but I know you can't resist me." He pulled away, gave me a smirk, and left the room.

A breath escaped me. Sliding down the wall, I scrubbed a hand down my face. He was right. God was he ever right.

(Luther)

"You did *what?*"

I almost laughed at my sister's outburst but thought better of it. "I revealed who I was. I told you I was doing that."

"I thought I had more time." Vanessa began pacing. "So what does this mean? Does she know you own this club? Does she know that the money we've been paying her has been coming back to us?"

I sat back in the leather chair. "No. But I'm sure she'll figure it out."

Vanessa shook her head. "I can't believe this. Her brother still owes money. What does this mean? You can't expect her to show up here again."

"I'll deal with it when the time comes."

"You'll deal with it when the time comes," Vanessa repeated. "This isn't right. She's innocent. Her brother—"

"You care for her." I sat forward. "Should I be jealous?"

Vanessa rolled her eyes. "Sorry big brother. I don't want your sloppy seconds, but I don't want her hurt. She doesn't deserve this shit."

"No. She doesn't." I had to figure out a way to make her forgive me. Was there something that could help me break down the walls she had built? The deli. An idea came to me. I just hoped it would help me get through to Lexi before it was too late.

NINETEEN

Lexi

IT HAD BEEN A week since Luther revealed who he truly was. Seven damn days since I found out he was my Master. And ever since then, I couldn't get him out of my head. It had been bad before I found out who he was, but it was even worse now since the big reveal.

I hadn't received a text from Miss Vee either since then. I had so many questions, but I was still pissed at Luther. I didn't want to contact him and let him think I had forgiven him. I sighed, rubbing the back of my neck.

"Uh…Lexi?"

I turned, finding Charlie standing at the entrance to the kitchen.

"You might want to come and see this." He headed to the back of the deli.

"Will you watch the counter?" I asked one of the waitresses.

"Of course." She gave me a small smile and took over cleaning and serving customers.

Heading to the back, I stopped suddenly. Two men were pushing a large stainless-steel fridge up against the wall. That was when I noticed the stove. My heart thumped hard behind the walls of my rib cage. The oven was huge. Larger than I had ever imagined it would be in person.

"What's going on?" I asked, stepping in front of it and running my hands along the sleek edges.

"These were delivered for you, ma'am," one of the men told me. He flipped through a clipboard. "You are Lexi Adams?"

I frowned. "I am but I never ordered these." What the hell was going on?

"We know." The younger man of the two opened the fridge. "We figured this might help answer your questions."

My heart raced. A large bouquet of red roses sat on the middle shelf inside the fridge.

"Lexi? Is that from Luther?" Charlie asked.

I ignored the accusatory glare from him and headed to the fridge. I thanked the men, left them a tip, and pulled the flowers from the fridge. The sweet scent of the roses wafted around me.

"There's a card." Charlie pulled a small envelope that had been placed inside the bouquet.

"Thank you." I took it from him. "Will you ask one of the staff to turn on the appliances in a few hours and make sure everything works, please? I just need a moment." I headed to the office before he could protest and ask any more questions.

Closing the door behind me, I locked it and placed the flowers on top of the desk. Opening the envelope, I grazed my thumb over the beautiful script on the small black card.

My dearest pet,
I'm sorry for everything. I hope the appliances and flowers will be a start to your forgiveness that I don't deserve, but crave just the same.
I will be awaiting your call.
Your Master

My stomach tumbled.

I was half tempted to throw the flowers out but I couldn't find it in my heart to do so.

Before I could think twice about it, I called Luther.

"Pet."

My body flushed at hearing his deep voice.

"Thank you for the flowers and the appliances but I can't pay you back."

"I don't expect you to pay me back, Lexi. It's my present to you."

I hesitated. "Why?"

"I care for you. I know you have questions. I'm willing to answer those questions but not over the phone. Come to The Club tonight. I'll be there, working."

"Working?" I repeated, gripping the phone tight in my hand.

"Lexi." He paused. "I own The Club."

Of course he did. "And Miss Vee?"

"She's my sister."

Pinching the bridge of my nose, I blew out a slow breath. "All this time—"

"Come to The Club tonight. I'm not answering any more of your questions over the phone. It's not safe, pet." Luther hung up, the sound of the call disconnecting, vibrating through me.

"It's not safe, pet."

What the hell was I getting myself into?

After Luther hung up, I read the card from him over and over. He was sorry. About everything. Could I believe him? I wanted to. God, did I want to. But these feelings I had for him scared the shit out of me. Did I want to take that chance?

I hardly knew him. But I found that I wanted to. I wanted to know everything. Where he grew up. What his childhood was like. I knew his father had passed but was he a good dad? Did he care for both Luther and Vanessa like he should? Why was Luther paranoid? And what the hell did my brother do to piss him off?

A hard knock on the door to my office startled me.

"Lexi." My brother knocked again.

"What?" I pulled open the door.

"What's going on?" He pushed me back and shut the door behind him. "You're sleeping with Luther, aren't you?"

"I have no idea what you're talking about." I was not having this conversation with my brother.

"Lexi, you do know who he is right?" Charlie's brows narrowed in the center. "You also remember how you met him? He kicked my ass. He wanted me fucking dead. He probably still does. But you don't give a shit about that, do you?"

"Excuse me?" I placed my hands on my hips, glaring up at him.

His pupils dilated, his body swaying.

I frowned. "Are you high?"

"No." He waved a hand in front of him. "I don't do that shit."

"Right." I grabbed his arm. "What's going on with you?"

Charlie shoved out of my grip. "Nothing. Why don't you go run along to your boyfriend seeing as that's all you care about."

"Me?" I laughed. "Who the hell has hardly been home the past few weeks? Who told me to contact The Club? Who keeps asking me if I've made payments and how much we still owe Luther? Who the hell is the one that put us in this situation in the first place? Oh yeah. That's right. It was you. So fuck you, Charlie. You can go to hell." I stormed past him, threw open the door, and stomped to the back of the deli. I sent one of the waitresses a text, telling her I was calling it a day and that something had come up. When really, I needed to get away from my brother before I was the one who murdered him instead of Luther.

I left the deli abruptly, walking the few blocks to The Club. Once I arrived at the alleyway leading to the building that held so many firsts for me, I paused. This would be the first time I would be here knowing who my Master was. Could I do this knowing that he was in fact Luther? Knowing that Luther had kept this huge secret from me?

My phone vibrated in my bag. Pulling it out of the inner pocket, I answered. "What do you want, Charlie?"

"I want to make sure that you're okay," he mumbled.

"I'm fine. Even though I have a dickhead for a brother."

"Listen, I'm sorry about that." He sighed. "The things I said. I just want you safe. It's fucking with my head knowing you're sleeping with the guy who's threatened my life."

"Well if you didn't give him reason to threaten you, I'm sure none of that would have happened." I could not believe I had justified Luther's reasoning for threatening my brother. God, what the hell was wrong with me?

"You really have no idea who you're sleeping with, do you?"

"I'm not talking about this with you." But I knew I was going to find out. One way or another, I would make Luther tell me about him.

"You're playing with fire, Lexi. Don't say I didn't warn you." Charlie disconnected the call before I could argue. Even though he was right, I was a big girl. I couldn't help the fact that my heart wanted more. That it wanted to figure out what made Luther tick. Or why he turned out the way he did. I wanted to know about his first tattoo. Everything that made up Luther Knight. I wanted it all.

When I reached the door, I lifted my hand to knock but it opened before I even got a chance to. My eyes widened at Luther standing in the doorway.

He crossed his thick arms under his broad chest, leaning against the doorjamb.

My mouth watered.

The tailored suit hugged every inch of him like a second layer of skin. The dark scruff on his jaw had grown in some since the last time I saw him.

"Pet," came his curt reply.

"Hi, Luther," I said, my voice shaking.

He smirked, stepping back. "Come in."

"I wasn't expecting you to answer. I thought it would have been Miss Vee." I stepped over the threshold.

"My sister is preoccupied," he said, closing the door behind me.

"I still can't believe she's your sister."

"Half-sister to be technical. We have the same father but different mothers. My mother died when I was little. My father met a new woman and they had Vanessa."

"Oh." My chest tightened. "That's sad."

"It is what it is." Luther took a step toward me. "You look good, pet."

I swallowed hard. "So do you."

He pinched my chin, placing a soft peck on my forehead. "Did you like your present?"

"Yes." I stepped back, my heart fluttering at the sweet scent of spice wafting into my nose. "But you didn't have to do that."

"I know. I wanted to." He held out his hand. "Let me give you a tour."

"Miss Vee did that already," I reminded him.

"She didn't give you a tour of the whole place." He paused. "I won't hurt you, Lexi. Not like before."

"You mean, not like when you kept who you were from me?"

"That's right." He leaned down to my ear. "But I know you like a little pain mixed with your pleasure. I have fucked your ass, remember? Your moans made me so fucking hard, pet. I never thought you'd be into that, but you were, and I plan on making you feel that sweet pain again. And again." He kissed my cheek, releasing me. "Coming?" he asked, holding his hand out again.

Heat spread throughout every inch of me. Blowing out a slow breath, I ignored the warning in my head. That little voice telling me that Luther was bad for me or that he would break my heart. Instead, I placed my hand in his.

A wicked grin spread on his face as he wrapped his fingers around mine.

My heart picked up speed.

I realized then that there were many sides to Luther and I had a feeling that I hadn't seen all of them. But this side, the side leading me down the hall towards the unknown parts of the club I hadn't been to yet, this side was lethal. Because I knew that one command from him and I would submit. No matter what.

TWENTY

Lexi

"THIS PLACE ISN'T LIKE your romance books or any of the movies you've seen," Luther explained, keeping hold of my hand in a firm but gentle grip.

"How do you know if I've watched those movies or read those kinds of books? I could like action or horror." It wasn't true, but he shouldn't have assumed.

"Right, pet." He chuckled. "And I like romantic comedies."

"You do?" I asked, my eyes widening.

His laugh deepened.

I giggled. "I like horror movies but yeah, romance is my jam."

Luther grinned, tapping my nose. "I know."

"I haven't read a good romance book in a while though. Or any book for that matter." Life got in the way when I needed those books the most. It wasn't fair if you asked me.

"Life's too busy sometimes." Luther cleared his throat. "Listen, whatever you see beyond these doors is private and confidential. I know you signed a waiver but I'm just reminding you. We have to protect our members. And that includes you."

I nodded. "I understand."

"Alright." Luther brushed the back of his hand down my cheek. "Ready, pet?"

"I just have one question first. What happened to the money I was paying you?"

"I've set it aside. I don't need it." He reached into his pants pocket and pulled out a wallet. "I know you won't accept this now, but you will. In time." He handed me a check.

I coughed, my eyes widening at the number staring up at me. "Y-You've kept the money for me?"

Luther nodded. "Of course. Like I said, I don't need it."

"I can't accept this." I handed it back to him.

"I know." He slipped the check back into his wallet. "But it doesn't matter because that money's yours. You earned it. So whenever you can accept it, it's ready for you."

"What about my brother owing you money?"

"Lexi." Luther's hard stare met mine. "I'll answer any questions you have about you and I and this place, but I'll be damned if I'm going to let a conversation about your brother ruin this evening. So answer my question, are you ready?"

"Fine." I stepped in front of him. "I will find out either way."

"I know you will," he mumbled. "I know."

(Luther)

I never wanted to show her the check, knowing she wouldn't take it in the first place. She was a good person like that. But I also hadn't wanted to taint tonight with talk of her brother. He was a dick. Through and through. I could deal with that shit later on. Right now, I needed to worry about making Lexi forgive me.

Having her with me in my club, satisfied me more than I thought it would. But it still didn't mean I would let my guard down. It wasn't her I was worried about. It was everyone else. Her brother. My men. The vile bastards who wanted me dead. Same shit, different day.

With Lexi at my side, we walked into the main part of the club where everyone mingled and socialized. To an outsider, it looked like any other social gathering. Some men wore suits while others dressed more casually in dress pants and polo shirts. The women wore dresses, skirts, anything that they deemed comfortable but professional.

Lexi laughed, her cheeks reddening.

"You were expecting leather and chains, weren't you?" I asked her, cupping her nape.

"Yeah." She shrugged. "I can't help it, it's what I've seen on the Internet."

"Ah but, pet. Just because there aren't any whips and chains in this room, doesn't mean you won't see them later on." I stepped behind her, leaning down to her ear. "I have a feeling you would like my whip," I purred, running my hands down her bare arms. "The feel of the leather tip slicing across your skin. It would give your tender flesh a gentle nip, not hurting too much but letting you know who your true Master is."

Lexi shivered.

"Would you like that, pet?" I kissed the spot beneath her ear. "Do you want to feel my whip?"

She swallowed, her throat working at the movement. "Yes. I-I think I want to try that."

My dick stirred, jumping against the fly of my pants. This woman was something else. She tested me and pushed her limits along with my own. She was willing to try anything once and I couldn't wait to explore those sexual desires with her.

"What would you say if I told you that I wanted you to whip me?" I asked, needing to test the waters.

"What?" She spun around. "I'm not dominant. At all."

"It's not about dominance." I slid my hand into the back of her hair. "It's about needing to give up control just for a moment. Give me half an hour and I'm good." I shook my head, not making any sense. "It's just a question, pet. That's all."

Her brows narrowed in the center. "If you need that...I..." She shrugged. "I guess I could try for you."

My dick leaked even more. This woman was damn near perfect. I wasn't a submissive man. Not that I had anything against it. It just wasn't how I was wired. But unfortunately for me, the way I received my scars turned me into a masochist at the same time.

"Luther?" Lexi placed her hands on my chest. "What do you need?"

"Why are you so fucking perfect?" I captured her mouth in a bruising kiss.

"I'm not," she whispered against my lips.

The fact alone that she wanted to help me with my damn sessions, stirred something dark and feral inside of me. But I was good. For now. It wouldn't need to happen. Not yet anyway. But something told me that it would eventually.

Before I fucked her out in the open, I grabbed her hand and led her to the bar at the back of the large room.

"One drink, Lexi," I told her, holding her hand as she slid onto the stool. "I need you sober for the things I want to do later on."

She nodded. "Okay."

"What would you like?" Geoff Cole, The Club's regular bartender, asked Lexi.

"Just a glass of your house wine please," Lexi answered, keeping her hand in mine.

"Red or white?" Geoff's gaze flicked to mine.

"White please."

Geoff nodded. "The usual, Luther?"

"Please," I told him.

He nodded again and went about making our drinks.

Lexi's jaw clenched, her eyes flicking back and forth in front of her. She shifted on the stool.

"Don't be nervous." I brought our joined hands up to my mouth, kissing her palm.

She blew out a slow breath, her cheeks reddening even more. "It's safe here? You said that being out in public is hard for you. Or that's what I got from it anyway."

"It's safe, pet." I brushed my thumb down the length of her jaw. "Nothing will happen to you."

"I don't want anything to happen to you either, Luther." She pressed her lips into a firm line. "I mean that."

My heart stuttered. Who the hell was this woman that I was becoming addicted to so suddenly? Something about her made me latch on. I couldn't get enough. No matter how much my sister told me it wasn't smart or right and all that shit, I wanted more. But I wanted to still kick Charlie's ass. Or maybe I should thank him first and then kick his ass.

My phone vibrated.

Geoff placed our drinks on the counter in front of us.

While Lexi drank her wine, I checked my cell.

Unknown: You with my sister?

I frowned.

Me: You get a new phone, Charlie? Does it make you feel like a man now? You know I can track you down no matter where you call or text me from.

Unknown: Just answer my question, asshole.

My jaw clenched.

Me: Your sister is keeping you alive. But don't push me. I don't like being taken advantage of.

Unknown: I'm not scared of you.

Me: Right. That's what you were saying when you pissed yourself after I held a gun to your head? That's what I thought. Stop being a pussy, Charlie. Why don't you tell your sister who you really are.

Unknown: Fuck you.

Me: Sorry. I only like pussy.

And your sister's pussy is the only one I crave.

Unknown: You better not hurt her.

Me: It won't be me doing shit.

He was going to hurt her. I would bet my whole life savings and everything I was worth, on that fact alone. Charlie was desperate and desperate people did stupid things and made mistakes. I just hoped I would be there to protect Lexi from it.

TWENTY-ONE

"ARE YOU OKAY?" I asked Luther.

He stuffed his phone into the pocket on the inside of his suit jacket and gave me a small smile. "I am now."

My cheeks burned. It had amazed me how one moment he could be lethal and the next, sweet and gentle. He looked at me like I was the only thing that existed in his world.

Finishing the last bit of wine, I placed the empty glass on the bar and slid off the stool. "Are you sure you're okay?" I asked Luther, running a finger along the tattoos on the side of his neck.

His dark eyes pierced into mine. "I don't like being teased, pet. If you want something, say it."

I glanced around the room. People milled about. The social gathering looked like any other party but if you really looked, you could see who the Dom was and who was the submissive.

Luther wrapped his arm around my middle. "Lexi, tell me what you want."

"You, Luther." I turned back to him. "I want you."

He stood, grabbed my hand, and led me out of the large room. We headed down a long hall that held scene rooms on either side. The curtains were closed but every so often you could see shadows moving about behind them. It didn't take a rocket scientist to figure out what they were doing.

"After three in the morning is when the curtains open if they so desire. That's usually when the voyeurs like to come out and play."

I looked up at Luther. "Voyeurs?"

"People who like to watch." Luther stopped outside a large window. "But this is one-way glass. They can't see us, but we can see them. So they won't actually know if they're being watched or not. It makes it more exciting that way."

"I'm not sure if I would enjoy being watched. I do like the idea of possibly being caught though."

Luther swiped his card through the key lock. "Don't worry, pet. Voyeurism isn't my thing. I'm a private man. And I also get jealous very quickly. I wouldn't want anyone watching you come apart for me."

"Good." I wrapped a hand around his forearm. "Because I wouldn't want anyone watching you either."

His eyes darkened. "Jealous, pet?"

"Yes," I said without missing a beat. "You're beautiful when you let yourself go."

Something flashed behind his eyes. "Let's go." He pushed open the door, pulling me along with him.

I followed behind him. My eyes widened when we entered the large room. It was red. The carpet. The walls. The ceiling. But the furniture was black. It held a large four-poster bed that sat against the far wall across from us. A cabinet sat to the right. And another door was on the left.

"That door leads to a bathroom. It has a shower, a bath, and everything else you need to clean yourself up."

"After you make me dirty?" I asked him.

He gave me a wicked grin. "Yeah, pet." He moved behind me, closing the door and clicking the lock into place. "After I make you filthy."

I shivered at the deep voice in my ear.

"Strip and get on the bed."

My heart jumped, and I did as I was told. I knelt on the bed, waiting for him.

"Close your eyes," he demanded, his voice low.

My eyes fluttered closed. I felt him before he neared me. The scent of his cologne was thick in the air, making my nose tingle. My body wept, ready and willing to take him however he wanted me.

A firm hand cupped my cheek. "You're so fucking beautiful."

I leaned into his palm.

Luther moved his hand to my nape, fisted my hair, and tugged my head back.

My knees spread at the rough movement, the touch forcing a moan from my lips.

A dark chuckle escaped him, washing over me. It was my favorite sound. This man. This person who knew every inch of my soul and made it his own toy to play with.

He was the Master and I was the puppet. He controlled the strings and I danced. Willingly.

A hot mouth captured mine in a firm kiss. His tongue slipped between my lips, forcing a groan from us both. His free hand trailed down the length of my torso, stopping just above my mound. His fingers tickled the sensitive flesh.

My chest rose and fell with ragged breaths. My knees spread even more. My fingers dug into the blankets I knelt on.

Moving his fingers lower, Luther ran them along my soaked center.

I panted, undulating my hips toward him.

"So greedy, pet." He placed a soft peck on my forehead. "Look at me."

My eyes popped open.

"Your safeword is *Charlie*."

I looked away.

In a quick move, Luther cupped my jaw, forcing me to meet his hard stare. "No. You will not look away from me."

"Don't be an asshole then," I bit out, shoving my head out of his grip.

"Ah, pet." He smirked. "You haven't seen anything yet. Keep being a little brat and I'll hold back all of your orgasms from you. Eventually it will hurt, and you will sob, begging me for a release. Is that what you want?"

"No but you don't need to be a dick." I pushed onto my knees. "You can be dominant without being an asshole," I whispered, running my fingers through his hair. "You can control me without—" I moaned when he thrust his fingers inside of me. "—being…"

Luther bit my chin. "Without being what, Lexi?" he murmured.

"God." I grabbed his hand that was between my legs, pushed it higher, and circled my hips back and forth. "I…Luther." I covered his mouth with mine, slipping my tongue between his lips and letting him control every waking thought. Every inch of my body belonged to him.

He was an asshole but God, I loved the way he made me feel.

He pumped his hand between my legs, thrusting hard and deep.

I reached between us, pulling his shirt from his pants and unbuttoning it. I needed to feel him. To see every inch of him come alive as he shoved us both over the edge to the point of madness.

Breaking the kiss, I pushed his shirt off his strong shoulders. My mouth watered. His inked torso flexed beneath my touch.

Luther pulled his hand from between my legs and tossed the fabric to the floor.

I reached for his belt and pulled him against me.

"Something you want, pet?" he asked, placing soft bites on my neck.

"God, yes. You. Every inch of you. Please, Luther."

Running his free hand down the length of my spine, he cupped my ass and pushed me onto my back. He stuck his fingers that had been inside me in his mouth and sucked them clean. "Fucking tasty." His dark eyes were wild with lust. Hooking his arms around my thighs, he pulled me to the edge of the bed. He bent over, picking up something off the floor.

My eyes widened when he straightened, holding a leather shackle in his hand.

Without waiting for me to say anything, he wrapped the leather around my ankle and grabbed my hand, doing the same with my wrist. Once it was locked and secure, I couldn't move.

With the back of his hand, he brushed me from my ankle to my inner thigh, skipped my center, and ran it up my other leg. He bent again, grabbed another shackle and repeated the movement with my left ankle and wrist.

"Absolutely perfect." Luther undid his belt and wrapped a hand around my ankle. Placing a soft peck on my calf, he brushed his lips up my leg.

The tiny hairs on my body tingled. My core clenched, becoming wetter the closer he got to where I wanted him most.

"I can smell you, pet." He sunk his teeth into my inner thigh.

"Please," I whispered, shaking beneath him.

Luther slid his pants down his legs, standing naked before me. His hard cock stood proud, pointing up to his belly button. Wrapping his hand around the thick length, he stroked it a few times before crouching to the floor once again.

"Luther," I whined.

"Patience, Lexi." He stood, holding what I could only assume was a vibrator in his hand. "Have you ever seen one of these before?"

I shook my head. "No."

"Trust me." A wicked grin spread on his face. "You'll enjoy this."

(Luther)

Lexi was spread open for me. She was wet, ripe, and utterly perfect.

Holding the Hitachi Wand, I turned it on and pressed it against her lower stomach. She gasped, her eyes widening. The wand wasn't even on full speed yet, but I'd bet my life savings that she could feel the vibrations throughout.

"Beg, pet," I demanded, wrapping my free hand around my cock.

"Fuck me, Luther," she whispered, her wide eyes darkening with lust.

Lining up the tip of my dick with her soaked center, I pressed the wand against her clit at the same time I thrust into her in a smooth move.

Lexi cried out, arching beneath me. Her pussy gripped me tight, sucking me in even deeper. Holding the wand against her, I turned up the power. I wanted her to break. I wanted her to be so far gone that with one thrust of my cock and she would explode. I wanted her to make a fucking mess.

"Luther," she whined, her chest rising and falling with ragged breaths.

I leaned over her and covered her mouth with mine.

She sighed, opening instantly to me.

"So fucking good, pet," I whispered against her lips. "Come for me. Squirt this sweet honey all over me."

She moaned.

Thrusting hard and deep, I forced her over that edge. "Come, pet."

Lexi gasped.

I swallowed her scream, her body trembling and shaking beneath me, but I didn't let up. I pressed the wand firmer against her clit.

"Luther." She cried out.

Leaning back, I pressed my other hand against her chest and fucked her hard and deep. "Come again."

"I can't," she whined.

"Baby, you've only had one orgasm. That's not enough." I slammed into her. "Come. *Now.*"

Her eyes rolled into the back of her head, incoherent sounds left her lips. Her body gushed, erupting with the release I let her have. Pulling free from her body, I kept the wand against her clit. She screamed, another powerful gush leaving her body.

"Oh God. Luther, please." A sheen of sweat coated her skin, her cheeks became flushed.

Turning the wand off, I placed it on the bed and lowered to my knees.

Her wide eyes watched me.

I winked and covered her core with my mouth.

Another cry left her.

The sweet acidic taste of her pussy coated my tongue. "So fucking good," I growled, thrusting my tongue in and out of her sex.

"Luther," she panted. "Please. I can't. I can't take anymore."

I released her with a wet smack and slid my cock back into her tight heat.

She whimpered, staring up at me.

Leaning over her, I rested my elbows on either side of her head. "You're beautiful," I whispered, placing a soft peck on her forehead.

Her cheeks reddened even more. She gave me a small smile. "You're…you…you make me feel so good."

"Good." I kissed her gently on the mouth.

"Come, Luther."

I smirked. "You want me to fill this tight cunt with my cum?"

She moaned. "Yes."

Leaning back, I undid the cuffs wrapped around her ankles and wrists. I wanted to feel her hands on my body. I wanted her nails digging into my skin as I forced her over the edge again, this time with me.

Once I had her out of the restraints, I kissed her wrists. "Touch me, Lexi."

With gentle fingers, she ran them down my chest, over my abs and around to my ass. "Fuck me harder, Luther."

Kneeling on the bed between her spread legs, I crushed my mouth to hers and gave her what she wanted. What we both wanted.

TWENTY-TWO

Lexi

I WOKE A WHILE later. My body was stiff and sore, but I had never been so relaxed in my life. Sitting up, I scrubbed my face and frowned. I was in an office and I was wearing a white robe.

"You're awake."

My gaze flicked to Luther's. He was sitting behind a large desk to my right. "Where am I?"

"In my office." He sat back, tenting his fingers beneath his chin. "How did you sleep?"

"Good." I rubbed the back of my neck. "Really good." I looked around me. Bookshelves lined the far wall. The furniture was dark, much like the owner himself.

Luther rose from the spot behind the desk and headed to a minibar across the room. "I brought you in here after you fell asleep." He poured a glass of water and brought it over to me.

"Thank you." I took it from him and brought it up to my lips. Taking a sip, the cool liquid eased my parched throat.

He sat down beside me. "Turn around."

I did as I was told.

With gentle but firm hands, he started messaging my neck and shoulders.

I sighed, leaned into his touch, and continued to drink the water.

"Come home with me tonight," he said, breaking the silence.

I turned to him. "Really?"

"I want more time with you." He cupped my cheek. "Tonight wasn't enough."

My heart jumped. "Luther."

He stared at me. "I want more, Lexi."

I pulled away from him. "What does that even mean?" I asked, heading to the minibar and pouring myself another glass of water.

"It means exactly what I just said." Luther stood, coming toward me. "Why are you making a big deal of it?"

"Because you're you and I'm me." I waved a hand between us. "This…are you wanting to make this work?"

"What if I am?" He closed the distance between us, brushing a finger over my collarbone and pulling the robe open.

"Because there's the whole issue of my brother still." I should have pushed him away but instead, I just stood there letting him undress me. Although I was sore, I could never get enough of him. I wasn't sure why or what it was about him that made me so damn compliant, but I found that I enjoyed it. Maybe I actually needed it. He took care of me. Although he did let me be in control in a way.

"I want you, Lexi." He took the glass from me and placed it on the bar before turning back to me. "I want more. Not just sex."

"You want a relationship?" I asked, raising an eyebrow.

He brushed a hand down the center of my torso and nodded. "I do."

I tilted my head to the side. "Why?"

His dark eyes popped up to mine. His jaw ticked. "I don't like being questioned, pet."

"Well, *Sir*," I mocked. "Excuse me for wondering what the hell is going on and why you would want a relationship when it doesn't sound like you."

In a quick move, Luther spun me around and pushed me up against the wall.

I swallowed hard, a nervous flutter racing through me.

"The thing is, *pet*," he growled in my ear. "I have no idea what the fuck I'm doing when it comes to you and it's throwing me off." He kicked my legs apart. "But I'm finding that I like it this way. You're unpredictable and you challenge me. I need it."

"I need it too." I turned in his arms and slid the robe off of my body. "I really need it and it's scaring me. Because…"

"Because why?" he asked, leaning his forehead against mine.

"Because I know no matter what you do to my brother—" I looked up at Luther, cupping his face. "—I'll still want you." Shame weighed heavily on my shoulders at my confession.

"Pet." Luther lifted me in his arms, carried me over to the couch, and cradled me against him like a child. "You have nothing to feel guilty about."

I wrapped an arm around his shoulders. Even though I was completely naked, and he wasn't, he never took it further. He rested his arm on my lap and that was it. Nothing more. It was almost unnerving the way Luther could go from being a dominant asshole one moment to the complete opposite the next.

"Will you tell me something about Charlie? You keep saying that he's a bastard, but I don't know why. I only know him as my brother." I brushed my thumb over Luther's bottom lip.

"Lexi," Luther's voice came out rough.

"Please. Just one thing." I needed to know. I needed to understand. I loved my brother, but I knew he had been acting different lately. "Please, Sir."

Luther's nostrils flared. "Fuck me, I love when you call me that."

I turned in his arms, straddling him. Brushing my fingers down the side of his thick neck, I traced them over the black ink marking his skin. "Please."

"Your brother came to me a while ago. He was desperate. He mentioned something about living in a shitty apartment and he also added that he still lived with his sister. The guys made fun of him."

"I'm not that bad," I mumbled.

Luther grunted. "It's not you, pet. It's all him. Anyway, he needed money. He said that he needed it so you two could get out of debt, fix up the deli and the apartment. If he never would have mentioned you, I wouldn't have cared but the way he went on about wanting to help his sister out, I felt sorry for him. A few months later, I caved and gave him a job. He had to make a delivery. I was working with a known drug lord. He helped me. I helped him. But Charlie never made that delivery and it made me look bad. That drug lord almost had me killed because of it."

"Oh God." I clapped a hand over my mouth. "I'm sorry."

"Lexi." Luther grabbed my hand. "Don't be sorry for the stupid choices your brother made. It has never been you. I dealt with it, but it cost me a lot of money to do so."

"What did Charlie do with the delivery?" I asked even though I was scared to find out the answer.

"He kept it for himself. It was money. A lot of money. I'm not a good guy, Lexi. I will do anything to stay as powerful as I am but to be fair, I was kind of forced into this situation." He shook his head. "Anyway, I don't want you to feel sorry for me. I'm not looking for that. Your brother isn't a good guy and like I said before, he will do anything to make ends meet. And that includes you."

"What about me?"

Luther paused, his jaw clenching. "Charlie showed the guys a picture of you. He was drunk and talking about you. The guys asked to see a picture, so he showed them. They were going on about how hot you are. I saw the picture and I agreed but I was more concerned about your safety."

"Nothing has happened." I told him.

"*Yet*, Lexi," he corrected. "Nothing has happened *yet*."

"Do you think something could happen?" I asked him, not really understanding what he was telling me.

"I do but not if you stay with me." Luther ran his hands down the length of my back. "You're safe with me, pet. I promise you that."

I pushed out of his hold and left the warmth of his lap. Picking up my clothes that were folded neatly on a nearby chair, I started getting dressed.

"What are you doing?"

I shivered as his deep voice washed over me. "I should go home. I should talk to Charlie and find out what the hell is going on."

"If you want to talk to him, talk to him here. Or at my estate but I don't want you going home."

"So, I'm just going to live with you, Luther?" I laughed. "Come on. We both know that's way too damn soon." I finished getting dressed when I felt him come up behind me.

"I meant what I said, Lexi." He kissed the side of my neck. "I want more."

"I like you, Luther. Even though I know I probably shouldn't, but I do. I can't help it, but I love my brother. Even if he is the cause of this whole thing, he's still family."

"He will do everything to make sure he gets what he wants, pet." Luther turned me in his arms. "And he won't care if he has to use you as bait."

"What?" I leaned back. "He would never do that."

"No?" Luther pinched my chin. "He could have gone anywhere after I kicked his ass, but he went home. He led me right to you, Lexi."

"You won't hurt me." I brushed my hand down Luther's chest. "I know you won't hurt me."

"I won't." Luther cupped my cheek, sliding his hand to my nape and tugging my head back. "But he doesn't know that."

"What are you saying?" I asked, gripping his shirt tightly in my hands.

Luther stiffened.

"Tell me," I demanded.

He took a breath and released me. He started pacing, rubbing the back of his neck.

"Luther," I pressed.

He paused, meeting my gaze. "I think he was hoping I would."

A laugh escaped me. "You have got to be kidding me right now. Are you serious?"

When he didn't respond, my stomach twisted.

"Luther." I hugged myself. "You can't be serious."

"I wish I wasn't." He came toward me and before I could protest, had me in his arms. His hand cupped the back of my head, holding me against him. "I would die first before I let something happen to you, Lexi."

I leaned back, staring up at him. "Really?" I said, breathlessly.

"Yeah." He placed a soft peck on my mouth. "Really."

"This is dangerous," I told him, wrapping my arms around his shoulders.

"It is." He pushed me back until I hit the wall. "But I'm sure you know by now, I live for danger."

I leaned my forehead against his chest. Taking a deep inhale, a flutter of peace washed over me. He smelled of spice and sex. God, he smelled good. So damn good.

"Come home with me."

Just as I was about to respond, a soft knock sounded on the door. "Luther, are you in here?" came his sister's muffled voice from the other side.

"I am," he called out. "You alone?"

"No."

A glance passed between Luther and I.

"Do you trust me?" he murmured, taking my hand and leading me to his desk.

"I do." But I still didn't know what the hell was going on.

"I need you to kneel here and stay hidden." Luther cupped my cheek. "Can you do that for me?"

"You want me to stay quiet?" I asked, my heart jumping.

"Yes, pet." He kissed my forehead.

"Everything okay?" I glanced between him and the door.

"I don't know. Just please do as I ask."

I nodded. "Okay." I knelt and moved beneath the desk.

"Good girl." Luther's praise did something funny to my belly.

I never needed to be coddled before but having him give me recognition over listening to him, warmed every inch of me. But something was wrong. Something was very wrong.

"What's going on, Vanessa?" Luther asked.

"I have a problem."

"What the hell is *he* doing here?"

My back stiffened at the harsh tone of Luther's voice. I was tempted to reveal myself but thought better of it. Something forced me to stay hidden.

"I think it's obvious why I'm here."

My eyes widened. *Charlie.*

What the hell was going on?

"Vanessa," Luther growled. "You better have a good reason as to why he's here."

"It doesn't matter why I brought him here," she answered.

"Yes, it does," Luther said. "Especially when all of our clients, including the submissives, go through a process. You know this, Vanessa. So tell me, why the hell is he here?"

"If you must know, he's my new pet and I started training him for me."

Charlie only chuckled.

"Vanessa," Luther barked.

"What the hell is your problem, Luther? I wanted to know if you have the keys—"

"Did you ask him who he is?" Luther demanded.

"Wh…no…why…" she stuttered. She was nervous. She was never nervous. Miss Vee had been the most confident woman I had ever come across. "Fine. Who are you?"

"You didn't care who I was the first time, or even last night," Charlie said, his voice laced with amusement.

"Listen, little boy. I don't give a shit what we did but clearly something is going on and you haven't told me everything. Luther," Vanessa demanded. "Who is he?"

"He's Lexi's brother," he answered.

"You have got to be fucking kidding me!" Vanessa yelled.

A moment later, Luther came back around the desk and sat in the large chair. He held out his hand, waiting.

I took it, pushing my face into his palm. I squeezed my eyes shut, trying so damn hard to take the strength from him that I needed.

"Luther, explain to me what's going on." I could picture Vanessa standing there, peering down at both men in the room with her hands on her hips.

Luther brushed his finger over my bottom lip.

My eyes fluttered open. Inching forward, I cupped his inner thigh, resting my head against his knee.

His hand slid to the back of my neck, holding me tight against him. "Charlie, why don't you tell my sister what's been going on. Or shall I? No? Okay. So Charlie here is the one who owes me money."

"And you brought your sister into it?" Vanessa asked.

"I never asked her to do that for me," Charlie said nonchalantly.

Luther stiffened in his chair. Sitting forward, he held my hand tightly in his. "You didn't have to ask her, Charlie. She did it because you're her brother and like the good person that she is, she would do anything to make sure I don't kick your ass again. Enough. I don't want to hear any more of your shit. You can leave."

"Luther," Vanessa said gently.

"Leave," Luther repeated. "*Now.*" The door shut a moment later. "They're gone, pet."

I pushed out from beneath the desk and stood. "What the hell is going on? Why is he here?"

"I think you know why he's here," Luther said, turning toward me.

"He's sleeping with your sister." I rubbed the back of my neck and began pacing. "But it doesn't explain…hell, I don't even know anymore."

"Lexi, come here."

I turned away from him. I couldn't do this. I needed to talk to Charlie. I needed answers. I needed to go home with Luther. I needed…God, I was so damn confused. Maybe I needed some time alone.

"Lexi."

I shivered at the threat hidden in Luther's deep voice. "I think I need some time alone." As soon as I got the words out of my mouth, he crashed into me.

"Don't say that to me." Luther cupped my face, tilted my head back. and placed a soft peck on my mouth.

"Luther, I don't know what's going on. Charlie is sleeping with your sister and I…"

"I don't think he's doing much sleeping."

I huffed, pushing away from him. "You know what I mean."

Luther scrubbed a hand down his face. "Lexi, I want you to spend the night with me."

"I need to talk to Charlie," I said instead of answering him.

"And say what?" Luther came toward me. "I don't trust him. I know you do but I don't. I don't give a shit that he's family. Something is going on and I have no idea what it is. It's pissing me off."

"Does it bother you that he's sleeping with Vanessa?"

"No," Luther answered automatically. "My sister is a big girl. Although I am kind of surprised that she went for him and not you instead."

I looked away, my cheeks heating. "I'm not into women."

A gentle hand cupped my cheek, turning me toward Luther. "I know, pet. I know. I don't want you talking to Charlie alone but..." His jaw clenched. "If you need space, as much as that'll drive me fucking insane, I'll give it you."

My eyes widened. "Really?"

He nodded.

"Why?"

"Because I need you to trust me. So I have to trust you just the same." He went back behind his desk and sat in the large leather chair.

"Why did you keep the money I paid you?"

He glanced up behind the computer screen. "I'm not a good man. I've never been a good man. But for once in my life, I felt that by keeping the money aside, I was doing the right thing." He looked back at his computer. "Even if you never take it, I refuse to spend it. Oh, when you leave, make sure you shut the door hard. It likes to stick."

I glanced between him and the door, wondering what just happened. One moment Luther was demanding that I stay and the next, giving me permission to leave.

"Luther," I murmured, taking a step toward him.

He glanced up from his computer screen. "Lexi."

I swallowed hard at the coldness hidden behind his eyes. Turning toward the door, I took a breath and made my way to it. With each step I took, I could feel Luther's anger growing and growing. But he was right. He had to trust me. I needed answers. And I was determined to get them one way or another.

TWENTY-THREE

Lexi

I SHOULDN'T HAVE LEFT The Club. I knew that, but did I listen to that inner voice? No. All because I wanted to be a big girl and figure out what the hell was going on. By myself.

Luther kept the money I had paid him. All of it. And didn't spend a single cent of it so he could give it back to me. As confusing as this whole situation was, it warmed my heart that he would do that for me.

Heading back to the deli, I realized rather quickly that I should have taken a cab but instead, I decided to walk. I had no idea if Charlie was still at The Club. I could only imagine that he was. I had so many questions that I wished I had answers for but mostly, I wished I would have stayed with Luther.

Once I saw the light from the deli a few blocks away, a breath of relief left me, and I picked up my speed.

It was pushing late into the evening, so the deli was still open, but that didn't explain why it was suddenly so busy. As I neared it, my frown deepened. Several men in suits sat at one table. There were about five of them ranging in all different sizes and ages.

I opened the door, entering the place that had been my home for as long as I could remember. As soon as I stepped over the threshold, I could feel all eyes on me.

Muttering a quick *hello* to my staff, I hightailed it to the kitchen and bumped into a hard body.

"Shit, Lexi."

I jumped back, staring up at Charlie. "What the hell? How did you get back here so quickly?"

"Back here?" He scowled. "You were there?"

"I was. What the hell is going on, Charlie? Why are you sleeping with Miss Vee?" Not that it was any of my business, but I couldn't stop the question from leaving my mouth.

"Same reason you're sleeping with Luther." He turned and headed to the office.

"Charlie." I followed him. "Something isn't right. I love you, but this doesn't make sense at all."

"Why the fuck does it need to make sense?" he snapped, shoving open the door to the office.

"Luther told me some things and I need to know if they're true. I need to know what your intentions are." I shut the door behind me. "Charlie, talk to me."

"What the hell do you want me to say?" He started pacing and rubbing the back of his neck.

Leaning against the wall, I crossed my arms under my chest. "Why did you come home that night instead of going to the hospital?"

Charlie stopped. "What are you talking about?"

"When Luther beat you up. Why did you come home?"

His brows furrowed. "What lies is he feeding you?"

"Tell me, Charlie. Why did you come home?" I didn't want to believe Luther. Charlie was my brother. He wouldn't hurt me. He couldn't be that desperate. Could he?

"I'm not dealing with this shit." He took a step toward the door, but I blocked him. "Get out of my way, Lexi."

"Tell me. If you don't want me to believe him, then tell me what's going on."

"I shouldn't have to tell you shit. You should believe me because I'm your brother." His jaw clenched, his cheeks turning red.

"Yeah?" I stared up at him. "Then tell me why you led him right to me. A man who owns half—maybe more—of this damn city. A man who threatened your life." A thought crossed my mind. "Did you lead him to me thinking I would seduce him? Was I a distraction, Charlie? Were you hoping that he would focus on me instead of going after you again?"

"I'd like to know the answer to that too."

I jumped, spun around, and found Luther standing in the doorway.

He was leaning against the doorjamb with his thick arms crossed under his broad chest. His black dress shirt hugged his large frame, the sleeves rolled up to his elbows. The veins in his tattooed forearms popped, making my mouth water.

He caught my gaze, a knowing smirk spreading on his face.

I looked away, finding Charlie glaring at me.

"Is this it, Lexi?" he asked, his voice laced with venom. "Are you choosing him over your own brother?"

"I want to know what's going on," I said gently. "Why would you pass a picture of me around to those men?"

"You know about that?" Charlie shook his head. "Doesn't matter. Nothing would happen to you."

"Nothing would happen?" I laughed. "Come on, Charlie. I'm not stupid."

"You're not stupid?" Charlie repeated. "You're fucking the most dangerous man in the damn city," he yelled.

"Careful." Luther stepped up behind me.

"Fuck you," Charlie spat. "This is your fault. Pitting my sister against me. Is that what you wanted all along, Luther?"

"No." Luther feigned a yawn. "I actually wanted her in my bed." He brushed a hand down my spine, sending a shiver along with it. "But that's none of your business. You see, I don't give a shit what you've done or what you will do but I do give a shit where your sister is concerned."

"Why?" Charlie frowned. "Do you have feelings for her?"

"Uh…I'm right here." I placed my hands on my hips. "Tell me why you led him to me."

Charlie's jaw clenched. "I wanted to see if he would take the bait."

"What?" My eyes widened. "What does that mean?"

Luther grabbed my hand, pulling me back a step.

"I wanted to see if I could get him to fall for you." Charlie's gaze flicked between us both. "You were a distraction. You're right about that. But I didn't want to hurt you."

"How did you know that he wouldn't hurt me?" I asked, not believing what I was hearing.

Charlie hesitated, rubbing his nape.

"Charlie, tell me," I demanded.

"I didn't know." Charlie blew out a slow breath. "I didn't know if he would hurt you."

"So you…you led the most lethal man in this city right to me, hoping I would distract him enough to get him away from you. Oh, and you did all this not knowing if he would hurt me or not. Am I right?" When Charlie didn't respond, I pushed him. "Tell me I'm right."

"Yes," he finally said. "You're right. I was hoping I could get him off my ass long enough to…"

"To what?" Luther asked, his voice rough.

Charlie met my gaze. "I'm sorry." He glanced over my head. "To take you out."

(Luther)

I dealt with a lot of bastards in my life. Lethal, vile men who wanted to take me out to gain a reputation. To make others think they were the *be all, end all* when it came to power. They wanted to take what I had and make it their own, letting others think they were so damn strong and scary. Fucking please. It was all bullshit if you asked me. But hearing Charlie say that he used his sister as bait, hoping she would distract me, pissed me off more than I could ever imagine.

Words passed between the siblings, but I couldn't hear them. Red-blooded rage sliced through me. As much as I knew it would upset Lexi, Charlie had to disappear or else I would take him out myself.

A gentle hand grabbed mine.

My gaze dropped to Lexi.

She chewed her bottom lip. Her cheeks were flushed. Her eyes filled with concern. She *should* be concerned. I wanted Charlie dead.

(Lexi)

Luther was on the verge of snapping. I had to do something. And quick.

Keeping his hand in mine, I did the only thing I could think of. "You need to leave," I told Charlie.

"What?" He laughed. "Are you fucking kidding me right now?"

"No." I released Luther's hand and opened the door. "Leave. *Now.*"

"You're making a big mistake, Lexi." Charlie's brows narrowed in the center. "A big fucking mistake."

"Don't you dare threaten me," I snapped.

"Threaten you?" Charlie threw his head back, laughing even harder. "Listen to me, my dear sister. If I was threatening you, you would fucking know it." He stormed past me but paused in the doorway, peering at Luther. "He better be worth it."

"Get the fuck out!" I yelled. "*Now!*"

Charlie left the office, taking every ounce of air in my lungs with him.

I slammed the door shut, turned the lock, and slid down the wall until I hit the floor.

"Lexi."

"Don't." I covered my face, my body shaking. So many emotions ran through me but the one that stuck out the most was fear.

Fear of the unknown.

Fear that I had just lost my brother.

Fear that I was falling for a man who wanted him dead.

Fear that I didn't care.

"Pet."

"Please don't." A sob escaped me.

"Hey." Luther grabbed my hands, pulling me into his arms.

"Luther." I struggled against him.

"Stop," he demanded, holding me tight.

"I...I can't..." My lungs burned, my chest aching with lack of air. Spots danced in my vision, my body trembling.

"Lexi."

"Stop." I pushed against him, but he was too strong for me. "Please. I just...I need...I can't..."

"Lexi," Luther's hard voice slid through me.

"I can't do this anymore." I wrapped my arms around his shoulders, holding him. Being with him. Touching him. I squeezed him so damn hard, it was like I was trying to burrow under his skin.

"Shit." Luther wrapped himself around me, reaching his hands beneath my dress. But he didn't take it further. He just touched me. When his fingers found the skin of my back, his stiff body relaxed. "I want him dead. I want to watch him suffer for putting you through this pain."

My eyes burned. "I know. God I know. I..."

"Baby." Luther cupped the back of my neck. "Lexi."

"I..." I pushed against him. "I can't do this. I can't be with you knowing you want to murder my brother. I'm so damn confused."

Luther stiffened. He leaned back, staring at me with those dark eyes of his.

I swallowed hard, looking away.

"No. Look at me, Lexi. Continue with whatever it is you want to say to me."

"Don't be an asshole." I shoved from his grip and stood.

Luther rose to his feet, towering over me. "Tell me."

"These feelings I have for you, scare me. I...I need some space."

He came toward me.

I backed up until I hit the wall, holding up my hands. "Don't."

"You think I *want* to murder your brother? No. I don't. Because I know that if I did, I'd lose you. But the fact that he used you as bait, pisses me off. I've done shit. A lot of bad shit. I've made mistakes. Stupid choices. I'm a fucking human. It happens. But the one thing I finally do right in life and it is backfiring on me."

"What's that?" I whispered.

"Falling in love with you, pet." Luther pinched my chin, forcing me to look up at him. "But I'm not going to beg for you to be with me. It's not how I'm wired."

My eyes burned, my throat working over the hard lump. "Luther."

"This...what we have, is so fucking right. We may not have met in the conventional way and as much as I hate your brother, I owe him."

"You do?" I placed my hand over Luther's heart, feeling the muscle beating beneath my palm. "Why?"

"Because I never would have met you." He leaned his forehead against mine, covering my hand with his. "I'm in love with you, Lexi."

"Don't," I sobbed. "Please don't say that to me." I couldn't deal with his confession knowing what he wanted to do to my brother. It wasn't fair. It wasn't fair at all.

Luther pulled away.

"Luther." I reached for him, but he backed out of my way. "Please."

"As much as this will hurt us both, I'm done. I'd rather leave you then have you hate me," he said, his voice thick.

"No." I rushed to him, grabbing onto his shirt. "We can work through this. I'll talk to Charlie. I'll find out what else is going on. Please. Please, Sir." I had pushed him away, confused and broken, not realizing how he felt for me. Once he confessed his feelings, nothing else mattered. I knew. I knew this was right. Just like he said. Even though I had to deal with my brother, I needed Luther by my side to keep me strong. To keep me sane. To just be with me.

"Don't, Lexi." Luther grabbed my hands, attempting to pull me off of him but I only latched on harder. "Let go."

"I'm confused. None of this makes sense but I need you. Please."

"You just said you were done." Luther pushed me back. "Did you lie to me? I'm too old for games. I've told you how I felt. I've revealed who I am. This is all me. I am Luther Knight, Lexi. Who the *fuck* are you?"

"I'm yours, Luther. I am yours." I pulled him against me. "Please. I can't do this without you. I can't face him alone."

"You wanted out." He grabbed my wrists, pulling me off of him. "I'm making it easy for you." He released me and headed to the door.

"No, Luther. Please don't leave. I love you. God, I love you too."

He stopped, peering down at me over his shoulder.

My heart shattered at the mere intensity rolling off of him in waves. "Luther."

"I confess my feelings only for you to throw them back in my face."

I backed up, the icy tone of his voice sending a flutter of fear racing through me. "No." I shook my head. "Never. I *do* love you. I do. Please believe me."

"Believe you?" he repeated. "Baby, this shit ends. This shit ends right the fuck now. Either you want me, or you don't. But you can't say that you want me one moment and then push me away the next. Be a fucking adult. Make a decision for once."

"I am making a decision," I insisted. "I want you. That's it. That's all I've ever wanted."

"No." Luther grabbed my hand and pulled me against him. Fisting my hair, he ripped my head back.

I yelped, strands of hair pulling free from my head.

"You wanted your Master. You fell in love with him first." Luther leaned down to my ear. "Isn't that right, pet?"

I whimpered. "I don't know what you're talking about."

"No?" Luther spun me around, slamming me up against the wall and kicking my legs apart.

"Luther." I struggled against him, but he was too quick. He hiked the hem of my dress up to my hips. "Please."

"Please what, pet?" he growled in my ear, landing a hard swat on my ass. "Please stop? Or please continue? Say it. Tell me now, Lexi."

I shivered at the anger in his voice, but I found that it also turned me on. God, what the hell was wrong with me that I wanted this part of him? This lethal, ruthless side. This side that reminded me of the first time he fucked me as my Master. He was angry then and now he was filled with rage.

"Fuck me," I whispered.

Luther spun me around, lifted me in his arms, and wrapped my legs around his waist. He crushed his mouth to mine. The sound of a zipper lowering made my heart jump. Dropping me onto him, he swallowed my cries and fucked me against the wall of my office.

"Harder," I pleaded, digging my nails into his shoulders. "Luther," I cried out.

He growled, sinking his teeth into my lip. "Take it, Lexi. Take all of it."

"Yes, please." I dug my heels into his ass, forcing him deeper. "God, Luther. Faster. Please. Faster. Fuck me faster."

"Shit, baby." He groaned, gripping my inner thighs and spreading me open even more for him. "I don't even have to do anything, and you become wet for me." His dark eyes met mine. "Isn't that right, pet?"

"Yes," I moaned.

Luther lifted my dress up and off of me, throwing the fabric to the side. "So fucking beautiful."

Undoing the buttons on his dress shirt, I brushed my fingers down his tattooed torso and watched him pump his cock in and out of me.

Leaning his forehead against mine, we watched us make each other feel good. So damn good. "I'm sorry," he whispered.

"F-For what?" I asked, breathlessly.

"For being an asshole." He kissed my forehead. "You leave me so fucking unraveled." He pinched my chin, tilting my head back. "Say it again," he demanded. "Tell me how you feel."

"I love you," I whispered.

"Again."

"I love you," I repeated, cupping his nape and covering his mouth with mine. "I love you, Luther," I said again against his lips. "Do I know what's going to come of this? No. But right now I need you to shut up and fuck me."

He grinned and dropped me on my feet. "You want me to fuck you, pet?"

"Y-Yes."

"That's what we were doing." He wrapped a hand around his thick cock. "But if you want more, I'm happy to oblige." He spun me around. "On your knees. *Now.*"

I dropped to the floor at the same time he pulled my feet out from under me.

In a quick move, he was back inside me. "Is this what you wanted, pet? You wanted to be fucked on the floor like a damn animal?"

"Yes," I whimpered, spreading my legs for him.

"Good." Luther reached a hand beneath me, coming into contact with my clit. "Come for me."

"Oh God. I can't." It was too good. The pleasure was almost too much. I couldn't handle it. A shiver trembled through me. "Luther."

"Come, pet." Luther sunk his teeth into the back of my neck, pinning me against the floor. "Come for me." His thrusts picked up speed, his finger pushing against the swollen nub.

An eruption of pleasure exploded through me. His name left my mouth on a hard cry.

"That's right, Lexi. Say my name. Say who's making you feel good right now. Say who's fucking you on the floor."

"Luther," I whined, covering his hand with mine and helping him force me over that edge again.

"You're a greedy little thing." His cock swelled, his release following soon after. "Fuck me." Warmth coated me, his cream leaking from my body. "So damn good." Luther spun me onto my back and slid back inside me.

I moaned.

"I could stay like this forever," he murmured against the side of my neck.

I wrapped my arms around him, holding him against me. I wasn't sure what would come of this, but I *was* sure about my feelings for him. Even though I knew I shouldn't be, I was in love with him.

Luther lifted his head, giving me a small smile.

"What now?" I asked him, running my fingers over the tattoos on his chest.

"Love me," he said, placing a soft peck on my forehead. "That's all I want."

"I do." I ran my hands through his hair. "But what about Charlie?" I slid out from beneath Luther, grabbed my dress, and put it back on.

"I'll deal with Charlie," Luther mumbled, righting his pants.

"Luther." I knew what he meant by that. Rubbing the back of my neck, I leaned against the wall.

He stood in front of me and grabbed my hand, giving the back of it a soft kiss. "I'm not going to kill him. Not right now anyway but if he does something to cause you harm, I can't be held accountable for what happens."

"I thought I knew him." I leaned my forehead against Luther's chest. "But I guess I was wrong."

Luther kissed my hair. "I'm sorry, Lexi. I'm so fucking sorry for everything."

"I know you are." I wasn't sure what would come of this, but I knew that I needed Luther. I needed him in ways I never thought I could need another human being before. Was this normal with love? Did others ever feel this way about the people they were with? I wasn't sure, but I did know that before this got out of control, I needed to keep my brother safe. Something told me that there was only one way I could do that. I just hoped Luther could forgive me.

TWENTY-FOUR

Luther

WITH LEXI'S HAND IN mine, I drove us to the estate. I needed her to myself. I needed to spend the night savoring every inch of her. I was selfish in the way I wanted to hide her from the world. To lock her away and be the only one who could see her or spend time with her. The love I felt for her bordered on obsession. No, I was already past that. I became possessed with the need to show her that she belonged to me. In every sense of the word.

"Luther?"

I passed a quick glance at Lexi. "Yeah?"

She turned toward me. "I'm scared."

My stomach twisted. "Me too, petite. Me too." I wasn't a man who revealed my fears. My father had taught me at a young age that it made a person look weak. And in our line of work, we needed to be as strong as possible.

The phone rang through the speakers of the car, startling us both.

I pressed the screen on the dash. "Knight."

"Luther," came a deep reply.

"Georgio, what's up my friend?"

"You alone?" he asked.

"No," I said, squeezing Lexi's hand.

"I'll make this quick then. Mr. Adams has been quite busy."

Lexi shifted beside me.

"Go on," I demanded.

"It seems he had no intention of ever delivering that money."

My jaw clenched. "We've already come to this conclusion."

"We have but there's something else." Georgio paused. "Rumors have been traveling underground."

"What kind of rumors?" That familiar feeling started brewing. Rage. Pure hard rage.

"He was going to give you his sister as payment."

"What?" Lexi's head whipped around. "No. That's not true. Luther, what the hell is going on?"

I rubbed my jaw. Hell. We were in fucking hell. That was what was going on.

(Lexi)

"Georgio, I'll call you back." Luther disconnected the call and pulled over to the side of the road. He killed the engine before turning to me. "I need you to trust me."

"Did you know all along that Charlie was going to give me to you?" I barked a laugh when he didn't answer. "You have got to be fucking kidding me."

"Lexi."

"Drive me home," I demanded.

"No."

"Drive me home," I repeated.

"Why?" Luther asked, raising an eyebrow.

"Because I'm going to kill my brother myself." I crossed my arms under my chest, blowing out a slow breath and then another.

Luther turned the car around instead of arguing.

I chanced a glance at him. His jaw was tight, that muscle in his cheek working hard.

We drove the rest of the way to my apartment in silence. I wasn't sure if Charlie would be there, but I had to take the chance that he was. I had known all along that he was desperate, but I had no idea just how far that desperation went.

Once Luther pulled up in front of my place, I left the car, not waiting for him to follow me because I knew he would no matter what.

He didn't trust Charlie. I thought I did but I realized then that being family meant shit to my brother.

Heading into the old building, I walked up the stairs to my apartment and found the door slightly ajar. My heart started racing.

"Lexi?"

I turned to Luther. "The door's open."

"Shit." He pulled me behind him and retrieved a gun from the back of his pants.

My eyes widened. "Luther."

He slowly opened the door and quickly shut it again before turning to me. "I need you to trust me."

"What's going on?" My skin became clammy, my heart picking up speed.

"Trust me, Lexi." He pulled a cell from his pocket and pressed a button before putting it away.

"What's going on?" I repeated. "Is Charlie in there? Is he okay?" I rushed past Luther when he hooked an arm around my middle. "Let me go."

"Lexi."

I struggled against him. "Please, Luther. Tell me he's okay." I shoved out of his hold, opened the door, and rushed into my apartment, but stopped suddenly.

A scream lodged its way in my throat. I fell to my knees, the world fading in and out around me. Blood. So much damn blood. I crawled to him. My brother. He was almost unrecognizable, but I knew it was him. I could feel it in the marrow of my bones.

"Charlie," I sobbed, gripping his hoodie. "Why?"

He didn't move. He didn't jump up and tell me he was only kidding. He didn't do anything. He just laid there.

"Lexi." A gentle hand cupped my shoulder.

"No." I shoved Luther off and pushed him. "You did this," I screamed.

Luther's eyes widened, pain flashing behind them as the words tumbled from my lips.

"This is your fault. If I never would have met you. If…If I never would have fallen in love with you." I covered my face, sobs wracking through my shoulders. "He's dead. Charlie is dead. My brother…"

Gentle arms wrapped around me.

"Don't." I tried shoving away from Luther, but he only held me tighter. "Stop."

"Listen to me." He cupped my face, brushing the tears from under my eyes. "I know you're hurting. I know you have every right to be pissed at me. And you're right. He probably would still be alive if you'd never met me, but his death was coming."

I looked away, my jaw clenching.

"You and I both know it." Luther pinched my chin, forcing me to look up at him. "I'm sorry this happened but I am not sorry for meeting you. And I sure as hell am not sorry for falling in love with you."

My chest ached. "He died with me being mad at him. The last words I said were mean." I looked at Luther, the vision of him blurring behind my tears. "He probably died thinking I hated him."

"Don't," Luther snapped. "Don't do that to yourself. You'll only make yourself sick."

"It's true," I yelled, jumping to my feet. I gripped my hair, pulling some of the strands free from my head.

"Lexi." Luther came toward me.

"You did this." I pushed him, beating my fists against his chest. "You made me lose him."

"Lexi," Luther repeated, cupping my head and holding me against him.

"You did this," I sobbed, my fists hitting his chest, but the fight was no longer there. I lost my brother and I lost him to the hands of a monster. "Oh Charlie."

(Luther)

"What do you know?" I asked Georgio, pacing back and forth behind my desk. It had been a few hours since we'd found Charlie dead in the apartment he shared with Lexi. A few hours since she spat those hateful words at me.

And a few hours since I dragged her out of there kicking and screaming. Literally.

"I had the laundry service clean up the mess. There will be no evidence that anything was out of place. At all," Georgio said from the video on my laptop.

The laundry service was another name for the cleaning crew we used that disposed of bodies and cleaned up crime scenes. Much to Lexi's protesting, I refused to go to the police with this. Even though I had some of them paid off, this was above their pay grade.

"What else?" I asked my long-time friend and business partner.

"Charlie wasn't a good guy, Luther."

I passed a glance at Lexi's sleeping form on the couch.

She stirred but other than that, she didn't wake up. I had given her a sleeping pill and a shot of bourbon. She passed out a few minutes later. That was over an hour ago.

"You care for her," Georgio stated.

That was an understatement. I rubbed the back of my neck, easing some of the tension rushing through me. "Send me everything you have on Charlie. I need proof, G. I need proof that he was a monster, so I can help my girl heal."

"I'm on it." Georgio disconnected the video chat.

"Luther?" Lexi sat up, rubbing her eyes and looking around her. "Where am I?"

"You're in my office." I went to her and pulled her onto my lap. Holding her against me, I ran my hand up and down her back.

"I can't believe he's gone." She sniffed, curling against me.

"I know, baby." I kissed her head. "I'm so sorry."

"I'm..." She lifted her head. "I'm sorry for what I said to you."

"Don't." I placed a soft peck on her mouth. "You were upset. I get it."

"I still shouldn't have said those things." She chewed her bottom lip. "I was going to leave you."

Her words were like a punch to the gut. "You were going to choose your brother over me."

She nodded, looking away. "Family comes first. Or I thought it did."

"Georgio is sending me information on him. We're going to figure out exactly who your brother was, pet."

"We should tell your sister," Lexi said softly.

"I did." That was a conversation I didn't want to relive either.

"You did?" Lexi tilted her head. "How did she take it?"

"My sister isn't like most people." I shrugged. "She didn't say anything really, but I know she's hurting." And she also blamed me.

"Oh." Lexi slid off my lap, a yawn trembling through her. "Take me to bed?"

Pushing from the couch, I led her out of the office and to my bedroom. Once we stood in front of my bed, I helped her out of her dress and threw it in the hamper.

"I don't have any clothes. I have..." Her eyes welled. "I have nothing here."

I rushed to her and she crumpled against me. I held her as she cried, wishing there was something I could do to take away her pain. As much as I didn't like Charlie, Lexi didn't deserve this. She didn't deserve any of this.

"Everything you need is here, pet," I whispered against her hair.

Her breath hitched but she didn't argue.

Helping her into the bed, I held her against me as she silently cried herself to sleep. My phone buzzed. Pulling it from the pocket of my pants, my body stiffened when I read the email from Georgio.

The more I read, the angrier I became.

Lexi stirred, wrapping her arm around my middle and snuggling her face into my chest. "Sleep, Luther," she whispered.

I placed my phone on the nightstand and laid down beside her, pulling the blankets up and over us. But I didn't sleep. How could I? Not when I'd just found out exactly who Charlie was.

TWENTY-FIVE

Lexi

I WOKE A FEW hours later to the spot beside me warm but empty. Everything that happened tonight came rushing back. My eyes burned, my throat working over the hard lump that seemed to be permanently lodged in it.

I couldn't believe that Charlie was gone. My brother. Dead.

Letting out a hard sigh, I sat up in the bed and looked around me. Turning on the light to the lamp that sat on the nightstand, I went in search of something to wear when I found a folded-up pile of clothes on the dresser. There were sweatpants, a tank top, and a sweater. I searched through each item, realizing quickly that no panties or bra were included. I smiled to myself. I wasn't surprised. But I *was* surprised that I had clothes in the first place knowing Luther would rather I walked around naked.

Once I was dressed, I left the room and went in search of him. When I reached the end of the hall, I found him pacing back and forth, holding a phone to his ear. He was dressed in gray sweatpants and a white t-shirt. I had never seen him dressed casually before. It almost made him look more…lethal.

Luther stopped, glancing at me over his shoulder. "I have to go." He hung up the phone and shoved it into his pocket. "I see you found the clothes."

I nodded. "Thank you." I noticed his stance was off, his body stiff. "W-Will you give me a tour?"

He came toward me then. Cupping my face, he leaned down until he was eye level with me. "I will do whatever you want, pet."

"Show me you." I covered his hand. "I want to know more about the man I'm in love with."

His nostrils flared, something dark flashing behind his eyes. He grabbed my hand, leading me down another hall. "My dad started this business when he was my age."

"How old are you?" I asked Luther, following beside him.

"Thirty-three." We stopped in front of a door. "You?"

"I'll be twenty-six soon." I thought a moment. "Wouldn't you know that already from the paperwork I filled out for The Club?"

"True but I wanted you to tell me anyway."

"Were you checking to see if I was lying about my age?" I asked, raising an eyebrow.

"Never." He winked. "But…" He brushed the back of his hand down the side of my cheek. "I do like that I'm older than you."

My stomach flipped.

"Anyway." He cleared his throat. "We need to talk about your brother, but I want to show you this first and then I'll give you a proper tour tomorrow." He pushed open the door and tugged me in front of him. "Tell me what you see," he said, turning on the light.

My eyes widened. The room held nothing but a cage. It sat in the middle of the floor and looked like a cage you would put an animal in, but it was bigger than that. Much bigger. No doubt made for a human.

"What do you see?" Luther cupped my shoulders.

"A cage," I whispered.

"Yes, pet." He kissed my cheek. "A cage. You want to know what I do with it? I'll tell you. Nothing. Because I haven't found the perfect pet. Not until now."

"You want to put me in the cage?" I asked, unsure how I felt about that.

"In time." Luther pulled me out of the room, turned off the light, and closed the door. "But not right now. I need you to trust me completely first and putting you in my cage is a step that neither of us are ready for."

"Why would you want to do that?"

"I like being in control. I told you in the beginning that I wanted to play with you. I want to eventually put you in my cage, so I can control you completely. When you eat. When you shower. When you use the washroom. But you wouldn't stay in the cage for long. Maybe a half an hour at first. And then an hour and so on. It's not to break you." He held his hand out. "It's to make you mine. In every single way."

"I—I don't understand." I took a step back. "Can't you control me in other ways?"

"I could." He stepped toward me. "But I don't want to. I have needs. Unconventional needs. I get that it's scary. But I promise that I won't do anything to you that you don't want. You'll enjoy every moment of it. I know you like pleasing me. Your pupils dilate when I give you praise. And you become so damn wet when I tell you what to do.”

“This is all new to me, Luther.” I leaned against the wall, hugging my arms around myself.

“I know.” He stood in front of me, placing both hands on either side of my head. “Trust me, pet. This is new to me too. I never realized what I was looking for until I found you. I wish I could thank your brother for that, but I can’t.” He kissed the top of my head before pushing away from me. “I need to tell you who your brother was.” He held out his hand. “If you’re ready to find out that information, then I need you to come with me.”

I tentatively placed my hand in Luther’s, needing to find out what secrets my brother had and exactly who he was.

Luther led me back to his office, keeping a firm grip on my hand. He unlocked the door and pushed it open before stepping aside.

I entered the room with him following behind me. The sound of the door closing made me jump.

“You’re safe here.” Luther ran a hand down my spine. “I promise you that.” He walked to the large leather chair behind his desk and patted his lap. “Come here, pet.”

I did as I was told and sat on his lap.

Hugging an arm around my middle, Luther inched a hand beneath the sweater and tank top and cupped my breast.

I shivered, the soft touch relaxing in a way. “Show me who my brother was, Luther.”

He wiggled the mouse, the computer screen coming to life. A man stared back at me. His dark eyes pierced into me. He ran his fingers along his black goatee before pulling his shoulder length wavy hair back into a low ponytail.

"Ah, you must be Lexi. I'm Georgio."

"Um…it's nice to meet you," I murmured.

"It's nice to meet you too." He smiled softly. "I wish I could say it was under better terms."

"What do you know about my brother?" I grabbed Luther's other hand, hoping he could give me the strength I needed.

"You already know that he was wanting to give you to Luther as payment."

"And I ended up selling myself to him anyway," I mumbled.

Georgio raised an eyebrow. "That's a story I'll need to hear."

Luther grunted. "Go on."

"Fine." Georgio brought a tumbler of amber liquid to his lips and took a sip before continuing, "Rumors went around that he was trying to take out Luther. He was actually planning it for a while. He had a whole team set up. He wanted Luther's companies. The estate. His power. All of it. He was fucking hungry for it."

"But someone took him out instead," I said. "Was this to protect Luther?"

"No, Lexi. It seems someone else got wind of what Charlie was doing and decided to take it upon themselves to do the same. But they had to take him out first. It was also brought to my attention that Luther's fingerprints were all over the fucking place. If you would have gone to the police, it would have looked like Luther had killed your brother."

My eyes widened. "What? But he was with me."

"I know, little one. He was. And thank fuck for that. Listen, whoever did this, is good."

"Who wants to destroy you?" I asked Luther. I couldn't believe someone would go through all this trouble to end him.

"Who doesn't?" Luther shifted beneath me. "Listen, pet. I have enemies. Besides you and my sister, Georgio is the only one I trust."

"Aww, shucks." Georgio blew him a kiss.

Luther rolled his eyes.

"How is your sister doing, anyway?" Georgio asked. "She still going for the little boys or is she ready to take on a man yet?"

"Not happening, G." Luther moved his hand covering my breast to my stomach, running his thumb back and forth over my hip bone.

"Not happening again, you mean," Georgio corrected. "I'm not into submitting to women and shit but fuck me, I'd beg at that woman's feet and—"

"On that note." Luther sat forward. "Call me when you find anything else. And leave my sister alone. She's going through enough right now."

"Fine, fine." Georgio waved a hand in front of him. "I'll give her time to mourn." He said his goodbyes and disconnected the call.

Luther shut the laptop and sat back in his chair, all the while keeping his hands on my skin.

"Do you think he'll call her?" I asked, wondering what their history was.

"He will but I know my sister, she doesn't forgive and forget. She gets revenge."

"Really? Did he break her heart?" It was nice talking about something other than us. Other than my brother and what happened. Although I felt guilty. Was it wrong to try and distract myself?

"He did. They were kids. Young. Foolish. His dad was friends with ours. Both powerful. Both hungry for more." Luther met my gaze. "But not like your brother. They would never use family the way he used you."

"Do you have proof?" I asked, needing to know if what I found out was in fact the truth or not.

Luther opened his laptop again. He clicked through a few folders before opening a PDF file. Image after image appeared on the screen. Luther. Georgio. Vanessa. All in their day to day activities. They were being watched.

"Was Charlie watching you guys this whole time?" I asked, my skin becoming clammy.

"He was paying someone to watch us, pet." Luther rested his chin on my shoulder, brushing his thumb back and forth over my nipple. That soft touch sent a shiver down my spine but gave me the strength I needed to find out what kind of monster my brother was.

"I didn't know him." My eyes burned. "I didn't know him at all."

"You knew the part that loved you." Luther kissed my shoulder. "Listen to me, Lexi. No matter what he did or what he was trying to do, he loved you. Even *I* know that he loved you."

"He had a funny way of showing it," I grumbled, wiping the lone tear that had fallen down my cheek. "Show me more."

"Everything I have on him is here, pet. But you won't like what you find out. This could very well make you hate him."

"I already ha…" I blew out a slow breath, stopping myself from saying those words. I didn't hate him. But God, did I want to. It would make things so much easier.

"I'll leave you alone with this." Luther placed a soft peck on the side of my neck and slid out from under me. "Lexi?" he said, stopping at the doorway.

I glanced up from the screen.

"I love you."

My heart stuttered. "I love you too."

Luther nodded once and left the office, leaving me alone to the research that was done on my brother.

I spent the next several hours going through each file.

My brain hurt. All of the information poked at my mind like tiny little needles. Basically, what I had learned was that my brother was not who he said he was. At all. I knew him as Charlie Adams. Others knew him as different. I wondered how he was with Vanessa. She was a Domme. I knew that much. Did he submit to her too? Not that it mattered. *God, Charlie.*

How the hell did he get to be this way? Did he just snap one day? Was he planning it all along? After reading up on him, I felt even more confused than I did before.

A part of me wondered if I should have been more upset. I had only just lost him and there I was, sitting at a computer, reading all this shit on him. All of his dark and dirty secrets. Everything that made up *him*.

Charlie was ruthless. Georgio had been right. He wanted to take over Luther's role. But a thought occurred to me.

Opening the video chat, I clicked on Georgio's name. I wasn't sure if he would answer but I had to try.

He appeared in the video a moment later. "Lexi, what's wrong?"

"Who set up Luther and how did my brother come to be this way? Did he wake up one day and decide to bring Luther down? I need more answers, Georgio."

"We don't know any of that yet." He frowned. "Where's Luther?"

"He left me alone to read Charlie's file. Why?"

"Because he won't like me talking to you alone." Georgio rubbed the back of his neck. "I love that fucker like a brother but he's possessive and mean as fuck."

"I'll deal with him." I opened the PDF file again. "The file doesn't say anything new. It's just proof that what you two told me is true. But I need more answers. I'm still so confused."

"And you'll get them when we get them, Lexi."

"Where's his body? I need to bury him. I need…" God I wasn't sure what I needed anymore but no matter who my brother was, he had always been good to me. Well, until I found out he was going to give me to a man who wanted him dead.

"His body is being held at a local morgue. I sent Luther the details. I'm sure he'll take you there if you ask him."

I nodded, pinching the bridge of my nose. "I need more."

"We'll give you more, pet."

My head snapped up, finding Luther gazing down at me. He placed a bottle of water on the desk, along with a plate that had a sandwich on it.

"It's not like your sandwiches but I thought you might be hungry." He nodded to the screen. "Did you call him?"

"I did." I stood. "Thank you for the sandwich." Which reminded me that I needed to let my staff know what was going on without giving them too much detail.

Luther sat, pulling me onto his lap. "What's going on?"

"I've read this file over and over again but I'm not getting any new information. Other than what you both have told me already. I need to know more." I picked up the sandwich and took a bite. It was turkey and swiss with mustard. It was perfect.

"Maybe it's for the best that you don't know everything," Georgio stated.

"What do you mean?" I asked after I swallowed.

"I mean…" Georgio looked behind me.

I glanced at Luther. "What does he mean?"

"He means that you could be in danger if you find out too much but, whoever killed Charlie knows where you live." Luther grabbed my hand and kissed my knuckles.

"So, I'm staying with you," I said, without him even asking me. He didn't need to. I knew how he worked. Even though we hadn't been together for long, there would be no way that Luther would let me go back to my apartment.

"I think that's a good idea," Georgio said. "But I need to ask you something, Lexi. Do you have any enemies?"

"What?" My head whipped around. "No. How could I? I don't do anything. The most excitement I've had in my life has been since meeting Luther."

"I'm not surprised there. Listen, I'm going to do some more digging. I have a contact in New Jersey. He's a retired hacker."

"You can trust him?" Luther asked, not taking his gaze away from me.

"I can."

"Good." Luther leaned forward, closed the laptop, and before I could process what he was doing, his mouth was on mine.

I opened instantly to him, taking his tongue deep between my lips.

He groaned, turning me toward him and running his hands up the back of my sweater.

"Luther," I whispered, undulating my hips against him. He grew beneath me, but he never hinted for more. He just kept kissing me.

"I love you, Lexi." He trailed his mouth down the length of my jaw. "And I'll do everything I can to protect you. I'll keep you safe. From them. From me."

I leaned back, frowning. "What do you mean? I'm not scared of you."

"I know you aren't." He leaned his forehead against my chest, hugging me tighter against him. "But you should be."

"Luther." I cupped his nape. "Hey. What's going on?"

Lifting me in his arms, he sat me on top of his desk and rested his head in my lap.

"Talk to me, please." I didn't know what was going on but the air around him suddenly became thick with tension. He needed something, and I wasn't sure what it was. Sex? My submission? Something more? "Let me help you."

"I'll take you to see your brother tomorrow and I'll help you set everything up, so you can give him a proper burial." Luther stood, towering over me. "And we can deal with the deli then too. I'm sure they're wondering where you are and if everything's alright. Okay?"

"Okay," I said, breathlessly. I cupped his jaw, staring intently into his dark eyes. "There's something else. What do you need?"

"It's not the right time." He kissed my forehead. "I shouldn't want you so fucking much." He kissed my nose. "I shouldn't want…" He leaned back. "I want you to surrender your will to me."

My heart raced. "Take me to your room. Make love to me. No playing. No toys. Just you and me. Just skin against skin."

His eyes darkened even more.

"Please, Luther. I don't want my Master. I want *you*. Just you. Help me out of my head." I placed a soft peck on his mouth. "Help me and I'll help you just the same."

Without responding, he stepped back and held out his hand.

I understood that to be one of his signature moves. It gave me control. It was a silent safeword. If I didn't put my hand in his, then we wouldn't continue, and we would probably talk about it. But I didn't want to talk.

Taking a deep breath, I slid off the desk and instead of grabbing his hand like I wanted to, I held out my own instead. And waited.

Luther came toward me. His gaze was hard. His stance was stiff. His nostrils flared. He lifted his head, taking a deep breath and glancing back at me.

I swallowed hard.

Although I had told him I didn't want to play and that I wanted *him* only, I had a feeling that I was about to learn exactly who Luther was.

In two steps, he was on me. His hands were in my hair. His mouth fused to mine.

"Luther," I whispered against his mouth, inching my hands beneath his shirt.

He broke the kiss, pulling his shirt up and over his head before tossing it to the floor.

I chewed my bottom lip, grazing my fingers down his chest. "You're breathtaking."

He pinched my chin, tilted my head back, and covered my mouth again.

I sighed, wrapping my arms around his shoulders and deepening the kiss. Everything that had happened tonight faded away around us until it was just Luther and I. I needed this. I needed him. And something told me that he did too. I didn't know what else happened or what had changed his mood so suddenly, but I would do anything to help him.

Luther pushed me back until I hit the wall. Releasing my mouth, he grabbed the hem of the sweater and pulled it up and off my torso. Licking his lips, he brushed his fingers over my collarbone, my nipples pebbling beneath his touch.

My chest rose and fell with ragged breaths, but I couldn't move. I stood still and watched. Much to my surprise, Luther lowered to his knees.

Without him asking, I took off the tank top and dropped it on the floor.

His eyes darkened. Hooking his fingers in the waistband of my pants, he lowered them down my legs. I kicked them to the side, standing naked before him.

Placing a soft peck on my lower stomach, he ran his hands up and down the back of my legs. His rough calloused hands made the tiny hairs on my body tingle. He kissed my skin, licked and sucked. Nipped and pecked. I was writhing against him by the time he was done. The need to beg was on the tip of my tongue but I found that I wanted to wait. To see what would happen next. The anticipation was turning me on even more.

Luther cupped my calf and kissed my hip bone before throwing my leg over his shoulder.

Running my fingers through his hair, a breath left me as I pulled him closer.

(Luther)

She smelled so fucking good. When Lexi asked me to make love to her, I almost fell at her feet and begged for her to do whatever the hell she wanted to me. I was never into love and flowers and shit but with her, I wanted it all and I wanted to show her the damn world.

Brushing my nose over her swollen clit, I inhaled.

She whimpered, her fingers latching onto my hair.

Acidic sweetness wafted into my nose. My dick was hard. So fucking hard. But I wouldn't take it further. Not yet. This was all for her. My Lexi. My pet. She didn't want to play. She didn't want her Master. She wanted me

instead. A part of me wondered if I was worse. But I complied anyway.

"Luther," she whispered.

My gaze popped to hers as I swiped my tongue over her clit.

Her mouth fell open, the red in her cheeks becoming more pronounced.

I repeated my movement. Slow, torturous movements.

Her chest rose and fell. Her eyes darkened. Her tongue licked along her bottom lip. I knew she wanted more. She wanted me to make her come but to take it slow just the same.

Her pretty little pussy wept for me. There was a light smattering of hair on it and it made me want to shove my face into her cunt and eat her raw. But I didn't. I wouldn't. Not yet. I reined in on that control and took a breath. And then another. And picked up the speed with my tongue.

"Oh." She pulled me harder against her.

I almost chuckled at how greedy she was but instead, I found that it turned me on. Flicking my tongue back and forth, I held onto her thighs, helping her ride out the wave of ecstasy. Her body trembled. Her legs shook. A release shattered through her, my name leaving her lips on a hard scream. And I didn't stop.

(Lexi)

I was hungry for him. Greedy. Ravenous. I wanted more. I wanted him. I wanted it all.

Luther Knight was the epitome of desire. And with his face between my legs, I surrendered my will and gave him everything that made up me.

He had me coming undone a second time before he stood. The scent of my desire was on his mouth. "Do you want more?" he asked, running his thumb along my bottom lip.

"Yes."

He leaned down, licking up the length of my neck. "You sure, Lexi?"

"Please, Luther." I circled my arms around him.

Lifting me, he wrapped my legs around his waist and carried me out of the office.

With him holding me, he brought me to his room and placed me gently on the bed. Pulling off his pants, he crawled between my knees and covered my mouth with his.

I reached between us, coming into contact with his swollen length.

He shivered, pumping his hips into my hand.

Spreading my legs wider, I guided him to where I wanted him most and once he was fully seated deep inside me, I realized that this was where I belonged. With him. In his arms. In his bed. In his life. In his *heart*.

TWENTY-SIX

Luther

IT HAD BEEN A few hours since I left Lexi in my bed. She was wrapped up in my black satin sheets with the scent of sex on her skin. As much as I didn't want to leave her, I needed to find out answers. Just like her, I needed to know what the hell was going on.

I contacted Georgio and asked him to meet me at her apartment.

"Does she know you're here?" Georgio asked, pushing away from the wall.

"No." And she wouldn't either. Not until I was good and ready to tell her.

"She's going to kick your ass when she finds out." He raised an eyebrow. "You ready for that?"

"Just unlock the door and leave my personal shit out of this." Lexi would understand. I would make sure of it.

"Fine." He picked the lock, the door opening a moment later. "The laundry service is good. There's no scent of bleach or anything."

"Did you have doubts about them?" They were paid a good chunk of change to clean up our messes. Although most of us left without a trace. The person who killed Charlie was good but messy. It was almost like they were desperate in taking him out. It didn't make sense. Not one fucking bit.

"No doubts. They just always surprise me." Georgio ran his finger along a table sitting by the wall. "Yup. Definitely surprised," he said when his finger came back dust free.

"I think this person wanted their shit found. They were probably hoping we would go to the police."

Georgio grunted, pulling on black rubber gloves before throwing me a pair.

I slid them on and walked down the hall. "There should be money in one of the kitchen cupboards. It might be in something," I called out to him as I headed farther down the hall. When Lexi had revealed that information to me several weeks ago, I was surprised at the time that it hadn't been spent. It was also at a time that she feared me. And now she didn't. She should. I wasn't proud of who I was. But this person who was trying to destroy me, needed to be caught. They should just turn themselves in because once I got a hold of them, I would make them suffer. They also killed Lexi's brother and in turn, hurt her. When she was in pain, I was in pain and I wouldn't stop until I brought them to justice like Lexi deserved.

Once I reached the end of the hallway of the small apartment, I tried a door, but it was locked. I glanced down the hall. There were two other doors. I could only assume that one was Lexi's bedroom and the other was the bathroom.

Something told me that the door I was standing in front of was Charlie's room. Pulling out my lock pick set, I grabbed a tool and jimmied the lock until it clicked free.

Stuffing the kit away, I went to turn the doorknob when a bang sounded from the other side of it followed by a muttered voice. Leaning my head against the door, I tried listening but couldn't hear anything else.

Georgio took that moment to come down the hall.

I held my finger to my lips, signalling for him to be silent.

He raised an eyebrow, coming toward me.

A bang sounded again.

He frowned, pushing me out of the way. Pulling a gun from the back of his pants, he grabbed the knob.

I retrieved my own gun and waited.

He held up three fingers and started counting down. Once all fingers dropped, he shoved the door open.

I followed in behind him.

The culprit jumped.

"Who the hell are you?" I demanded, aiming my gun at them. Dressed in all black, they had their back to us. The hood of the sweatshirt they were wearing was pulled up and over their head.

They held up their hands, dropping a bag at their feet.

"Answer him," Georgio added. "*Now.*"

They slowly turned around, pushing the hood back.

At that moment, everything I had come to know, everything I had lived for, fell out from under me. The estate. The fucking empire, all of it, was nothing. None of it mattered. Not when the person staring back at me stole all of the trust I had ever felt toward anyone and replaced it with pure hard rage. No. It wasn't rage. It was worse.

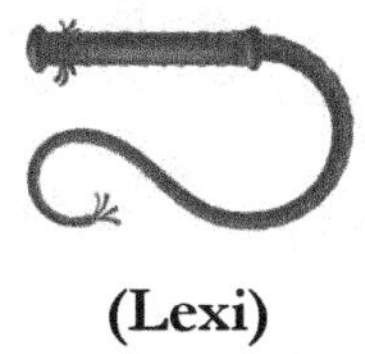

(Lexi)

I wasn't expecting to see him. I shouldn't have been surprised but I was. I stared at the two men aiming guns at me.

Georgio looked confused and shocked beyond belief while Luther looked like he was ready to—

"Tell me why the fuck you're here," Luther growled, his voice laced with venom.

And there it was. The man I had come to know.

I took a step toward him. "I can explain."

"How?" He cocked his gun. "How the *fuck* are you going to explain this shit to me?"

I was vaguely aware of Georgio leaving the room, the door closing softly behind him.

"Lexi," Luther barked. "You better tell me what the hell you're doing before I put a bullet between your eyes."

I closed the distance between us and grabbed his hand. Lifting it, I pressed the end of the gun against my forehead. "Do it, Luther."

He was caught off guard momentarily before he pushed the end of the pistol against my forehead. "Don't fucking test me, woman."

I swallowed hard. "I can explain everything."

"You have five seconds."

"Right." I laughed, pulling away from him and went back to my bag. "Because we both know that I can get all of that information out in that short amount of time."

"What the hell is going on? Why are you here? You were in my bed. I left you in my fucking bed. How did you get here so quickly?" His eyes moved back and forth over my face. His stance was ridged, his body stiff. His shoulders were pulled tight. He was ready for a damn war.

I couldn't blame him.

"I'll tell you if you lower the gun." I placed my hands on my hips when he didn't budge. "Luther."

A snarl erupted from him before he charged for me. With his hand wrapped around my throat, he pushed me up against the wall and aimed the gun at my head.

"Tell me what you're doing here. Tell me who you are. Tell me something. Anything. Because the thoughts going through my head right now are not going to help you live through the fucking night."

I shivered at the threat. "God, I love this side of you."

Luther's jaw clenched, his hold on me loosening. "Lexi."

"I'm sorry." I placed my hands on his chest, my fingers splaying over his heart. "For everything. I am. I needed information on my brother. Both you and Georgio led me right to him. As soon as you left your room and thought I was sleeping, I got dressed and headed here."

"Did you know I was coming here?"

"No, not exactly but I was hoping you were."

"I don't understand." Luther released me but kept the gun aimed at me. "Was all of this a fucking lie?"

"What?" My eyes widened. I shook my head. "God, no. Not at all. My feelings for you are very real. I love you. My relationship with my brother was off."

"What do you mean?"

"I was contacted about six months ago."

"By who?" Luther's jaw clenched when I didn't answer. "Who the fuck contacted you, Lexi?"

"I did."

Both of us turned at the sound of the voice.

"What?" All of the color drained from Luther's face when he started putting the pieces together. "Georgio."

"Let's go into the living room." Georgio pushed away from the wall. "I think it's time we all sit down and talk."

(Luther)

My long-time friend and business partner, a man I trusted, along with the woman I loved, sat on the couch, staring up at me like I would bolt. No. I wasn't running. I wasn't running anywhere. Not until I got the answers I was looking for.

"Did you want to sit?" Lexi asked gently.

I glared at her.

She jumped, looking away.

I had never been this enraged with someone. It was like she reached inside my chest, ripped out my heart, and ate it while I crumpled to the ground.

Betrayal. It was an ugly thing.

"This is my fault, Luther." Georgio sat forward. "If you want to blame someone, blame me."

"Oh, don't fucking worry. I am blaming you. I'm blaming both of you. All of this time, you said not to have any secrets," I told Georgio. "We've never had secrets and yet, you've kept the biggest one from me. You were supposed to be my friend." I held up my hand when they both went to speak. "Tell me how you know each other."

"Luther, how about you put that gun away first," Georgio suggested.

"Oh sure. I'll put it away so you two can plot my death. Is that what you've been planning all along? You took out Charlie and then you were going to take me out next. Tell me how the *fuck* you know each other."

"Fine." Georgio jutted his chin. "Go ahead and tell him, Lexi."

"I met him at one of his clubs," Lexi answered instead. "Officially anyway."

"What?" My stomach twisted. "Explain that to me."

She blew out a slow breath. "I needed help. I was in a bad place. Charlie hadn't been easy to live with. I loved him. I did but he was not a good guy. Which you told me that. You just confirmed my beliefs on who he actually was. The deli was going under and I was on the verge of bankruptcy."

"That's why you headed to The Club. That's why you sold yourself to me." I slammed a fist against my chest. "Or was that a lie too?"

"No, that was very much real." She wrung her hands together in her lap. "Charlie had a temper. He was drinking one night, and we got in a fight. He was mixing drugs with alcohol and it was going downhill from there. He was becoming a mess. I called him out on it and he hit me. This happened at the deli and Georgio saw everything."

"So, you were her knight in shining armor," I said, my voice flat.

"No. It wasn't like that. It was never like that. I want your sister. I never lied about that fact." Georgio stood and started pacing. "I made sure Lexi was safe and then I left. A week later, I went to the deli again and asked her if she would make some pies for one of my clubs. I was obsessed with them. I couldn't get them out of my head. I swear, it was just pie I wanted from her."

"That's not making me feel better right now," I grumbled, shoving the gun in the back of my pants. "So you meet at a club. Officially. You obviously know more about BDSM than you let on then, isn't that right?" I asked Lexi.

Her cheeks reddened.

"Answer me," I yelled. "I deserve this much. Give me the answers I'm fucking looking for."

"Yes, I know about BDSM," she said, her voice calmer than how I felt. "Only because I've done research. That was before you. I thought maybe you wouldn't want me because I knew about it."

I grunted, rolling my eyes. "Right. Tell me why you contacted her." I demanded of Georgio.

He reached inside his jacket and pulled out a black item before flipping it open.

FBI. FBI. FBI.

The three letters screamed at me.

Before I knew what I was doing, I dove at him.

TWENTY-SEVEN

Lexi

"LUTHER," I SCREAMED, TRYING with all of my strength to pull the men apart. I understood he was pissed. I got it. I really did. But he needed to understand that I had no choice. "Please stop. I'll explain more. It wasn't his fault. It wasn't either of our faults." I wrapped my arms around his shoulders and pulled him back against me until we fell to the floor.

"How the hell could you be FBI? We've done shit together. Illegal shit, Georgio." Luther shoved away from me and jumped to his feet before getting in his friend's face. "How could you not tell me that you're with the fucking feds? We've been friends since we were kids. Our fathers were best friends. How could you?"

"They contacted me." Georgio rubbed his jaw. "Fuck, I forgot how hard you hit." He shook his head. "Anyway, Charlie was closing in on you. He was going to set you up."

"Is Charlie actually dead or did you two lie about that as well?" Luther fixed his jacket. "Well?"

"He's dead," I told him, pushing to my feet. "Georgio contacted me asking for help to get information on my brother. I let Charlie believe we still needed the money when we didn't. I wanted him to become desperate. I wanted to see what he would do to get the money he thought would help us." I wasn't proud of the fact that I had used my brother, but I had tried to stop him before his desperation got him killed. Even though it didn't work, I hope he died knowing that I was trying to make things better for him. For us.

"Did you get the information you were looking for?" Luther asked Georgio. "Well, did you? Was all of this fucking worth it?"

"Charlie…" Georgio glanced at me.

I looked down at my feet, shame weighing heavily on my shoulders over the shit my brother had done.

"Charlie was good at sales and a mastermind of the dark web. We'd been following him for a while but could never prove that it was, in fact, him running the show. Not until he made a mistake. He had different aliases but one true tell between all of them." Georgio reached into his jacket and pulled out his phone. He clicked a button before showing Luther the small screen. "All of these names have one thing in common."

"Knight," Luther muttered. His gaze popped to Georgio's. "Was he making it look like it was me this whole time?"

"I'm not sure yet. Lexi was getting me all of the information she could find from Charlie's room. That's why she was here."

"He drove you," Luther said, peering down at me. He turned back to Georgio. "You drove her. You picked her up from my place, drove her here and then waited out in the hall for me." He pushed Georgio. "I'm right. Aren't I?"

Georgio rubbed the back of his neck. "Yes."

"Fuck." Luther stepped away from us and began pacing. "What's my role in all of this?"

I stepped up beside him. "I had no idea that he would lead you to me. I had no idea about any of this."

"Who killed him?" Luther asked. "If he's actually dead like you say he is."

"I killed him," Georgio stated nonchalantly like he was just talking about the weather.

"Did you set me up?" Luther got in his face. "Did you stage it, so it would look like I killed him?"

"No. That was a lie. Your prints weren't here at all." Georgio cupped Luther's nape. "You have to believe me. Charlie wasn't a good guy. We were trying to bring him down."

"Then why did you lie and say that it was made to look like I killed him?" Luther threw at him. "Why the hell would you say that to me?"

"Because I needed to keep you away. I know you. You would have brought Lexi back here so she could grab her things. I needed to keep you both away to protect you. We're not the only ones involved in this shit." Georgio put his phone away. "I'll explain when I get more information but it's taking longer than I would like."

"You used me." Luther pushed him. "Both of you used me."

"Luther." I reached out for him, but he jumped back.

"No. I've been betrayed by a lot of fucking people but none of those hurt like this does." He shook his head, heading to the door of my apartment. "I'm done. All of this is fucking done."

"Luther," I cried, rushing to him. "Please. Take me home with you. Let me explain. Let me make this up to you."

"Explain?" he shouted, gripping my shoulders and shoving me up against the wall. "Explain what, Lexi? Explain that you made me fall in love with you. That you gave me everything that I needed, only to throw it back in my face."

"No, that's not true." A sob escaped me. "Please believe me."

"Fuck you," he spat, shoving away from me. He slammed the door open, storming down the hall.

"Luther," Georgio called out.

I ran after Luther. "Please, Luther. Sir. Master. Please fucking believe me," I screamed. "I didn't want this. I didn't want any of this. I had no choice. Charlie was evil. He was using the dark web to sell things. Weapons. Drugs. People. He was going to make it look like it was all you. He was going to destroy you."

"You didn't know me when this shit started," Luther snapped, spinning on me. "You didn't know me at fucking all, so you can't say that shit to me. You can't tell me that you actually cared because you didn't know me."

"I *did* know you. I saw pictures of you. Georgio had me read up on you. Please." I gripped his jacket. "Please believe me."

"You gave her information on me?" Luther asked, staring over my head.

"I had a feeling that Charlie would try and backstab you. I wanted Lexi to have as much information as she could. My job was on the line for bringing in someone who wasn't even remotely close to being FBI. I was desperate. I needed help." Georgio swallowed noisily. "You have to believe me."

Luther's jaw clenched, that muscle beneath his ear ticking. He stared down at me, grabbed my wrists and leaned down to my ear. His hands tightened, squeezing until the bones rubbed together.

I whimpered.

"If you know what's good for you," Luther's voice was calm and even and it utterly terrified me. "You won't follow me." He pushed me away and headed down the hall, taking my heart and soul with him.

TWENTY-EIGHT

Lexi

"LUTHER! PLEASE." BEFORE I could run after him, an arm wrapped around my middle and I was lifted off my feet.

"Trust me, Lexi, you don't want to go after him."

"This is your fault." I pushed Georgio. "I didn't want any of this to happen."

"I wasn't expecting you to actually fall in love with him," he threw at me.

"Fuck you." I shoved away from him and before he could catch me again, I ran after Luther.

Once I reached outside, a black car sped by me. I hailed a Taxi. Luckily it was still early at night, so the cabs were moving constantly.

"Lexi," Georgio called after me.

A cab stopped in front of me.

I jumped into the back. "I need you to follow that car."

"Which car?" the driver asked, frowning.

"Just go!" I yelled. "Please!"

He grumbled a curse but listened to me. "Do you have an address?" he asked a moment later.

I gave it to him and pinched the bridge of my nose. What the hell was I doing? I was about to face Luther. By myself. Without Georgio. He could at least back me up but no, I was stupid and rushed off. I just needed Luther to hear me out. I needed him to understand. I needed him to know that I had no choice.

Once we pulled up in front of the gate leading to Luther's large estate, I threw money at the driver and jumped out of the cab.

Luck was on my side when I saw the gate was still open. I wasn't sure why. It wasn't like Luther. He clearly wasn't thinking straight. And it was all my fault. Everything was all my damn fault.

I ran up the gravel driveway, my heart jumping when I saw Luther's black car. Bounding up the steps, I tried the door. It opened. Thank God.

"Luther," I yelled. "Luther, we need to talk. Please let me explain."

He appeared around the corner, a tumbler of amber liquid in his hand. "Talk. You want to talk?" He placed the glass on a nearby table. "How about I talk instead?" He took a step toward me. "I fell in love with you. I fell in love with you fucking hard. I felt guilty for not telling you who I was right away. And you were pissed. I understood that. And then I find out that you've actually known my best friend for months. Did you even care that he killed your brother? Did you know that he set me up?"

"I cared. Of course I cared. I'm not a monster. But no, I didn't know he told you Charlie's death was made to look like you did it. I had no idea Georgio would go that far." My hands itched to reach out to Luther but instead, I kept them to myself.

Luther took another step toward me. "I have so many fucking questions. So many. But I'm tired and right now, I just don't give a shit anymore."

I backed up, not liking the way his hate was directed at me. "I know you're mad but please don't hate me. I'm sorry. I'm sorry for everything."

"Sorry." He laughed, the sound cold and evil.

Before I could comprehend what he was doing, he charged toward me.

I jumped, running in the opposite direction.

"That's right, Lexi. Run away from me. I know every inch of this house. I will find you. I will catch you. And I will break you. I will make you pay for the shit you've done."

My eyes burned, my chest tightening. I ended up down a hall that looked familiar, but I hadn't been down it often, so I wasn't sure if I had seen it before. Hell, I hadn't been in many parts of the house, aside from the office and bedroom.

A warm body stepped up behind me.

"Luther," I whispered, tears falling freely down my cheeks.

This was it. I would face his wrath. I would get the side of him he thought neither of us was ready for. I knew when he moved to the door in front of me and pushed it open. I knew when I walked past him, yet when I stepped into the room, my eyes widened.

"No." I spun on him. "Not here. Take me to the other room. Whip me. Spank me. Unleash all of your anger on me. I don't care. But I'm not ready. You're not ready. Not for this."

Luther pushed me back into the room. "Fuck being ready."

"Please." I beat my fists against his chest. "We can talk."

"I'm done fucking talking," he yelled, grabbing my wrist. He headed to the cage, dragging me behind him.

"Luther," I cried. "Please don't do this."

With my wrist in his hand, he leaned down and opened the door to the cage. "Get in."

"No." I tried prying his fingers off of me. "I'm sorry but I don't deserve this. And neither do you." I knew this could hurt both of us. Not just me, but him as well.

"Get the fuck in," he growled, his hate fueled eyes glaring daggers into me.

I lowered to my knees before I could stop myself. Sobs wracked through me and I crawled into the cage. The door slammed shut, followed by a click of the lock.

"Luther," I cried, turning to him. "Please. I'm sorry. I'm so sorry. Please let me out. We can talk."

"Talk?" he boomed. "Talk. You fucking lied to me. All of this time. All of it. Lies."

"I lied to you." I laughed. "You fucking lied to me too," I screamed. "You never told me who you were and that you were my Master. Remember that, Luther? Do you remember?"

But he didn't say anything as he stared me down.

"God, please. Just let me out and we can talk about this." Defeat rested heavily on my shoulders, weighing me down to the point I couldn't breathe.

"No," came his curt reply.

"Please let me out of here," I said anyway, silently pleading with him to hear me out.

"It's funny." He crouched in front of me. "I said I didn't want to put you in here yet because I didn't want to break you."

My heart started racing.

"Well now, I don't give a fuck if I break you or not." He pulled away.

"No, please, Luther. Please, let me out." I shook the bars. "I'm sorry. I'm so fucking sorry."

As he neared the door, my screams grew louder. When he left the room, my guilt turned into hate. How would we get past this? How would we find each other again? I didn't have the answer to either of those questions but what I did know, was that this was going to hurt Luther far more than it hurt me.

(Luther)

Lexi's screams shattered my heart. I slid down the wall, hitting the ground with a thud. I had no idea what the hell I was doing but the rage had taken over and the next thing I knew, she was in my cage.

When her screams quieted, I blew out a slow breath of relief.

Dropping my head in my hands, I thought over the revelations that had come to light in the past couple of hours. I had every intention of going to her apartment to get answers about Charlie. Well I fucking got answers alright. Just not the ones I was looking for.

She was right though. I did lie to her and I apologized for it. She forgave me and we moved on. Now she lied to me, apologized just the same and I was fucking punishing her.

I leaned my head back against the wall, pulling my knees to my chest.

This new feeling washed over me. It was something I had never felt before. *Peace.*

Lexi's betrayal poked at a side of me that had wanted to throw her in the cage weeks ago. But I hadn't. Because I wasn't sure either of us could handle it.

I stood from the floor, brushed off my pants and popped the collar of my jacket. I wasn't ready then but now I was.

Lexi would understand rather quickly exactly who she had betrayed, and I couldn't wait to show her.

TWENTY-NINE

Luther

THE PAIN SLICED THROUGH me, forcing me to my knees. I tried crawling away from it, but the agony only followed. No matter where I went, it was there. Embedded in my skin. Seared into my flesh. It was all throughout me. Inside my soul. In my blood. In the marrow of my bones.

"Luther."

I winced, a breathless gasp escaping me.

"He's had enough."

"He can take some more." As soon as those words slid into my ear, the bite of the whip stung across my skin.

A low moan left my mouth, my body falling to the ground beneath me.

"I told you he could take it."

"It seems more that he likes it."

"This will help him. He may not like it the way you think. He'll have no choice but to take it. To take all of it."

I squeezed my eyes shut, trying to ignore the voices surrounding me. I did like it, but I wasn't sure why. My father had taught me to be in control but the pain forced me to my knees every damn time.

"Luther."

My eyes fluttered open, landing on my dad. A man who had unleashed himself on me. A man who I had looked up to for as long as I could remember. A man I trusted.

"I'm not doing this to make you hate me or because I want to."

"I know," I croaked. I may have been young, but I wasn't stupid.

"You will need to find someone some day who can help you." His face softened. "Someone who can take you out of your head."

I nodded. "What if it never happens?"

"It will, son." He clapped my shoulder, careful to not hit the lashes across my upper back. "These won't scar too bad. The cuts aren't deep."

I blew out a breath of relief. "I'm sorry."

"For what, Luther?" He sat on the floor, leaning against the wall across from me.

"For not being normal." I picked at an invisible fuzz on my black sweatpants.

"I never asked for a normal kid, Luther." My father sat forward. "Listen to me. You will be taking over my business soon enough. But this other side of you, this darker side, you will need to find someone some day that can help you through it. That can show you that it's okay to like the darker side of life. They will help you gain control."

"I am in control," I insisted.

"Yes, you are. At times. But not always. I've seen you lose it and kill a man with your bare hands because they looked at you funny." He held up his hand when I opened my mouth to say something. "I'm not judging. At fucking all. But I also need to make sure that you don't just suddenly snap and I lose all of my

clientele because you're having a bad day." He stood. "So, you will need help with these sessions. As you get older, this will turn into something more. Something that I can't provide you or help you with."

I nodded in understanding.

"I won't always be around, Luther." He gave my shoulder a light squeeze. "But I will teach you everything I know so you can live the life you deserve. I will also need you to take care of your sister."

I nodded again.

"Work together and you will own the fucking world, son. I guarantee it." When his hand slid from my shoulder, a sense of loss fluttered through me. That was the last time I had seen him. The last time I had talked to him.

I lost a piece of myself that day. And I was damn determined to get it back. No matter the cost.

(Lexi)

Minutes went by. Hours. Maybe even days. I wasn't sure anymore. Time was lost to me as I was holed up in that damn cage. It could have even been just seconds. But I didn't know. My will was tested the moment I crawled into what would be my new home for who the hell knew how long. I had so many things to take care of. The deli. My brother's funeral. Even though he deserved what he got, he was still family. My mom wouldn't have wanted it any other way.

But while I waited to meet my maker, I wondered what would have happened if I would have told Luther what was going on from the very beginning. I still had so many questions and I was sure he did as well.

"Luther?" I called out, hoping beyond hope that he had time to cool off so we could talk, but all I got was silence. My eyes burned, my chest aching over what I had done. I was stupid to think he would have forgiven me so damn easily.

Laying on the floor of the cage, I curled into myself. I wasn't sure how long I had been locked up for, but it couldn't have been too long. I wasn't hungry yet and I didn't have to use the washroom. Either way, this sucked. This sucked a whole hell of a lot.

Rolling over onto my back, I leaned against the bars of the cage. I could do this. I could get through this and come out stronger than ever. Luther said in the beginning he didn't want to break me. Now I wasn't so sure, but I prayed that it was just due to anger that forced those words from his mouth.

Hate. So much damn hate. All because I had trusted a man who needed help bringing down my brother. But I never expected to fall in love with Luther. I never expected to need him in ways I never even knew existed before meeting him.

Tears fell freely down my cheeks, taking every last bit of energy I had with them. We would get through this. We had to. There was no other way. I had questions that I needed answered and so did he.

"Luther," I called out again. "Please talk to me."

The door opened that time.

I sat up, moving to the corner of the cage and hugged my knees to my chest. "I'm sorry."

Luther closed the door behind him and sat on the floor, leaning against the wall. "Why are you sorry?"

I swallowed hard at the accusatory glare rippling from him. "For everything."

"Be fucking specific, Lexi. Tell me why you are sorry." He sat forward. "Do you not remember what you did?" He checked the watch on his wrist. "It's only been a few hours." His dark stare met mine. "Are you broken already?"

"Fuck you," I bit out through clenched teeth. "You have to do more than throw me in a cage to break me, Luther."

He chuckled, the sound cold and threatening. "Oh, little girl. You haven't seen anything yet. Now tell me why you're sorry."

"For hurting you. For lying. For everything." I scrubbed a hand down my face. "But like you, I'm not sorry for falling in love with you." I moved to the other end of the cage, gripping the bars tight in my hands. "As much of an asshole as you are…"

He moved to all fours and stuck a hand between the bars, cupping my face. "You still love me, pet?" His mouth covered mine.

"Please," I whispered, a shiver sliding over my skin at the soft contact. "Take me out of here. I'll make it up to you. I'll do anything. Please, Luther."

"No." He pulled away from me.

I whimpered at the loss. "Why are you doing this?"

"I haven't decided yet." He rubbed the dark scruff on his jaw.

"What do you want with me? I have to bury my brother. I have to call the deli at least and tell them what's going on and that I won't be there for a few days."

"I think it's going to be a little longer than that, pet." Luther pulled his phone out of the inner pocket of his jacket and handed it to me. "Call them. If you so much as even think of calling the police, I'll do more than just keep you locked up in my cage."

"You don't scare me, Luther." I snatched the phone from him and dialed the deli. "But keep trying. It's sexy as hell."

He muttered a curse and sat back against the wall. I was getting to him. Good. Because as much as I was pissed that he locked me away, I understood. I wasn't sure why, but I did. And I knew that once he let me out, all bets were off. He needed to be in control. Well I would show him just how badly I needed to feel his wrath.

I called the deli, keeping my gaze locked with Luther's. When one of my waitresses answered, I quickly told her that I had been under the weather and I wouldn't be there for a few days. I also mentioned that there was a family emergency. I didn't tell her about my brother's death. That could wait until I buried Charlie and everything was finalized. I needed to make sure everything was in order before I let that information be known because something was still off about the whole thing.

Saying my goodbyes, I disconnected the call and tossed the phone through the bars of the cage.

"Satisfied now?" Luther grabbed the phone and put it away.

I didn't answer. I only stared at him.

"What?" he asked, a deep frown settling between his dark brows.

"What happened to make you this way?" We had been together for a few months, but I still didn't truly know him. Something told me that it would take quite a while to find out everything there was to know about Luther Knight.

"What do you mean?" he asked, crossing his tattooed forearms under his chest.

I waved a hand in front of me. "This. You. I've heard of Doms wanting to control their submissives but this is a bit much. Isn't it?"

Luther smirked. "I almost forgot that you know more about BDSM than you let on. My little pet is smart. Isn't she?"

"No." My cheeks burned. "That's not what I'm saying."

"It's not?" He raised an eyebrow. "Then tell me, pet. Tell me everything you know about BDSM."

"Tell me what I'm doing in here first." I lifted my chin defiantly.

Luther chuckled and crawled to the door of the cage. Much to my surprise, he unlocked it. He reached in and grabbed my ankles, pulling me toward him.

"Luther." I gasped, slapping my hands against his chest.

He towered over me, fisting my hair. "You're in here because I feel like keeping you in here. You betrayed me, Lexi. No one betrays me and gets away with it. If you were a man, you would be dead already. But you're not. So I have to find other ways to punish you."

"Please, Luther." I struggled beneath him.

Reaching between us, he cupped me over my leggings.

My eyes widened, a flush of heat spreading through me. It had felt like years since he had touched me when it had only been a day.

"Luther," I whispered.

His fingers tightened around my throat, his dark eyes becoming black with lust. His hand between my legs pressed against me, rubbing me over the fabric.

My body hummed, my legs spreading even more of their own accord. I gripped his hand that was around my neck, arching beneath him.

He leaned down, his breath fanning my face. His palm connected with my clit, pushing and rubbing, igniting a burn I had never felt before.

The cotton of my panties became soaked the faster he rubbed against me. A moan escaped me.

My core ached, clenching with the need to have him inside me. Reaching between us, I grabbed onto his pants and lowered the zipper.

His nostrils flared, tightening his hold on my throat. "One word and this ends. You know that, Lexi. But you won't use your safeword, will you? You like this." He kissed the corner of my mouth. "You like it dark."

His words were true. But I never knew I liked it this way until I met him.

"Tell me," he murmured, licking up the side of my face. "Tell me how you like it when I take full control."

"I do," I whispered.

"I know you do." His palm pushed against me. "You're probably wondering why this feels so damn wrong but right all at the same time. Aren't you?"

I swallowed hard, nodding.

"Good." He lifted his head, staring down at me. His thumb brushed back and forth over the side of my throat. "One word, Lexi."

But I refused to use it. For most, this would be too much. Too far. But for me, for us, it was damn near perfect. I hurt him. And I'd meant what I said when I told him that I would do anything to make it up to him. He had my full consent. He always had. Although this was dark, dangerous even, I would never want it any other way.

Once I had his pants undone, I reached inside and pulled out his straining cock.

Luther released my throat, grabbed the crotch of my leggings and with a rough tug, tore them apart.

My heart hammered against the walls of my rib cage.

Leaning over me, he licked along my bottom lip. Brushing the back of his knuckle over my soaked panties, he hooked a finger inside them and pulled them to the side.

"Safeword," he growled.

"Ch-Charlie," I whispered at the same time he thrust forward. I swallowed a scream, arching beneath him.

Luther wrapped his arms around my knees. Pushing them to my chest, he thrust hard and deep while he fucked me on the floor of the cage.

"Luther," I moaned, taking him further inside me. My body was half in, half out of the cage and although most wouldn't think it was normal, it was damn near perfect. It was ours. It was everything. It was erotic. Delicious. And damn near violent.

Luther growled, slapped his hands against the floor on either side of my head, and bucked his hips forward. "So fucking good."

"Come, Luther. Please come inside me."

"Fuck." He slammed his mouth against mine, shoved his tongue between my lips, and devoured the hell out of me.

I moaned, grabbed onto his hips and pulled him forward. I broke the kiss, unable to breathe. "Harder," I cried out. "Please, harder."

His mouth trailed down the length of my jaw, raining tiny bites on my skin. Licking along the shell of my ear, he powered forward and back. "You like this. Being fucked on the floor of my cage. You enjoy being my little pet, don't you, Lexi?"

"Yes." I inched my hands beneath his shirt, running them up the length of his spine. The bumpy ridges reminded me that I had never asked him how he got the scars. I would. In time. But now, I needed him to take me away. To show me his full wrath. To make me his. Every inch of me.

"You're so fucking beautiful." Luther leaned back, falling free from my body and crawling out of the cage. Wrapping his hands around my ankles, he dragged me out with him. Pulling me to my feet, he bent me over the top of the cage and slammed back into me.

The scream that was lodged in my throat broke free as he fucked me harder and faster. The metal of the cage dug into my hips. His hand gripped my hair, pushing my head face first against the top while his other hand landed hard swats on my ass.

I whimpered, my knees shaking at the rough hold he had on my body.

"You wanted me, Lexi. You wanted all of me. Do you regret it yet?"

"No," I screamed, a release rocking through my body. His name left my lips until my voice gave out.

Luther pulled out, spread me open even more and thrust into the tight rim that had only ever been claimed by him.

Another scream broke. My body burned, the pain from him fucking my ass turning into a pleasure I had never felt before.

The thrusts slowed, his cock emptying inside of my body. Finally, Luther pulled out. Holding me against him, he cupped my jaw and placed a hard peck on my lips before pushing me to my knees.

Without even asking me, I knew, and crawled back inside the cage.

(Luther)

With my marks on her skin and my cum deep inside her ass, I closed the door of the cage and locked it. I had no intention of fucking Lexi. Not like that. But my control had snapped. It took everything in me not to continue but my orgasm had stopped me. She was lucky.

"Do you hate me?" she asked, her voice small.

"No, pet." And that was the truth. I didn't hate her. At all. I hated what she did, and she would make up for it. She would have to earn my forgiveness but hate her? Not one fucking bit.

"Then why did you fuck me like you did?" She curled into a ball, a tear falling free from her eye.

I walked around the cage and crouched, cupping her head. Her hair was a wild mess around her head. Her leggings torn. But she was flawless and damn near perfect. I wouldn't have her any other way.

"You owe me for your betrayal. I will make you pay for what you did. And I will get the answers I'm looking for, but right now you need to rest. I'll come collect you in a while and give you a bath, feed you and let you use the washroom."

"Will you ever let me out of here?"

I was taken aback by her question. I wasn't a good man, but I also wasn't a monster. "What do you think, pet?"

She pushed to her forearms. "I think you're showing me just how mad you are over everything that happened."

"Rest." I stood. "I'll come get you in a bit," I said, heading to the door.

"Luther?"

I stopped, staring back at her. "Yes?"

"You can fuck me, hate me, do whatever you want to me…" Her breath hitched. "But it won't stop me from loving you."

Instead of responding, I left the room and locked the door behind me. I realized then that I had truly met my match. Lexi was placed in my life when I needed her most. Although we hadn't met the normal way, she was mine and I was hers. What we shared was ours. I could be rough with her and she welcomed it with open arms. She begged for it.

Heading to my bedroom, I stripped along the way. Once I reached the large room, I was naked. Throwing my clothes in the laundry hamper, I trudged to the bathroom. The scent of Lexi was all over me. She was embedded in my skin. In my damn senses. The love I had for her scared the shit out of me. Because I knew, no matter what happened, I would go to the darkest place of my soul to keep her. And I hadn't been there since I was a kid. I just prayed she would join me.

THIRTY

Lexi

EVERYTHING IN ME TOLD me that Luther was trying to get me to hate him. I wasn't sure why. I knew I screwed up. I trusted a man who would help me bring down my brother only to lose another man I loved in the process.

It had felt like days since I was forced to crawl into Luther's cage. Even though I knew that wasn't the case, time seemed to stand still. I lost all sense of reality the longer I was stuck between these four walls of bars.

Luther had fucked me two more times against the cage, only to throw me back inside it. As much as I wanted to hate him for it, I couldn't. He had warned me that there was a side to him that I wasn't ready for. That neither of us were ready for but I found that I enjoyed it. Every bit of him.

Just when I thought Luther had left me alone for what I could only assume was the same night, the door opened.

My body thrummed, hoping he would use me for a fourth time. Although my hips were bruised from being pushed up against the metal edge of the cage, my nipples peaked and my core clenched with anticipation.

Luther came into the room and crouched in front of the cage. Unlocking the door, he reached inside.

Before he could speak, I was in his arms with my body wrapped around him. I feared he would push me away but instead, he lifted me and carried me out of the room.

He held me against him, running his hand up and down my back.

I squeezed him, snuggling my face into the crook of his neck and inhaled the heady scent of our sex. He hadn't showered, and I could smell me all over him. My desire. The faint scent of my perfume tickled my nose.

Once we were in his room, he brought me to his large bathroom and placed me gently on my feet.

"I'll run you a bath," he said, brushing his hand down my cheek.

I nodded, glancing at the toilet. My bladder suddenly screamed for release.

"I'm not leaving, Lexi, so you might as well get used to relieving yourself in front of me." Luther sat on the edge of the large tub and turned on the water.

Doing as I was told, I used the toilet, the embarrassment vanishing quickly when my bladder got the relief it needed.

"Are you going to join me?" I asked him when I was finished.

"Do you want me to?"

I nodded, coming up to his side and taking off my clothes. Standing naked before him, I waited. For what I was no longer sure.

"You have bruises." He brushed his thumb over my hip bones, his dark eyes popping back to mine. "Do you hurt?"

I shrugged. Physically, not really. But emotionally? Yes.

His jaw clenched. Pulling off his own clothes, Luther placed them in the laundry hamper.

My eyes widened.

With his back to me, that was when I truly saw them. I had seen him naked before but never in this light. And I sure as hell didn't see the tattoos on his back.

"Luther." I walked up to him, brushing my hands over his back.

He stiffened. "Lexi."

"What happened?" The tattoos marking his skin had been slashed. Almost like he had been whipped repeatedly.

"I was punished." He turned around, grabbed my hand and kissed my knuckles.

"For what?" I asked, my heart jumping.

"I like pain, pet. But it wasn't by choice. That's why when I revealed myself to you and you slapped me, my cock only became harder."

I shivered, remembering that moment when he had let it be known that he was my Master.

"I don't understand," I murmured. "You can be dominant but enjoy pain as well?"

"Yes."

"How?" I frowned, trying to understand.

"I don't know, Lexi." He pulled me to the tub, helping me into the hot water. "I've liked pain for as long as I can remember but I would have these moments where I would black out. I would do things during these blackouts but have no recollection of it. The pain, my sessions, would help me learn to control them. And it's worked so far. But it's been a while."

"Is that why you asked me how I would feel about whipping you?"

"Yes." Luther stepped into the tub behind me.

I sat, leaning against him.

He wrapped his arms around me, kissing the side of my neck. "I won't ask you to do anything that you don't want to do but I trust you. Even though we have shit to work through, I still do trust you."

I turned in his arms, leaning against the side of the tub. "I am sorry. I'm sorry for everything."

"I know you are." Luther grabbed a cloth, dipped it into the water and ran it over my shoulders and upper back. "I'm sorry for throwing you in my cage. I also shouldn't have fucked you like I did tonight."

"I liked it," I muttered. "Is something wrong with me?"

"No." He cupped my face and placed a soft peck on my temple. "You liked it just as much as I did." He leaned his forehead against mine. "I shouldn't have done that though. I…fuck. I'm truly sorry."

"I know," I whispered. "Have you talked to Georgio?" He'd fucked up something fierce and I had no idea if he would ever be able to earn Luther's trust again.

"No." Luther leaned back. "I should. I know I should but I…" He hesitated. "I've known him since we were kids. And as much as it pisses me off, I understand why he couldn't tell me he was with the FBI. I get that part. But what I don't get is how he could drag you into this."

"I could have said no." I turned back around and leaned against Luther's chest. "I should feel more guilt for what happened to my brother. Maybe I will. Maybe it hasn't truly hit me yet. I didn't know Georgio was going to kill him. I had no idea at all." I sat forward, curling my knees against my chest. "I wish I could have talked to Charlie first before this shit went down."

"I know, pet." Luther ran his hands up and down my back, easing some of the tension rippling through me. "My sister is going to stop by later today."

"Maybe she can give me some insight into who my brother was as well."

"Maybe but I don't think she knows anything more than we do." Luther brushed my hair off my nape. "I think she was his way out of his head."

"He used her." I leaned my head to the side, giving Luther better access to my throat.

"Mmmhmm…" Luther ran his fingers beneath the underside of my breast. "I think he let her play. Do whatever she wanted. Some people who are in control of everything around them, need to submit in the bedroom."

"Like me," I whispered.

"Yeah, pet." Luther kissed my shoulder. "Exactly like you."

"I'm still so confused about everything but there's one thing I'm not confused about." I looked up at him then.

"What's that?" he asked, his voice husky.

"My feelings for you," I said, breathlessly.

"Yeah?" He turned me in his arms, pulling me onto his lap. "And what are your feelings for me?"

"Hmm…" I tapped my chin. "You're an asshole but—" Luther pushed me back until I was submerged in the water. I pushed him, came up for air, and coughed.

He chuckled.

"I can't believe you did that," I said between coughs.

"That's what you get for calling me an asshole, pet." He placed a soft peck between my breasts. "Even though it's true." He winked.

I sighed, brushing his bangs out of his hair. "So…" I didn't want to ruin the moment between us, but I needed to know. "Can I spend the night in your bed?"

"I'm not putting you back in the cage. Not tonight. If that's what you're wondering."

"It is," I said, blowing out a slow breath.

"As pissed as I am…" He rubbed the back of his neck. "We can't move forward if we don't deal with this shit. But I promise you, I will fuck you against my cage again." He ran his thumbs over the bruises on my hips. "I know you enjoy the bite of the metal in your skin. You may not need pain to get off, but you certainly become wetter."

My body heated. "I *am* sorry," I murmured. "For everything."

"I know." His eyes darkened. "But I don't want to talk about it anymore."

"What did you want to talk about?" I asked, my body heating. I knew what he wanted. His dick had hardened between us in the past couple of minutes. "This?" I wrapped my hands around him.

"Hop on, baby," he growled. "Earn my forgiveness."

And I did.

THIRTY-ONE

Luther

"PLEASE." FUCK. I SHIVERED, my body heating as the pain sliced through me. I needed more of it. I needed to bathe in the agony and let it wash over me. I needed it to control me, so I could learn to control my lust for it. It wasn't right. This need for more. This hunger to hurt. This yearning for torture.

"One more."

I winced, bracing myself as the slice of the whip cut into my back.

My body exploded, a hard cry leaving my lips as the orgasm ripped through me.

A wet cloth was shoved into my hands. The sound of a door closing a moment later grated on my nerves.

It always ended this way.

She whipped.

I came.
She left.

I shot up in bed, my skin covered in a cold sheen of sweat.

"Luther?" A gentle hand cupped my shoulder.

I grabbed it, brought it to my mouth, and laid back down beside Lexi. Pulling her into my arms, I brushed my face into the crook of her neck. A sense of calm washed over me as I laid with her in my arms.

"You okay?" she asked, pulling my arm tighter around her.

"I am now." I kissed the spot beneath her ear.

"Bad dream?"

"Yeah," I murmured. I hadn't had a dream like that in years. I had been good. Things had been *good* but clearly my time for another session was coming. And soon. *Fuck.*

"Want to talk about it?" Lexi asked softly, rolling onto her side until she was facing me.

I reached over her and turned on the lamp before scrubbing a hand down my face. I didn't want to talk about it, but I knew I should. I should tell Lexi everything that made up me. That made me who I was today.

"There was a woman," I croaked. "I'm not sure what you would want to call her. I never talked to her. I never met with her outside of my…sessions."

"Sessions?" Lexi raised an eyebrow, keeping her hand locked in mine.

"Yeah, pet." I rolled over onto my back, staring up at the ceiling. "She helped me deal with those blackouts I told you about."

"Oh. What else did she help you with?"

"Just that." I pinched the bridge of my nose, warding off the impending headache threatening to consume me. "She would whip me, and I would…fall apart." Which was putting it politely.

"You would have an orgasm?" Lexi asked, her voice small.

"Yeah."

Lexi rested her head on my chest. "If you need my help, I'm here."

I met her gaze. "Really?" She had told me before that she would help me, that she would whip me if that was what I needed, but hearing her say it again stirred something inside of me.

"Just tell me what I need to do," Lexi said. "I might not like it but if it's therapy or helps you or whatever, I'm…I'm willing to try. For you."

I pushed her onto her back, kneeled between her legs, and crushed my mouth to hers.

She gasped, letting me in and arching beneath me.

"I fucking love you," I murmured against her mouth.

"Mmmm…" She snaked her hands around my neck, deepening the kiss. "I love you too, Luther."

(Lexi)

Instead of answering me, Luther made love to me for the rest of the night until we both passed out. I wanted answers from him. I wanted to know what was going on and why suddenly he seemed more stressed than usual. I also wanted to know who the woman was that he used to see or let unleash her full wrath on him. It didn't make sense to me that he was dominant but a masochist just the same. I had no idea that was even possible.

Luther let me sleep for a few hours before slipping back inside my body. It had been gentle and sweet, nothing like the man on top of me. It contradicted with his actions but made me fall even more in love with him just the same.

Later that morning, a ringing jarred through me.

With my eyes still closed, I reached out and snatched my phone off the nightstand. "Yeah."

"Lexi?"

My eyes widened. I sat up, glancing at the clock. It was almost noon. "Oh God. Britney. I'm so sorry." I had left her in charge while I wasn't at the deli, but I forgot to call her directly and let her know what was going on.

"I'm just glad you're okay. I was worried sick. All of us have been."

My chest tightened. I was momentarily surprised that Charlie's death never made the news but then I quickly remembered that the men in my life preferred to keep it a secret.

"There's been a family emergency, everything's fine," I added quickly for fear she would ask questions I wasn't ready to answer. "I just need a couple more days and then I'll be back there. Anything you need to stock up, just use the business account." I stood from the bed and began pacing. "Has anything else happened?"

"No."

"Good." I blew out a breath of relief. "I'm glad."

"Oh, wait. There is one more thing." Britney paused.

"What's that?"

"Uh…there's a man who's been by a few times."

My heart jumped. "What does he want?"

"He never says. Just asks where you are. We tell him that you're away due to a family emergency and then he leaves. But it's weird though. He stops by. Has a slice of apple pie, a cup of coffee, asks where you are, we give him an answer, and he leaves. It's been going on for a few days."

Georgio. But he knew where I was, why would he be stopping by the deli? "Okay. Let me see if I can find out what's going on. If he stops by again and asks where I am, just give him the same answer you've been giving him already."

"Okay," Britney said. "Will do."

"Thank you. I'll be in touch."

We said our goodbyes and I placed my phone back on the nightstand. Blowing out a slow breath, I scrubbed a hand down my face. So many questions were still unanswered. I needed to speak to Georgio. I needed to find out what the hell was going on. And I also needed to know if Luther still kept in touch with that woman. I waited for the jealousy to hit but it never did. Knowing he asked me to help him proved that he wasn't using her for his sessions. But it didn't mean he still didn't see her.

Quickly getting dressed, I left the room and went in search of Luther. It was the middle of the week, so the house was busier than what I was used to. Staff milled about. Construction crew walked around with their tools, muttering to each other about whatever it was they had to fix up. I couldn't imagine what that would be. The place was perfect if you asked me.

"Lexi."

I jumped, spinning around and finding Luther leaning against the wall. His dark eyes peered into my soul. He was dressed in light beige khakis with a white dress shirt. The sleeves were rolled up to his elbows. The tattoos on his forearms flexed with each movement. His hair was unkempt but God, he was beautiful.

"How did you sleep?" he asked, pushing away from the wall and closing the distance between us.

"Fine. I spoke to Britney just now. She's who I left in charge at the deli."

"Everything okay?"

I nodded. "I need to get back there. Make an appearance at least. And I'm not sure what to do about my apartment."

"Rent it out. Move all of your stuff here and put Charlie's things into storage."

I gaped at Luther. "You want me to move in with you?"

He tilted his head. "Why wouldn't I?"

"I…" I looked around us. It wasn't like there wasn't the room but was I ready to move in with him?

"Lexi." Luther pinched my chin, forcing me to look up at him. "I love you, pet. I need you by my side. You can take one of my cars, so you have a way back and forth to the deli, but I don't want you in that apartment alone."

I didn't want to stay there anyway after finding my brother dead. It held too many bad memories, but I was still shocked that Luther would want me moving in with him and so soon.

"Please, pet."

"You really want me to move in with you?" I asked, brushing my hands down his broad chest.

"I do." He kissed my cheek, running his lips down the length of my jaw. "We fit well together. I think you would look good ruling my home."

"You want me to be your Queen?" I whispered.

Luther lifted his head, a small smirk spreading on his face. Without answering, he placed a soft peck on my forehead. "I have work to do. Make yourself at home, pet. We'll stop by the deli later and then I have to make an appearance at ToKnight." He kissed me one last time before releasing me and heading back down the hall he had come from.

I looked at the room before me. The sound of a door closing a moment later jarred through every inch of me. Something was off. And I had a feeling I was going to find out very soon just how off it actually was.

(Luther)

My cell rang and rang. The house phone rang. My email popped up, indicating a new email. Even Facebook notified me that I had a new message.

But I only sat back in the chair, tenting my fingers under my chin and ignoring it. All of it. It was Georgio trying to get a hold me. But I didn't want to hear him out. He had betrayed me and brought my girl into this shit. Under normal circumstances, I would have killed him already. Before I met Lexi, he would be dead at my feet, but I found that she brought out the best in me. So I wouldn't make him suffer. Not yet at least. Not until I had all the answers I was looking for. But I hated waiting.

A soft knock sounded on the door to my office. A tremor of anger rushed through me at being interrupted but I pushed it back. "Come in."

The door opened, revealing my sister.

"Vanessa." I stood. "Did you see Lexi?"

She shook her head. Her once bright eyes, now dark and vacant.

"What's going on?" I rushed to her side, pulling her into a quick hug before guiding her to the couch.

"Georgio's been trying to get in contact with me." She searched my face. "He killed Charlie. Didn't he?"

My chest tightened. "How could you know that?"

She shrugged. "Just a guess. I know this has nothing to do with me——"

"When it comes to Georgio, it always has something to do with you." I shook my head. "Listen." I grabbed her hands. "Charlie wasn't a good guy. I'm sorry you got caught up in this shit."

"How's Lexi doing?" she asked, ignoring me.

"As good as can be expected." I stood from the couch and went to the door. "I'm sure she'd like to see you."

Vanessa laughed. "Is that your subtle way of kicking me out?"

"I have work to do." I needed to figure out how deep I was in this shit since Charlie died. He owed people money. A lot of money. And I had to make sure they wouldn't come after Lexi because of his mistakes.

"Fine. I'll go find your girlfriend. Maybe she can entertain me." Vanessa rose from the couch, smoothing down her sweater and fixing her ponytail.

"Touch her and Charlie's death won't be the only thing you'll have to cry over," I growled.

"Yeah, yeah." Vanessa patted my chest. "Trust me, big brother. She doesn't want me. She only has eyes for you. I don't get it." She shook her head. "Have you introduced her to your sessions yet?"

"Goodbye, Vanessa." I pushed her out of my office and slammed the door shut before leaning against it. Blowing out a slow breath, my skin crawled at what I would eventually have to do. I just prayed Lexi was strong enough for it.

THIRTY-TWO

Lexi

"HELLO, PET."

My eyes popped up, landing on Vanessa. I gasped, shoved to my feet, and rushed to her before pulling her into a tight hug.

She let out a hard sigh, squeezing me back.

"How are you doing?" I asked, the scent of her rose shampoo tickling my nose. "I'm so sorry. I'm so sorry for everything."

She leaned back, frowning. "Why are you sorry?" She cupped my cheek. "Did *you* kill Charlie?"

"Well…no. But—"

"Then don't worry about it." She released me and walked to the large patio window. "You know, I used to hate this place."

"Really?" I moved to her side, staring out into the backyard. "Why?"

"It felt like hell." She reached her hand out.

I slipped my fingers in hers, waiting for her to continue.

"I'm not sure what all Luther has told you about our father but he was a controlling bastard. And because I had a different mother than Luther, it only made things worse."

"I'm sorry." I paused. "I didn't know my father and our mother died a while ago. It's been my brother and I ever since and now…" My chest tightened.

"You're not as torn up about Charlie as I thought you'd be." Vanessa's gaze burned into the side of my head. "Why is that, Lexi?"

"Because he was just like our father. Money hungry and desperate for more. He sold me to your brother, Vanessa. I'm sorry if I don't feel more guilt over his death." I turned to walk away when her hand tightened around mine.

"That's not…" Her lips pressed into a firm line. "I didn't know him that well but I fell for him fast. He had been the only man who could ever do that to me. He showed up at The Club one night and I felt sorry for him. I didn't know he was your brother. I swear I didn't know."

"I know. I believe you." And I did but I still needed to know… "Have you…have you talked to Georgio?"

She laughed, rubbing the back of her neck. "No, but he's tried contacting me. Why he thinks that I want anything to do with him after what he did to Charlie, is beyond me."

"You know about that?"

"I'm not stupid." She sighed. "Georgio and I have a history. He and Luther have been friends for as long as I can remember. Although, that friendship has always been rocky."

"What do you mean?"

Vanessa opened the patio door. "Let's go outside."

I followed beside her, letting her lead the way.

When we stepped out onto the back deck, she looked up at the evening sky. "Georgio always wanted more. Just like your brother. But it's how he and Luther were raised. Our father never expected me to take on that roll, so he focused all his time and energy on Luther. Maybe I was jealous. Maybe I still am. I don't know." She looked down at our joined hands.

My cheeks heated, forgetting that my hand was still in hers.

"I don't blame Luther. For anything. Not for being our father's favorite. Not for taking you from me. And not for falling in love with you."

"What?" I gasped, my eyes widening.

She gave me a small smile. "I never had a chance with you. I knew that then and I know that now. Between you and your brother, I don't know who's worse." She laughed lightly. "There's something about you both that can make the strongest Dom fall to their knees."

"Oh." My cheeks heated even more.

"God, what I wouldn't give to keep that blush on your skin." Vanessa shook her head, releasing my hand. "I'm sorry. You don't belong to me. But I'm glad we're friends."

"Of course we are," I told her. We had bonded rather quickly during the weeks she trained me.

"Good but if my brother does something stupid to make you leave him for good, I'm always here." She waggled her eyebrows.

I laughed, hooking an arm around her shoulders. "Thank you."

"For what?" She cupped my arm, leaning her head against mine.

"For making me laugh and for being my friend." I didn't grow up having girlfriends but was thankful for Vanessa. Even if she crossed the line a bit.

"Let's sit." She pulled away from me and sat at the nearest patio bench. "Tell me about everything. Whatever you know."

I sat beside her and let the words spill from my lips.

(Luther)

The video chat on my computer popped up, indicating an incoming call. As much as I didn't want to answer it, I did anyway.

"What do you want, Georgio?" I asked, sitting back in my chair and tenting my fingers under my chin.

"I need to explain."

"Explain what exactly?" I sat forward. "How you used my girlfriend to bring down her brother? How you betrayed me? Or how about the fact that you're still alive?"

"Listen to me, Luther. Lexi didn't have to agree."

I barked a laugh. "Right and you would have let her go freely? Come on, Georgio. I'm not fucking stupid. I know how you work. Just because you're a man of the law, doesn't mean you don't do shady shit as well."

"How the hell could you know that?"

I chuckled. "Because I would do the same thing. Now if you're not going to explain what the hell is going on, I'm done."

"Have you talked to your sister?"

"What the hell does she have to do with this?" She was innocent in this whole fucked up situation.

Georgio rubbed his jaw. "You should ask her that question," he said and disconnected the call.

I shot up from my chair and stormed out of the office. "Lexi," I called out. "Did my sister—" My steps slowed to a stop when I found Vanessa and Lexi standing by the patio door.

Lexi caught my gaze. "Hey, it started raining so we came back inside." She gave me a soft smile.

My heart stuttered. God, she was beautiful.

Her cheeks reddened.

"Vanessa," I said, my voice coming out rougher than I had intended.

My sister turned toward me, crossing her arms under chest. "What?"

"I talked to Georgio."

She frowned. "Yeah? And?"

"He asked me if I talked to you." I scratched my jaw. "I feel like he was implying that you're hiding something. Are you hiding something, Vanessa?"

Her lips pressed into a firm line, her back stiffening. "I should go. I'll see you later, Lexi," she said, her gaze not moving from mine.

"Oh. Okay," Lexi said softly.

Vanessa quickly left, and I let her. I would get out of her what was going on but until then, I would let her wonder what all I knew. And then when she finally caved, I would get the information I was looking for. No matter the cost.

THIRTY-THREE

Lexi

I HAD NO IDEA what was going on with Vanessa and Luther. She left, he went into his office, and I remained in the living room. She was hiding something.

I had every intention of leaving Luther alone when a thought came to me. Heading to Luther's office, I knocked lightly on the door. "Luther?" I peaked inside. "You have a moment?"

"What's wrong?" he asked, peering up from behind the computer on his desk.

"Nothing." I stepped farther into his office. "I need to go to my apartment."

"No," he said, his voice firm and final.

"Luther, we could get some answers as to what your sister is hiding. I have a feeling her and my brother were more than just Domme and sub." I approached him tentatively.

He sighed, sitting back in the chair and pinched the bridge of his nose. "I don't want you going there by yourself."

"Then come with me," I said, kneeling at his feet. "Please. I need answers just like you do, and I also need to get the apartment ready to rent out anyway."

"You're so beautiful," he said, cupping my cheek.

"Please." I leaned into his palm.

"Fine." He sat back and patted his lap. "Let me get some work done here first and then we'll go to your apartment."

I rose to my feet and sat on his lap. "Shouldn't I leave then so you can work?"

"No." He inched a hand beneath the hem of my shirt, his fingers brushing beneath my breasts.

I shivered at the soft touch. "Luther." I squirmed on his lap.

"Stop moving, pet," he bit out, that delicious part of him growing beneath me.

"Hmm…" I hooked an arm around his shoulders, placing a soft peck on his cheek. "You like that, Sir?"

He chuckled. "Careful, Lexi. I don't like being teased."

"Aww." I pushed my ass harder against his lap. "But I like teasing you."

In a quick move, Luther bent me over his desk. "Is that so?"

"Yes," I breathed, my heart racing.

"Interesting." Luther ran a hand up the back of my leg before landing a hard swat on the seat of my ass. "Tell me more. What else do you like to do?"

"I like seeing if you'll snap. I like when you lose control and take what you want from me." I pushed back into him, my rear rubbing over his crotch.

Luther sat back in the chair and lowered my pants to just below my ass. "Well I like when you submit to me and when your body does exactly what I want it to."

"Yeah? That's all you like?" I asked, looking at him behind me.

He smirked, running his hands over my ass. "I love you, Lexi."

My heart warmed. "I love you too, Luther."

His eyes darkened even more, his jaw clenching.

"What's wrong?"

"Nothing." His hands continued to roam over my ass, but something told me that he wasn't actually in the moment with me.

I lifted off of the desk and turned toward him. Slipping out of my clothes, I straddled his lap. "Talk to me," I whispered, running my fingers over the scruff on his strong jaw.

"There's nothing to talk about," he bit out, pushing me off of him. "I have work to do." He turned around toward his computer.

"Oh. Okay." I picked up my clothes and got dressed. I wanted to press and demand for him to tell me what was going on but that tick in his jaw made me decide against it.

"Lexi."

I ignored him and headed to the door.

"Lexi," he repeated, coming up behind me and cupping my shoulder.

"What do you want, Luther?" I covered his hand with mine.

"You. That's it."

I turned around, placing my hands on his chest. "Really? Are you sure? Because right now I feel like you're pushing me away."

"I'm trying…" He took a breath and then another. "I'm trying to figure out what's going on with my sister."

"Then let me help you. I had started looking through Charlie's room before…"

Luther pulled away and began pacing. "Before Georgio and I interrupted you."

"Hey." I closed the distance between us and grabbed onto his dress shirt. "Why don't you take a break and we can go to my apartment. I need answers just as much as you do and I'm sure we can find something there."

"Not tonight." Luther went back to the chair behind his desk.

"Then I'm going to go by myself." I opened the door when a heavy hand slammed it closed.

"No, you aren't."

"What am I supposed to do while you're working, Luther?" I spun on him. "I need to go to the deli. I need to go to my apartment. I need to do something because clearly you don't want me."

He raised a dark eyebrow. "I don't want you?" He grabbed my hand, placing it on the crotch of his pants. "Does this mean that I don't want you? My cock is motherfucking hard for you. Always so damn hard."

My eyes widened, my hand closing around him.

"Fuck." He shivered.

"You didn't want me a moment ago when I was naked and sitting on your lap," I said, brushing my thumb over the tip of his cock and kissing his jaw. "Do you want me now?"

"Shit, Lexi," he growled, slapping his hands against the door on either side of my head.

"Why are you fighting this? You've never fought this before." I cupped his nape, trailing kisses along his jaw. "Tell me."

"I'm losing control here." He leaned his forehead against mine. "I've never lost control before and I don't know how I feel about it."

"Well let me help you." Before he could say anything more, I covered his mouth with mine. "Please," I said when he hesitated. "We can work later. Right now, I need you and I know you need me just the same."

"I always need you," he murmured.

"Then use me, Luther." I gave his lip a gentle bite.

He growled, pushing me back against the door and deepening the kiss. His hands roamed down the sides of my body before cupping my ass. He lifted me, wrapping my legs around his waist. "I need inside you."

My stomach tumbled, a flush of heat washing over me at the desperation in his voice. "More. Tell me more."

"Fuck, Lexi." Luther released my mouth, trailing kisses and tiny bites down the length of my jaw. "I need to feel your hot pussy squeezing me. I need to feel you trembling as I fuck you as rough as I want."

"Hmm…" I gripped him hard. "You say the sweetest things."

Luther leaned back, cupping my jaw and sliding his finger between my lips. "You're so fucking incredible."

My mouth closed around his finger. Licking over the tip, I released it with a pop. "Fuck me, Sir."

(Luther)

Lexi was utterly breathtaking. I dropped her on her feet and spun her around. In a rough move, I had her pants below her ass and my hands all over her lower body. She moaned, panted, and begged for more. My palm connected with the cheeks of her ass. My fingers slid inside her, getting her hot, ready, and wet.

"Please, Luther," she pleaded, pushing back into my hand.

Cupping the back of her neck, I held her head against the door. Releasing her lower body, I undid the zipper of my pants and pulled out my straining cock. Beating the heavy flesh against the seat of her ass, I ran the tip of my cock over her drenched center.

She moaned.

I repeated the movements, teasing us both.

"Please, Luther," she whined, pushing back into me. She was greedy, her pussy hungry for my cock to fill it.

I leaned back, keeping my hand against her nape and sliding into her but not enough to fill her.

"More," she whimpered. "Please more."

I pulled out, not giving her what she wanted.

Lexi cried out in frustration. "Luther."

Pumping my cock between her legs, the tip hit her swollen clit.

"Oh God." She shook. "More."

"Are you hungry for me, Lexi?" I asked, my voice low and guttural. "You want my fat dick inside you?"

"Yes," she moaned.

Thrusting between her thighs, I watched the flush in her cheeks become more pronounced. Her eyes fluttered closed. Her breathing came out in short bursts of air. Her fingers dug into the door and her lower body met me thrust for every teasing thrust.

"I'm going to come," she whispered.

I picked up speed, helping her ride out that orgasm she craved. "Come on my cock, Lexi."

"Please fuck me," she whined.

"Nah, pet. I want you to come all over me. I want your thighs coated in your cream. I want you so fucking messy, all you can smell is what I do to you."

"Yes, please." She threw her head back, leaning it against my shoulder.

Cupping her jaw, I kissed her temple. "Come."

She cried out. "Luther."

I took that as my chance and thrust inside her.

Her cries of pleasure turned into screams. "Harder."

My thrusts picked up, slamming in and out of her. Reaching around her, my palm connected with her clit.

She gasped, her eyes shooting open.

I repeated the movement, my hand slapping against the swollen little button.

"Holy shit." She shook against me, her body heating at the pain and pleasure I was feeding it. "Again."

"You're a dirty little thing, aren't you?" I slapped her pussy, pushing my dick as deep into her as it could go.

"Yes," she screamed. "Fuck, Luther. Sir. Master."

I chuckled, connecting with her pussy again.

Slap. Slap. Slap.

"More," she cried out.

Slap. Slap. Slap.

My name left her lips on the loudest scream I had ever heard from her. I pulled out of her, slapped her clit again, and felt her release spraying over my dick. Thrusting back inside her, I prolonged her orgasm until she begged for me to stop. And only then did I fuck her harder and faster.

THIRTY-FOUR

Lexi

AFTER OUR MOMENT IN Luther's office, he decided not to work and brought me to my apartment instead. I made a quick appearance at the deli, telling everyone who was working that Charlie had passed and that I was moving.

"You want to rent your place to me?" Britney asked, her eyes shining.

I patted her hand. "I do. But I just need a couple of days to move stuff out of it. I'll leave the furniture of course but any personal items, I'll bring with me."

She nodded. "Of course." And much to my surprise, she gave me a hug. "Thank you. I really appreciate this."

"You're very welcome." I hugged her back. I said my goodbyes and met Luther out in the hall leading to my apartment.

"You good?" he asked, throwing his arm around my shoulders.

"I am but I really don't want to look through Charlie's stuff even though I know that we could find answers." I sighed. "I just want this done and over with."

"I know, Lexi." Luther kissed my cheek. "I'll help you. I just have to make a phone call first."

I caught his gaze. "Georgio?"

His jaw clenched. "As much as I don't want to talk to that fucker, I need to know what's going on."

"You forgave me. Why can't you forgive him?"

He opened his mouth to answer but scowled instead. "Let's go and get this done and over with."

I saluted him. "Yes, Sir."

"Careful." He swatted my ass. "I don't like being mocked, pet."

"Yeah, yeah." I blew him a kiss and headed to Charlie's bedroom. Opening the door, I let out a slow breath. Nothing was different from when he was last in it. Although, I had been looking through everything not too long ago, it still looked like Charlie had slept in it the night before. "Oh, Charlie." I wished things could have been different. I loved him. I did. But he loved power more than me.

"Lexi?"

I jumped as Luther came up behind me. "That was a quick call."

"It's been half an hour." He kissed the top of my head. "You good?"

"Not really." I didn't even realize that much time had passed already. I pushed away from the door and forced myself to enter the room. Charlie's room had been smaller than mine. He didn't have a lot of personal items I realized. A bed. A dresser. A nightstand with a lamp on top of it. A few movie and music posters. A floor to ceiling bookshelf and a safe. I sat on the floor in front of it.

"Do you know the code?" Luther asked, sitting on the edge of the bed behind me.

"I do. Charlie never gave it to me but it wasn't hard to crack either. It's like he wanted me to have access to it without me even knowing." It was our mother's birthday, Charlie's age, and my birth month. Any expert would be able to figure it out. "When you and Georgio found me in here, that's what I was looking through. But I wasn't able to find anything." I rubbed the back of my neck. "He had so many secrets."

"Georgio and my sister are coming over."

My head whipped around. "Really? Is it safe for them to be in the same room?"

Luther shrugged. "I don't give a fuck. You need answers. That's all I care about."

"What about you?"

"I don't care about me, Lexi." Luther moved to the floor behind me. He sat close, the heat from his body giving me the courage I needed to look through Charlie's things.

I opened the safe. There wasn't anything out of the ordinary inside it. Nothing that I wasn't expecting anyway. Money. A couple different passports for other countries. Jewelry. "I feel like maybe he watched too many movies with all this stuff."

"I wonder if this is to hide the fact that there's something else in here."

"What?" I frowned. "There's nothing in here." I pulled out large manila envelopes and handed a couple to Luther.

He took them from me and began looking through each envelope. "Uh…Lexi?

"Mmmhmm." I pulled out pictures. They were black and white and of people I had never seen before.

"Lexi."

I turned at the abrupt demand.

Luther was holding up a black and white picture of…*us*.

"I don't understand." I took the image from him. "Why would my brother have a picture of us? Or of these people?" I looked back down at the pile in my lap.

"I'm not sure, Lexi, but I will find out. Something tells me that he wasn't just taking pictures because he enjoyed it."

"Why would he have these?" I demanded, shoving the photo back into Luther's hands.

"I don't know, pet, but something is fucked up."

I scoffed. "You think?'

"Careful." He leaned forward and cupped my cheek, lowering his mouth my ear. "I know you want answers, but your sass will not help. It'll only make me throw you back in my cage."

"I just want answers." I shivered.

Luther leaned back, cupping my face. "I'll get you your answers, Lexi. No matter the cost."

"I don't like how that sounds." I grabbed onto his dress shirt, pulled him closer, and crushed my mouth to his. "You will not put yourself on the line for me."

"Lexi." His brows narrowed.

"No." I shot to my feet, storming out of Charlie's room.

"Lexi, don't walk away from me."

I spun around as Luther crashed into me. "I can't lose you. I only just found you."

"You won't lose me, baby." Luther wrapped his arms around me, holding me tightly and lifting me off my feet.

Wrapping my legs around him, I held on like he was my lifeline. Like he was everything I needed to survive. Which he was. I didn't have my brother anymore. I had no family. No one. I had no one. The revelation slammed into me. I struggled out of Luther's hold and began pacing. "I have no one. Charlie is dead. My brother, my only family, is dead and gone."

"You have me," Luther said gently.

I stopped pacing. "What are you telling me?"

"I love you, Lexi. I've never used those words before. Not to my parents. Not to my sister. No one. Not until you came along and slid into my heart like a damn drug." He closed the distance between us and cupped the back of my neck.

I sighed, stepping into his embrace. "I can feel you all through me. You're in my veins." I tilted my head, looking up at him. "You've given me everything I never knew I needed."

He placed a hard peck on my mouth.

The sound of the door opening followed by muffled voices, ruined our little moment.

"Until later, pet." Luther kissed the side of my neck and gave my ass a light swat. "I'll make you feel better."

My body heated at the promise.

"Why does this fucker have to be here?" Vanessa demanded, charging into the room with Georgio hot on her heels.

"To keep you on your pretty little toes, of course." Georgio smirked, his gaze landing on Vanessa's ass.

She let out a frustrated cry and came toward me. "I've missed you." She pulled me in for a hug. "Is my brother treating you well?"

"Yes," I answered. "But you saw me earlier today."

"Doesn't matter. I still missed you." She held me at arm's length, her brows narrowing in the center. She gave herself a shake and released me. "Brother."

Luther gave her a quick hug before stepping in front of both of us. "Before we begin, I need to know I can trust you." He rose a hand when Georgio went to speak. "I don't want to hear about how sorry you are for betraying me. I don't give a shit about that. Not anymore. Right now, we are here to find answers for Lexi. That's it." He headed down the hall. "Follow me," he called out.

Georgio looked between us, let out a grumbled curse, and followed Luther.

"You sure you're good?" Vanessa grabbed my hand.

"Yeah. You?"

She shrugged. "No matter what happens or what we find out, I cared for your brother. A lot."

"I know." I headed to Charlie's bedroom, pulling Vanessa along with me. "I don't know what's going on with you, but you will tell us. Won't you?"

"Yeah, I will."

I stopped just outside Charlie's room. "If you tell me first, I can keep Luther calm. What are you hiding?"

Vanessa searched my face. "I'm pregnant."

THIRTY-FIVE

Lexi

"IF YOU COULD HAVE kids, would you?" I asked, kicking my foot back and forth.

Charlie puffed on his cigarette. "I guess." He exhaled, the sweet scent of his smoke wafting around us. "I don't know. I don't really have the means to take care of a kid though."

"Neither do I but if it happened, I would be ecstatic."

My brother chuckled. "You need a man for that, Lexi."

"I know that, asshole," I threw back at him. "I'm just saying, if it did happen…I don't know. I guess I always pictured myself having a husband, two point five children, a dog, and all that wonderful stuff." I rolled over onto my stomach, pulling a magazine off his nightstand.

Charlie lifted his one knee to his chest, leaning back against the headboard.

"Shit like that doesn't happen to people like us, Lexi."

"Why do you always have to ruin my dreams?" I threw the magazine at him. "I'm going to meet a guy one day. We're going to fall in love and he's going to give me everything I deserve and take me out of this hell."

Charlie snorted. "Right."

"You're…you…what?" I stammered. I couldn't help it. Charlie wasn't sure if he ever wanted kids.

"I'm pregnant." Vanessa lifted her sweater, revealing a tiny bump.

"Oh…" I cupped her stomach. "Is it…"

She swallowed nosily. "It's Charlie's."

My eyes burned. "I'm going to be an aunt."

She laughed lightly. "Yeah, you are, pet."

"But I don't understand." I pulled away from her. "Luther found pictures of him and I. I thought you had a bigger secret than that. I thought…I don't know what I thought but it definitely wasn't that."

"I know," Vanessa said.

"What's going on?" Georgio asked, coming out into the hall and glancing between us both.

"Nothing." I pushed past him, finding Luther sitting on the edge of Charlie's bed. I looked back at Vanessa.

"Luther." She came toward us, ignoring Georgio's hard stare. "There's something I need to tell you."

"Do you know anything about this?" Luther asked, ignoring her and lifting the image of him and I.

"Yeah…" Her cheeks reddened. "About that." She blew out a slow breath. "Charlie was paranoid and desperate. He was trying to get enough money to…"

"To take care of you," I said.

"Yes, and you. I know he did some shady shit. I know you've had a hard time trusting him after you sold yourself to my brother." She sat down beside me and cupped my hands. "But I also know that he loved you. He loved you so much. This is all confusing. I get that.

But…" She glanced back at Georgio. "Maybe he can explain."

"What do you mean?" Georgio frowned. "I know shit all. I have no idea why the fuck I'm even here."

"Tell them about the plans you made." Vanessa stood. "How you were going to set Luther up. Make it look like he was stealing money from all of these big players he worked with. Or how about all the—"

"Shut the fuck up," Georgio snapped. "None of that shit is true." His gaze flicked to Luther's. "It's not. I promise it's not."

"Then why would she say it?" Luther rose from the bed. "Explain yourself to me. Were you trying to sabotage me? Did you recruit Lexi, hoping she would seduce me? Or did you plant it in Charlie's head that he needed all of this power? Power that got him fucking killed. By you."

Vanessa gasped. "You…you what?"

"Vee." Georgio stepped toward her. "Listen, I'm—"

"No!" She screamed, diving for him but Luther caught her around the middle. "You killed him. How could you? He didn't deserve this." Sobs wracked through her.

I pulled her from Luther, hugging her to me. My eyes welled, my throat burning past the hard lump lodged in it.

"You have one second to explain what the fuck is going on," Luther growled, shoving Georgio up against the wall.

I shivered at the mere intensity rolling off of Luther in waves.

"He was supposed to take care of me and…" She sniffed. "And you." She leaned back, cupping my face. "I know he had his moments. I know he could be a dick, but I promise you, he's not the monster you were made to think he is."

Luther glanced at me over his shoulder, raising an eyebrow.

I nodded, giving him encouragement. I was so damn confused. Hopefully Georgio could shed some light on what the hell was going on.

He turned back around to someone who used to be his partner, best friend, the only person he could trust.

"Tell me," he demanded.

"Vanessa's pregnant," Georgio finally said.

Luther passed a glance at his sister. "You're pregnant?"

Vanessa nodded, cupping her stomach.

He released Georgio and walked up to her, placing his hands on hers. "This baby will want for nothing."

She sniffed, nodding.

"You were upset," Luther said to Georgio.

"Of course I was fucking upset. I found out and lost my shit." Georgio shrugged like it was no big deal. "There, are you happy now?"

"Nope." Luther walked back over to the safe. "Not one fucking bit."

"He didn't just lose his shit." Vanessa scoffed. "Is that why you killed him? Were you jealous?"

"Of course I was fucking jealous," Georgio yelled. "But I didn't kill him because of that."

"Then why would you?" Vanessa's chin wobbled. "Why would you take him from me?"

"Because of this."

All of us turned to Luther sitting on the floor, holding up an image of Georgio standing with a man.

I frowned, recognizing the other man from seeing him in the paper or on TV. He had been every bit as powerful as Luther.

"That's…" Georgio looked between all of us. Suddenly, he spun on his heel and charged out of the room.

"I know something that might help crack your case."

I turned, finding Luther on his cell.

"I have no idea what's going on right now," Vanessa muttered.

"Neither do I." I stood at the same time Luther did.

"I'll be at your office in half an hour." He hung up, stuffing the cell back in his pocket.

"What's going on?" I asked. "Georgio recruited me to bring you down. Was that…I feel like that was all a lie."

"I have a feeling it was, pet." Luther cupped my cheek. "While I've had Georgio at my side for years, little does he know that I've actually been keeping tabs on him. But I never had any proof. I actually contacted Charlie after he started working for me. I paid him to help me find out whatever he could on my business partner. Charlie was good. He got a little too close though. Georgio found out and that's why he killed him. Charlie was innocent, Lexi. I promise he was and I'm sorry he lost his life because I asked him to help me. I'm also sorry that I never told you and that I made it seem like he came to me."

"So he never came to you? At all?"

"He did but not to the point I let you believe. I promise everything will be explained but I need to take care of Georgio first." Luther shoved his cell in the pocket of his dress pants.

"Who are you going to go meet up with?" I asked, unsure what to believe anymore.

"A federal agent I've dealt with on and off again throughout the years." Luther reached for my hand, bringing it up to his mouth and placing a soft peck on my knuckles. "I promise, I will explain."

I shook my head, the new revelation finally making sense. "So…Charlie wasn't bad like Georgio said?"

"No, baby." Luther gave me a soft smile. "I actually have something for you." He glanced over my head. "For both of you."

"I don't know what's going on right now," Vanessa said, her voice dripping with contempt. "But I swear if that man…" She took a sharp inhale. "I'll kill him myself."

"It won't come to that," Luther promised.

"Should we go after Georgio?" I asked, still not understanding what was going on.

"He'll turn up." Luther kept a firm grip on my hand and led me out of Charlie's bedroom. "He'll feel guilty and that guilt will force him to turn himself in."

"How do you know that?" Vanessa demanded. "I still don't know what the hell is going on. I don't like this. Luther, please tell us something. Anything."

"I know it because it's how he is." Luther paused in his steps, forcing us to come to a halt. "He acts all lethal and shit but he's truly not. Georgio is a pussy."

I snorted. "Well, he did ask me for my help." I couldn't believe this was all happening.

"Let's head home and we'll talk and show you what it is I need to show you." Luther brought my hands up to his mouth. "Okay?"

I nodded. "What about the person you spoke to on the phone just now?"

"I'm still meeting with them. They can wait worst case. They know my word is gold. But I need to show you and my sister something first."

I passed a glance at Vanessa.

She shrugged.

I wasn't sure what was so important that Luther refused to go after Georgio or even to the authorities like he said he was going to. I was confused. So damn confused. But also elated at the same time that Charlie wasn't as bad as I thought he was. Looked like Georgio set us both up.

God, Charlie. My eyes pricked with unshed tears, my nose burning. Guilt sat heavily on my shoulders. Knowing there was nothing I could do now that he was gone, all I could do was hope that he died, not blaming me.

THIRTY-SIX

ONCE WE ARRIVED AT our home, Vanessa left the vehicle first. When we were alone, Luther cut the engine and turned to me.

"Lexi."

I sighed, meeting his gaze. "I'm confused."

"I know, pet," he said gently. "All of your questions will get answered. I promise. But I wanted to tell you..." His dark eyes burned into me.

My body heated. "What is it?"

"After all of this…" He cleared his throat. "I need you. In every way. I can wait. This isn't the right time, but I need you, Lexi."

"I don't know what that means but I'll…I'll do whatever it is you need."

"You're fucking incredible." He cupped my cheek. "You do know that right?"

"I don't think I am. Not really anyway." I covered his hand. "But I'm willing to try for you."

A soft knock on the window made me jump.

Vanessa opened the door. "I hate to ruin this moment, but I would like to know what the hell is going on and the baby wants a gyro."

Luther slid from the car. "I can have—"

"Nope." Vanessa shook her head. "I don't want your cook to make me anything. Thank you though. There's a place by me that makes the best fucking gyros known to man." She groaned. "So good. That's what I want anyway. Although, I think I would drive hours just to get one with how bad this craving is."

I laughed, hooked my arm in hers, and led her up the steps. "How far along are you?"

"Almost four months." She placed a hand on her stomach. "I asked if I was further along because I didn't think I could be showing this much already."

"Four months. I didn't know you and Charlie…" I hesitated. "Anyway."

"I met him before you, pet." She stopped, stepping in front of me.

Luther walked by us, his hard gaze watching her.

I raised an eyebrow.

Our eyes locked.

"Give us a moment?" I asked gently.

He nodded, heading into the large house.

"He's jealous." Vanessa laughed. "I would say that he has no reason to be but if you weren't his, I'd snatch you up."

My cheeks burned.

She cocked her head to the side, giving me a small smile. "I can understand what he sees in you though."

She brushed her fingers down my cheek. "So submissive."

"Tell me how you met Charlie." I needed to change the subject off of me. It was weird. Way too weird. And I could feel Luther watching us. I didn't bother turning around, knowing I wouldn't see him anyway. He was probably watching us on one of the security cameras.

"Charlie came into The Club." Vanessa shrugged. "It was no big deal at first, but he was stressed about something. And I was intrigued. So I went up to him and well…I loved him. I know Georgio and I have a rocky history but what I had with Charlie was nothing like that."

"I wish I would have known."

"I know. I'm sorry for not telling you but Charlie was adamant about keeping it a secret. I'm not sure why but I have a feeling that it has to do with all of this shit that's going on." Vanessa rubbed the back of her neck. "I don't know but we need to find out."

"Let's go see what this thing is that Luther wants to show us." I went to walk up the stairs when Vanessa grabbed my arm. Before I knew what was going on, she pressed her lips against mine. My eyes widened.

The kiss quickly ended.

She gave me a lopsided grin. "Yup. I would definitely go for you if you weren't with Luther."

My face heated.

She laughed, placing a soft peck on my forehead. "I loved your brother even though he's gone but there's something about you, pet."

I stepped away from her and headed up the steps. Well that was weird.

As soon as I went to the door, it slammed open.

Luther stared down at us with his arms crossed. "Enjoy your little talk with my girlfriend, Vanessa?"

Vanessa scoffed, walking past him. "Please. She's all yours, brother dearest. I was just seeing what the fuss was about."

He grunted. "Meet us in my office."

She huffed. "Fine. I know when I'm not wanted." She gave me a wink and headed through the foyer and down the hall to the left.

"Pet."

I met Luther's hard stare. "I'm sorry. I don't know what happened."

He cupped my face, tilting my head back. "I'm not mad at you. My sister is a little…much sometimes."

My cheeks burned. God, I couldn't stop blushing around these two.

He smirked, placing a soft peck on my mouth.

Snaking my arms around his shoulders, I pulled him against me and deepened the kiss.

A soft growl escaped from somewhere deep in his chest. "Lexi," he murmured against my lips.

Running my fingers through his hair, I dove my tongue even further into his mouth. I wasn't sure what had come over me, but I knew that I needed to just feel him. To have him hard, swollen, begging for that release I always wanted to give him.

Luther ran his hands down my back, cupped my ass, and pushed me up against the wall. "Stop." He broke the kiss, brushing his thumb over my bottom lip. "My little minx."

"I'm sorry," I said, breathing hard. "I just…"

"You need me," he whispered, licking up the length of my neck. "Just as much as I need you."

I nodded, a shiver rippling down my spine.

"I don't think you'll ever need me as much as I need you," he muttered. His voice had been so low, I wasn't sure if I heard him correctly or not but either way, he was wrong. I would always need him. Just as much. Maybe a little more. He grabbed my hand, linking our fingers and placing a kiss on my knuckles. "Let's go before I fuck you right here."

"That wouldn't be so bad." But I stepped out of his hold.

He chuckled, giving my ass a light swat. "You got me nice and hard, pet." He kissed my cheek. "I'll make you pay for that later."

"I look forward to it." I stepped in front of him, reaching out to cup him over his pants. Standing on tiptoes, I placed a soft peck on his chin. "*Sir.*"

He shook his head. "Let's go and get this done and over with."

I didn't know what was going on but when Luther sat both Vanessa and I down in front of his computer, the nerves fluttering around in my belly only became worse as time ticked on.

Vanessa grabbed my hand which earned us a growl.

"Stop," she said to Luther. "I need…"

"We need each other," I told him.

He looked between us both. "Fine. Press play." He moved behind me, placing his hand on my shoulder and running his thumb back and forth over my nape.

I curled my fingers in Vanessa's and pressed play on his laptop.

Charlie suddenly came into the camera.

A gasp sounded from the room. I wasn't sure if it was from me or from Vanessa or from both of us.

"This…this fucking sucks. A lot. Because if you're watching this, obviously I'm dead." Charlie chuckled, running a hand through his shaggy brown hair. "I know you have questions. And I can only assume that both of you are there. My sister and my…" He swallowed hard. "My girl."

Vanessa's breath hitched.

"First, I just want to say how sorry I am. To both of you. I know you have questions and I promise I'm going to answer them." He sat back. That was when I realized he was in his bedroom at our apartment. "I'm just going to come out and say it. Georgio is a fucking bastard. I'm assuming it was him who killed me." His face paled. "Fuck, saying that out loud is…anyway." He cleared his throat again. "There's no easy way to say this so I'm just going to come right out and say it." He inhaled a deep breath. "I'm with the FBI."

My eyes widened.

"Holy shit," Vanessa exclaimed.

"Lexi, remember that job I had applied to a long time ago but didn't think I got it? Well this was it."

"I remember that conversation," I murmured.

"I don't think I got the job," Charlie grumbled.

"Well, maybe you're too good for them."

He never gave me any more information or told me what the job was that he actually applied for.

"When I applied, I was told I couldn't say that I was even applying for the job. That's why I made it seem like I never got it. It was very hush-hush. Once I was hired, I definitely couldn't say anything at that point. I had one job. To take Georgio out."

My heart started racing. "Is he…"

"Whatever you're thinking, Lexi, is probably correct. I was hired by the FBI to kill Georgio." Charlie leaned forward. "But it clearly didn't work, and he got to me first. He's good. He's really fucking good. Vee, I know you and Georgio have a history but please promise me that you will never go back to him. I don't want that fucker anywhere near our baby or you."

"I promise," Vanessa whispered.

I squeezed her hand.

"I made this video so you would have proof. There were so many times I wanted to tell you both what was going on, but I couldn't. I didn't want to put either of you in danger. So I asked Luther for help. I had seen pictures of them together. We also had so many files on them but they're good boys and haven't been caught yet."

Luther grunted, pulling a chair up beside me and sitting.

"Lexi," Charlie continued. "Georgio recruited you to get to Luther but I don't think he expected you to fall in love with him."

My cheeks burned.

Luther cupped my knee.

"I also assume you found the pictures," Charlie said.

I nodded even though Charlie couldn't see me.

"I took those pictures of you two to throw Georgio off my trail. Although, it didn't work." Charlie let out a heavy sigh. "Listen, bottom line is I'm not who I said I was and I'm sorry for that. I'm also sorry for being a dick and making it so you couldn't trust me in the end. But I promise, everything you were told about me was all lies. I never passed around a picture of you, Lexi. I never sold you to Luther. The Club set up was real, before you ask. It was very real but that was all your choice. And that shit about me being a dark web master was all lies. I had help. Again, to throw Georgio off. He's into some dangerous shit. He was trying to set Luther up. Some business partner you have there, buddy."

"Asshole," Luther muttered.

"But I get it." Charlie sat back, leaning against his headboard. "It's hard not trusting someone who's been with you your whole life. But enough of that. Georgio is a dick and needs to be put down. And the bottom line is, I'm dead and Georgio isn't. Luther, I know you're watching this. I need you to take care of my girl. To take care of my sister. To be the best damn uncle my baby has ever had. Lexi, I need you to be the best aunt they could ever have." Charlie's breath hitched. "Alright, I need Lexi and Luther to leave so I can talk to Vanessa."

"Oh God." Vanessa wiped under her eyes.

I stood, grabbed Luther's hand, and pulled him from the office. "Luther, I—"

"I'm sorry." He wrapped me in his arms, holding me against him. "I'm so fucking sorry. For everything." He cupped my nape.

"It's not your fault." I leaned back. "It's Georgio's. I'm glad. I'm so fucking glad that Charlie isn't who I thought he was. But I feel guilty because I thought the worst of him."

"That's not your fault either." Luther placed a soft peck on my head. "We'll figure this shit out. But I want you to know that I'm not going to the authorities with this."

My eyes widened. "You're not? But you said—"

"I know what I said. I had a package couriered to them with no return address. They'll get all the info they need but when it comes to Georgio…" Luther pulled away from me. "Georgio will die by my hands and my hands only."

"Luther." I went to him, but he only stepped away. "Are you sure that's a good idea?"

"Men like him will only get put in jail and released right away because of who he knows." Luther chuckled. "I can't believe this. After all this time. I'm the one who helped him get to where he is today. I'm the one who made him become big and powerful. Me, Lexi. And what does he do? He tries to fucking ruin me and kills my girlfriend's brother and my sister's boyfriend."

"What are you going to do?" I asked, my voice small.

"Don't worry about it, pet." Luther's big body shook. "But I will warn you. I won't be the same after. I'll need your help to get me through it."

"To get you through what?" I asked even though I already knew.

Luther closed the distance between us and cupped my face. "To get me through killing my best friend."

THIRTY-SEVEN

Luther

"WE'RE BROTHERS."

My eyes shot up as Georgio sat beside me. "Not by blood."

He scoffed. "Doesn't matter. You're the closest thing I have to a family anyway. Even though being in a mafia family is fucked up."

I grunted. "We're not mafia."

"Your dad is a powerful businessman who has his hands in everyone's pockets. Sounds like mafia to me."

I only rolled my eyes. We weren't mafia, the mob, or anything of that sort. Just power driven and hungry for more.

"Do you think we'll always be brothers?" Georgio asked, pulling me from my thoughts.

"Are you trying to tell me something?" Maybe I was being paranoid, but his question threw me off. My father had taught me to be cautious. Georgio and I had been best friends for the past five *years. We were now pushing eighteen. My father also taught me that the only person I could trust completely, was myself.*

"No." Georgio's dark gaze met mine. He shook his head. "You're too much like your father."

"Thank you." My father hadn't been the easiest person to get along with, but he taught me everything I knew.

Georgio grunted. "That wasn't a compliment."

I knew that. Even though my father had taken Georgio under his wing, there was still some tension there. I never knew why though. On the outside, you would think nothing was wrong. Or if you didn't know either of them like I did, you wouldn't be able to tell. But I could. I could feel it. Something was wrong. Something was very wrong.

"Do you have training today?" Georgio asked, changing the subject.

"I do." I stood, closing the journal my father had given me.

"Where you off to?"

"I have to get ready. I'll see you later this evening at dinner." Without waiting for a response from him, I left the study and headed to my bedroom to get ready for the training that would eventually break me.

I slipped the leather-bound journal back onto the bookshelf in my father's study. I had used this room as my own personal office ever since he had died, but it never truly felt like mine. So many years had gone by where I wondered if maybe I was doing the wrong thing. Making poor choices all because I trusted the one man who was supposed to be there for me. My father had been right. I couldn't trust anyone but myself. I trusted Lexi in the beginning and look what happened.

Letting out a hard sigh, I stroked a finger over the spine of the journal. So many passages written by my father on his life in our family. In our fucked-up world. I had ignored the journal for so long, I forgot what it had said. But something about today reminded me that it was there. That my father had spoken to me through his words.

My chest tightened.

A soft knock sounded on the door. "Luther?"

I turned, finding Lexi coming toward me with a tumbler of amber liquid. "I haven't seen you since this afternoon. Vanessa left. She needed some time alone." She handed me the glass. "You okay?"

"No." I took it from her and downed the drink in one gulp. The burn of the liquor settled deep in the pit of my stomach. It did nothing to curb this itch. This need for more. This need to fight and survive. Georgio was mine. I just had to find him first.

I would make him pay for the shit he did. For the pain he had caused both my sister and girlfriend.

"I'm sorry for everything," Lexi said, running her hand down my arm before linking our fingers. "I really am."

"I know, pet." I placed a soft peck on her forehead. "I need to find Georgio. Will you excuse me?"

She nodded. "Of course," she said and left my office.

I went to my desk, picking up the phone and dialed *one* on the speed dial. When a click sounded, indicating that someone had picked up, a slow grin spread on my face. "It's time," I said and disconnected the call.

I popped the collar of my suit jacket and went in search of Lexi. "Lexi," I called out. This house was too damn big.

Once I reached the living room, Lexi came down the hall that headed to the kitchen.

"Hey." She smiled at me. "I heard you call my name. What's up?"

"I have to head out for a bit," I said, closing the distance between us. "But when I get back…"

She frowned. "You're going to look for Georgio, aren't you?"

"Yes, but I'm not going to dwell on it. If I can't find him tonight, I'll look tomorrow and then the next day. Either I find him or he'll show up himself." I shrugged. "He's a pussy that way." If it were me, I would have left the country already.

"I feel like I don't know everything," Lexi said, her voice small.

I cupped her face, leaning down and placing a soft peck on her mouth. "You will. In time. Both you and my sister will know, but right now I need to do this."

"Come back to me," Lexi said, her voice firm. "Come back to me the way you are. Not as a changed man."

"Pet." I tilted her head back. "I've done this before."

"I know but it has never involved your best friend."

I pulled her against me, pushing my face into the crook of her neck. "I'll explain everything and answer all of your questions. In time."

"I know you will," she whispered, wrapping her arms around my waist. "Come back to me, Luther."

"Do they know anything?"

I grunted. "No. And you're lucky I like you or else this shit would have been exposed already."

"Aww." Charlie batted his green eyes. "You do love me."

"No but my girlfriend and sister do. That's the only reason I agreed to this in the first place."

"I shouldn't have made that video, but I was worried Georgio would actually kill me. So, I guess I was covering my ass," he said, not that I ever asked him to explain. He never needed to. I got it. He was covering his tracks. Making it look believable.

Charlie sighed, scrubbing a hand down his face. "I know and they're going to kick my ass when they find out."

"Yup. As they should."

"They're going to kick your ass too you know," Charlie so eloquently pointed out.

"Don't care. This was all your idea anyway." I leaned forward, my brows narrowing. We had been sitting outside of Georgio's condo for the past hour and nothing, absolutely nothing was happening. "He probably knows we're here."

"As fucking if."

I shot Charlie a glance at his choice of words.

"What?" He shrugged. "Anyway, Georgio may be a sneaky bastard but he's not the smartest. He didn't even know that I wasn't dead. You would think he would have checked my pulse or shot me in the head." Charlie shook his head. "That's what I would have done."

"Georgio was desperate," I told him. "That's probably why he never checked. He's a messy fucker." Although he never used to be.

"You know, you owe me."

I turned. "How do you figure?"

Charlie rubbed his jaw, faint bruises marred his skin. "I still fucking hurt from that beating."

"We had to make it look real." I was brought back to the first time I met Charlie. After I kicked his ass and followed him home only to find the woman that I would eventually fall in love with. "Did you know that Lexi was going to be there that night?"

"Yeah." Charlie dropped his hands in his lap. "She's always either home or at the deli. She works too damn much but I'm glad, as much as it hurt, that she met you."

My heart swelled. "I'm glad too. But…" My blood boiled through me. "I hate fucking waiting."

"I know." Charlie leaned forward. "I think something's going on."

I followed his gaze.

The front light lit up, the door to the house opening shortly after. A woman dressed in a black trench coat exited, stopped, and turned back toward the house.

Georgio appeared, grabbed her hand, and pulled her against him before slamming his mouth down on hers.

"So I guess the thought of being with my sister, no longer exists." Fucking asshole.

Charlie's head whipped around, his gaze burning into me. "He better never fucking touch her again."

"Trust me, Charlie. She only wants you." And my girlfriend if I weren't in the picture, but that was a conversation for another time. "Don't get your panties in a bunch."

"That fucker…"

I glanced at Charlie then. "She loves you. Most of the time, I'm not sure why. But she does."

"Yeah, well, she might not love me too much when she finds out that I'm in fact very much alive."

"Semantics." I turned back around. "We'll deal with that when the time comes." I knew Lexi was going to be pissed. But it had to be done to protect her. To protect both of them. Georgio took advantage of my girlfriend and killed her brother. Even though it was all a set up, it didn't mean shit to me. "How did the laundry service treat you?"

"Good. But being put in a body bag is not something I want to experience ever again." Charlie shook himself.

I could respect that. I had called the laundry service ahead of time, letting them know to be gentle with Charlie's body and I also paid off the coroner to keep the fact that he was alive, on the down-low.

"You think our girls will forgive us?" Charlie asked, bringing me out of my thoughts.

My jaw clenched. I wasn't sure, so I couldn't answer. But either way, I would spend the rest of my life making it up to Lexi. Whether she forgave me or not, putting men like Georgio to justice, would be worth it.

"I'm done waiting." I slipped from my vehicle, quietly shutting the door behind me.

"This is a bad idea," Charlie said, coming up beside me. "We should wait. Especially until that woman leaves."

"I don't give a shit anymore." I shoved my hands in my pockets and walked toward the house.

Georgio and the woman had gone back inside the house, clearly for round two or however many times he decided to get his dick wet before he died.

I was normally cool and collected. I always had my shit together but now I was on the verge of snapping. I needed this night to be done and over with. We needed all of our secrets revealed, so we could all move on. Then I could begin the process of doing everything I could to make Lexi forgive me.

"Luther." Charlie cupped my shoulder, stopping me. He nodded toward the house. "Is that..."

I followed his line of sight. My brows narrowed. Lexi was walking up the street, toward us. Her head was bowed, her shoulders slumped like she had the weight of the world resting on her small body.

My jaw clenched, my hands tightened into fists at my sides. "What the hell is she doing here?"

Did she come to warn Georgio? No. She wouldn't. Would she? I wasn't sure anymore, but I needed to stop her before she did something stupid. Georgio was a ticking time bomb and once all was revealed, I would bet my life savings that he would snap.

"Should I go back to the car?" Charlie murmured.

"No." I braced myself for Lexi's wrath and picked up my pace. I stopped in her path and waited.

(Lexi)

I wasn't sure what I was doing. After Luther left, I couldn't stop pacing back and forth. I called Vanessa but she wouldn't take my calls. I understood that, but it also pissed me off at the same time. I knew Luther was meeting Georgio to take him out. I also knew that I shouldn't be here, but I was a part of this just as much as him. Luther would need me after, and I was willing to do anything to help him through this. Even if this was a bad idea. Luther was going to be pissed.

Something moved in the corner of my eye. My head lifted. I stopped suddenly.

Luther stood a few feet away.

"Luther?" I knew that he was coming to meet up with Georgio but I wasn't expecting him to still be there. My eyes flicked to the side, finding another man coming toward him.

He caught my gaze, gave me a small smile and waved.

A sound escaped me that was a cross between a laugh and a sob.

"Charlie?" I shook my head. Was I dreaming? This didn't make sense. How the hell could Charlie be alive? I took a step toward them, faster and faster until I stood directly in front of Luther and my brother.

Before I knew what I was doing, I shoved Charlie. "How could you do this to me? How the hell are you still alive? You were dead. You are dead. You…" Sobs wracked through me. I pushed him, landing hard blows on his chest. "I hate you."

He didn't say anything. He just took my wrath. Embraced it. Made it his own.

"Lexi."

My head whipped around. "And you." I shoved Luther, taking my wrath out on him instead. "You knew about this? You held me while I cried. You took care of me. You were there for me. And Vanessa." I covered my face. "God." I stabbed a finger in Charlie's chest. "She's fucking pregnant, asshole, and you do this shit to her?"

"I can explain," he said softly.

"We both can." Luther grabbed my hands, stopping me from hitting them further. "But first, you're going to tell me why you're here."

"I came to offer moral support. I needed closure." My gaze flicked to Charlie's. "But obviously that closure is staring me right in the face."

Charlie looked away.

Luther's dark eyes peered down at me. "We'll continue this later. I also don't suggest arguing with me on the matter."

I swallowed hard at the threat hidden in his deep voice. "Fine." I pulled away from him and shoved past them.

"Lexi." Charlie rushed up to my side. "You shouldn't be here."

I spun on him. "You shouldn't be here either since you're supposed to be dead. I've been trying to bury you but I…"

"That's my fault," Luther said. "I distracted you so you wouldn't think of it. I didn't want to bury Charlie when he was still alive."

"Wow." I laughed, but there was no humor behind it. "This is unreal."

"I took a drug that slowed down my heart. I know you're pissed and that you want answers, but this isn't safe for you." Charlie looked over my head. "She shouldn't be here."

"Sorry." Luther walked past us. "I don't tell her what to do."

I scoffed.

Luther shot me a look over his shoulder. "I don't. What happens in the bedroom is different. I don't control you outside of it." And with that he walked up the steps to Georgio's house.

Charlie huffed. "I'm sorry, Lexi. I really am. I want to explain everything but he's right, we have to wait. We need to deal with Georgio first."

"Fine," I said once again and followed Luther. None of this made sense. I was looking at a ghost. I didn't give a shit if he used a drug to make it seem like he had actually died. When I found him lying there in a puddle of his own blood, it looked so real. I would never get that image out of my head and now that I knew he had been alive the whole time, that guilt I felt for how we left things when I thought he died, simmered.

Charlie had a lot of making up to do but he was right. This shit needed to end.

Tonight.

THIRTY-EIGHT

Luther

IT SHOULDN'T BE HAPPENING like this. Charlie shouldn't be with me and Lexi sure as hell shouldn't be with me either. But life had a funny way of changing things up on you. Keeping you on your toes and all that shit.

The sweet scent of lemon and vanilla wafted into my nose. A gentle hand slid into mine. "I don't understand what's going on right now," Lexi said softly. "But I want to."

"I love you, Lexi," I told her, not meeting her gaze. "I hope you remember that." Especially when she saw what I had to do. Georgio wouldn't make it through the night. My father had taught me that once a person had betrayed you, they would do it again and again. Although, Lexi had betrayed me once already. Should I have killed her too? No. It wasn't her fault she was duped by the enemy.

Lifting my hand, I knocked hard twice. After a minute, I banged on the door again. "I know you're in there, Georgio. I can smell your betrayal."

A moment later, the lock clicked free, followed by the door opening. "I have company."

"Make her leave," I told him.

"Come here to kill me?" Georgio asked, passing a glance between Lexi and I. His gaze landed between us. The color drained from his face. "I killed you."

"Yeah." Charlie scratched his head. "You see, you weren't actually successful. Obviously, you're not as good as you think you are. If it were Luther, he would have shot me in the head. But you're a pussy and you felt guilty, so you slipped up. Also, I see you're not that upset over Vanessa not being with you."

"I have no idea what you're talking about," Georgio grit out.

"Make her leave," I repeated, ignoring their banter.

"You think I'm stupid enough to do that?" Georgio laughed. "Come on, brother."

"Don't fucking call me that," I growled. "Charlie, get rid of her."

"On it." Charlie pushed his way into the house. Muffled voices sounded followed by a door closing. Charlie came back a moment later. "She went out the back. Looks like you know how to pick them, Georgio. I gave her a hundred and she ate that shit up." He shook his head.

Georgio's jaw clenched.

I pushed against the door, shoving him back a step. "You're lucky my girl is here. I had some nice plans for us this evening."

Lexi scoffed. "Don't hold back on my account."

My eyes flicked to hers.

She nodded once, crossing her arms under her chest. "Do what you gotta do, Luther. I'm here."

Meaning, she would be there to clean up the pieces of my mental stability after I killed my best friend. Fuck, I loved her.

"What do you want?" Georgio demanded, ignoring our little exchange.

"I want you to pay for what you did," Charlie said, answering for all of us. "I want you to pay for taking me away from my girl and my sister. For bringing Lexi into this shit in the first place."

"She was in this shit long before either of you were involved." Georgio walked away, heading down the long hall that led to his living room. With the dark colors and cherry oak furniture, the place looked warmer than the person who lived there.

"I came here to talk to you tonight," Lexi said, stepping in front of both Charlie and I. She kept her hand in mine. "I wanted to talk to you about Vanessa. About everything. Maybe I was coming here to warn you. I'm not sure. But we both know that you're not walking out of this alive. I may not have known Luther for as long as you have but I'm not stupid either."

No, she definitely wasn't that. At all.

Georgio stopped at a minibar sitting by the far wall. He poured himself a drink and walked in front of the patio doors that led to the backyard. "Will you give us a moment?" he asked, keeping his back to us.

I glanced between Lexi and Charlie, giving them both a nod.

Charlie grumbled something that I couldn't quite make out and headed back toward the front of the house.

"Luther," Lexi whispered, tugging on my hand.

I looked down at her and cupped her cheek. Brushing my thumb over her bottom lip, I leaned down to her ear. "After all of this is done, I need to put you back in my cage. I need your submission, pet. I need it like I need air to fucking breathe."

She shivered. "I want…" She turned her head, her mouth grazing over mine. "I need that too, Sir," she murmured, her pupils dilating. "I'll help you through this."

As much as I tried denying it, I needed her help.

Wrapping my hand around her throat, I ran my thumb over her jugular. "I want you to wear my collar." I wasn't sure if she knew what I meant but before she could ask questions, I released her. "Go."

She nodded, gave us one final look, and headed to where Charlie stood at the front door.

Turning back around, I undid the buttons on my jacket and slipped it off my shoulders before resting it neatly on the back of the couch.

The sound of the front door shutting, sent a shiver racing down my spine.

I went to the minibar and poured myself a drink. I wasn't sure what it was, but I shot it back anyway. I took another shot before turning the cup over and placing it on top of the bar.

Stepping up beside Georgio, I shoved my hands in my pants pockets.

"Can I ask you something?" Georgio asked without looking at me.

"Sure."

"Can you make it quick?"

Under normal circumstances, we didn't listen to requests. Georgio knew that. But this wasn't one of those times. This went far past being normal. Although Georgio betrayed me, I respected him enough to do as he asked.

"I can." I rolled up the sleeves to my white dress shirt. "This will probably hurt me more than it hurts you."

He grunted. "Unlikely. At least you have someone who can help heal you from this. I don't think anyone can bring me back from the dead."

My lips twitched. "You know that if it were the other way around, you would do the same thing," I told him, pulling black leather gloves out of my back pocket.

"I know." He turned to me then. "I loved you like a brother but unfortunately for me, I underestimated you."

"You thought you would get away with this. With everything you've done. Because we're best friends. Because we grew up together. Trained together. Were partners."

"Yes." Georgio turned back around. "Can I make another request?"

"Depends." I headed back to the minibar and opened the top drawer, finding a revolver along with a silencer, staring up at me. "You should change your hiding places."

"I guess it doesn't matter now."

"Nope. It doesn't." I pulled the gun from the drawer and stuck the silencer on the end, spinning it into place.

"You're going to kill me with my own gun." He shook his head. "I should have known."

"What's your request?" I asked, ignoring him.

"Tell your sister that I love her. That I've always loved her and that I'm sorry it couldn't work out, but I hope she's happy. I want her to be happy. With Charlie."

"Even if you didn't want her to be happy, it wouldn't matter," I told him. "My sister has a mind of her own and she definitely doesn't take too well to being told what to do."

Georgio grunted. "That's why we broke up. I couldn't handle her dominance."

I thought a moment, wondering what it would be like to submit to Lexi. A tremor of unease shivered over me. Nope. That shit would never happen. At all.

"I'll tell her for you," I finally said.

"Thank you." Georgio faced me. "I love you."

I took a step toward him. "I love you too, brother." I closed the distance between us, cupped his nape and pulled him against me. Pushing the end of the gun against his stomach, I pulled the trigger. Once. Twice. A third time.

Pop. Pop. Pop.

Georgio grunted, falling against me.

"Shhh…" I held him, dropping the gun on the ground and wrapping my arms around his shoulders. "I got you," I told him, holding the man I had looked up to for as long as I could remember. A man I had referred to as a brother even though we weren't related. A man I respected.

When Georgio took his final breath, I lowered us to the ground and pushed him onto his back. Brushing my hand over his eyes, I closed them and kissed his forehead. "When we meet again, brother."

THIRTY-NINE

Lexi

I COULDN'T HELP BUT stare at Charlie. He looked good. For someone who just recently died that is.

"I can feel you staring at me, Sis," he murmured, sitting against the hood of Luther's car.

"I can't help it. You see, my brother is supposed to be dead but yet, here he is, in front of me. And he was with my boyfriend. So are you guys actually friends and this whole thing between you was a ruse? You don't actually hate each other?" I knew I was throwing question after question at him, but I needed answers.

"We'll answer your questions, I prom—" Charlie glanced behind me.

I turned around, finding Luther coming toward us. His hands were shoved in his pockets, his head bowed. His stance was strong and stiff.

"Luther?" Charlie pushed away from the hood.

Luther came up to me, pushed his hand to the back of my head and fisted my hair before covering my mouth in a hard, bruising kiss.

He swallowed my gasp, shoving his tongue between my lips and taking the very control from my fingertips.

All too soon the kiss ended.

"We're going to drop Charlie off at my sister's place," Luther told me, keeping his fist wrapped around my hair. "And then we're going to go home and I'm going to use your body to make me feel better. Do you understand me?"

I swallowed hard. The intensity of his stare burned through me. As much as I knew we should talk, it would have to wait. There was no way Luther was even remotely close to being able to discuss what happened or what he had to do.

"I asked you a question," he said, his voice laced with venom.

"I understand." I pulled away from him and slipped into the passenger seat of the car.

Charlie didn't say anything until he was sitting in the back seat. "Do you think this will break him?"

"No." Not if I had anything to do with it. I was determined to make Luther feel better. One way or another. I didn't care that he needed to use me, knowing I would get something from him in return...

His complete and utter control.

After we dropped Charlie off at Vanessa's place, it was on the tip of my tongue to stay and help her through it. But Luther was having none of it. He sped the car out of there faster than I thought was possible.

"Luther," I said when we were about ten minutes from his place. "We need to talk. About everything. About the fact that Charlie's alive and how you kept it from me. We need to talk about all this shit before you…before we…"

"Before we what, Lexi?" Luther pinched my chin, turning it toward him in a rough move. "Before we fuck? Before I spend the rest of the night using your body, fucking every hole you have to offer me? Before I take out my pain on you?"

My stomach tumbled, my mouth going dry at the delicious promises he made. I grabbed his hand and slid my fingers between his. Kissing his knuckles, I stared at him. "You asked me if I could handle it. Whatever it is. Whatever you need to make you feel better. To help you through this. Are we still doing that?" I asked, my body heating when I remembered how he suggested I whip him. That felt like so long ago, I had almost forgotten that we'd had that conversation.

"Sorry, Lexi." He pulled his hand from mine and cupped my inner thigh. "This goes far beyond my therapy. My need for pain. My need to submit to the agony. I need you. Your submission. That's what I need right now. We can talk later. Tomorrow. Next week. I don't give a fuck. I'll use you until I'm good and ready to discuss what happened tonight. But until then, I suggest you brace yourself."

Rough hands moved along my body. They massaged, kneaded, bringing me to that point of passion I couldn't resist.

A purr escaped me the longer the hands touched me.

A deep chuckle sounded in my ear, but no words were said.

Luther ran his hand down my back before landing a hard swat on my ass.

I gasped, my teeth clenching down on the rubber ball in my mouth.

Swat. Swat. Swat.

My ass burned and although the agony sliced through me, my center heated, clenching with need for the man standing behind me.

As if he could sense my desire, Luther ran his finger between my legs.

I bucked against him, hinting, silently begging for him to take it further. To bring me to that point where all I felt was him.

"I love you, Lexi. But right now, this has nothing to do with love."

I knew. God did I ever know. As soon as we stepped into the house, his demands started flying.

"Take off your clothes."

"Kneel."

"Crawl for me."

"Don't speak."

"Glare at me again, pet, and I'll take it out on your ass."

This was for him. It was all for him. I realized then that I was his therapy. I was the beginning to his healing. We had come so far from what we started with.

Pain. Heartache. Passion. Lust. Fear. *Tragedy.*

But he was mine and I was his. And all of our pain was worth it in the end because it brought us together.

Luther moved around me, swiping his thumb over the drop of drool that had slid from the corner of my mouth. He brought it up to his lips, licking the tip. "You taste so fucking good, pet."

I breathed through my nose, watching him. Taking him in. He was beautiful. In a feral, terrifying way. Like a wolf. He stalked me like I was his prey. Like I was what he needed to eat to survive.

"Do the binds hurt?" he asked, reaching up to touch the leather cuffs wrapped around my wrists.

My heart warmed that he was concerned for me while he was battling through his own personal demons.

I shook my head.

A slow grin spread on his face. "Good." He leaned forward, placing a soft peck on my forehead.

My eyes fluttered closed. I breathed him in, taking the scent of his spicy cologne down deep into my lungs.

He kissed my forehead again and walked behind me.

Suddenly, something covered my eyes, cutting off my sight. My heart jumped.

"I want you to feel," Luther whispered, brushing his mouth along my ear.

Something warm, slid over my skin. It ran down between the crack of my ass, no doubt dripping onto the floor beneath me. I squirmed, the sounds of the chains binding me, clinking in the air.

"Do you trust me?" he asked, running his thumb over the spot between the cheeks of my ass.

I nodded, my breathing picking up.

"Good." His thumb entered me in a smooth move.

I jumped, the burn of him penetrating a spot that hadn't been used often, erupting through me.

Luther thrust his thumb in and out of me and it was soon replaced with a finger and then another.

I moaned, the delicious pain sliding over my skin like melted honey.

He chuckled, brushing the back of his other hand down the length of my spine. "So responsive, pet." He pushed his hand against me as deep as my body would allow.

I gasped, my heart racing at how deep he was inside my body.

"This is going to hurt, pet. But I want you to embrace the pain for me."

Something hard pushed into me. Luther removed his hand, but it did nothing to help the heavy weight I felt in my lower body.

"Breathe, pet. Breathe through the pain and let me make you fucking explode," he said, his voice low and husky.

I swallowed hard, steadying my breathing like he told me to do.

He wrapped something around my waist. It felt like a belt, sitting low on my hips. After a few seconds, the burn in my ass only seemed to grow.

I whimpered, the pain turning into a dull agony.

"Shhh…you're doing so well, pet. Such a good girl. You make your Master so damn proud."

My heart swelled. The pain simmering to a thrum of pleasure. It burned, testing me.

"Almost there." Luther reached up, grabbed my wrists, and released me from the hook in the ceiling. He placed his hand on my upper back and pushed me forward until I was bent at the waist. "Grab onto your ankles."

I did as I was told. I teetered, almost falling forward when my back landed against a hard surface.

"Absolutely beautiful." Luther kissed my cheek and walked back behind me. "So damn beautiful."

The back of my thighs burned at being bent forward. I tried bending my knees more, but it only heightened that sharp pain at my rear.

"A few more seconds." The burn exploded through me as those words left his mouth.

I gasped, my body shaking.

Luther gripped my hips and slammed into me, fucking me hard against whatever it was I was leaning against.

I screamed.

"That's it," he growled. "Fuck, pet."

He was animalistic in the way he had control of my body.

My pussy dripped, the cream running down my inner thighs the more he thrust in and out of me. The harder he moved, the wetter I became. And the wetter I became, the happier he was.

He grunted his approval, digging his fingers into my hips. His hold on me was so tight, I could feel the bones beneath my skin grinding from his touch.

Luther leaned forward, fisted my hair in his hand, and pulled me back against him. "I'm going to fuck you until you can no longer move."

(Luther)

While Lexi slept soundlessly beside me, I ran my hand up and down her back. I had used her for hours. Taking all of my wrath and pain out on her. It wasn't fair. I knew that. But I never considered myself to be a man of morals.

"Do you feel better?" Lexi asked me, staring up at me through her heavy eyes.

"Yeah, pet. I do."

But I would feel even better once she had my ring on her finger and my collar around her throat.

Lexi stirred, rolling over onto her stomach. "Luther," she whispered.

I leaned down, kissing the corner of her mouth. "I don't deserve you, pet. But I'll do whatever I can to make sure you know just how much I love you. You'll never want for nothing. Ever again."

Her mouth turned up into a smile. "I know, Sir." She yawned. "And I love you too."

I pulled back, finding her staring up at me. "Marry me."

Her eyes welled. "It's about damn time."

"I take it that's a yes?" I chuckled, pulling her into my arms.

"Definitely." She cupped my face, placing soft pecks on my lips. "But…when are you putting a collar on me?"

"Whenever you're ready." I reached up, cupped the back of her neck, and ran my thumb back and forth over the side of her throat. "So, you know what it is."

"Your sister told me." Lexi gave me a small smile. "I want to be yours. In every way you need me to be. In every way that I can."

I sat forward, holding Lexi against me. "You already are, pet." I kissed her softly on the mouth. "You already are."

EPILOGUE

Luther

Sometime later

MOANS SLID INTO MY ears. A wet, hot, pussy gripped my dick like a vice.

"Shhh…" I whispered, nipping Lexi's earlobe. My hand wrapped around her throat, my thumb running back and forth over the black leather collar. I pinched the heart shaped lock between my fingers. My dick swelled, knowing I was the only one who had the key.

"I can't help it," she panted, digging her heel into my ass and taking me even deeper.

A growl escaped me. "Careful, pet. I'll tie you the fuck up if you keep trying to take control."

She barked a laugh. "Please. Fuck, I don't give a shit what you do, Luther." Her head fell back, exposing her slender neck. "I haven't seen you all week. I need this. You. Your cock. Fuck."

I chuckled, leaning down to the soft spot just beneath her ear. I sucked and nibbled, sliding my tongue along her beautiful neck. "It's been a long week without you. My cage misses your beautiful little body."

She moaned, arching against me.

After the first time I put her in my cage, it became a normal thing for us. It usually consisted of a few hours before I let her out, basking in her ultimate submission.

"I'll do anything to help you," she panted. "You know that."

"I do, pet. Fuck do I ever." And I loved her even more for it.

Inching my hands between us, I spread her open even more. My hips sped up, my cock thrusting in and out of her.

Lexi shivered against me. She grabbed onto my dress shirt, pulling me even closer. "Please, Sir. I need you…I need to…"

Fisting her hair, I tugged her head back and crushed my mouth to hers. I slowed my hips, driving her past the point of madness.

She cried out in frustration. Although she hated the anticipation, I knew she liked the powerful orgasm in the end.

Lexi had been right. It had been way too damn long. We had both been busy all week, our only foreplay was a high five in the hall way and a kiss at night. When we first got married, I would normally wake her up when I got home by slipping into her tight body but now that we had kids, that was a little harder to do. My wife needed her rest and I had to control the raging beast inside of me.

"Luther," Lexi moaned, pulling me from my thoughts.

Just when I was about to pull out of her and drop to my knees, a soft knock sounded on the door.

Both of us stiffened.

"Yeah?" she called out.

"Mama, Uncle Charlie won't let me watch cartoons."

"Tattletale!"

"But you promised," our daughter, Faith cried.

"Daddy, can I watch fire trucks?" Emilia asked.

"No! I'm watching cartoons."

"But...but..." A scream sounded, followed by a laugh. "You whore!"

Lexi gasped, her eyes widening. "Where did she get that from?"

"They're your kids." I shrugged. "Who knows?"

"As fucking if." Lexi grabbed onto my shirt, pulling me lower. "They're our kids, Mr. Knight."

I grinned.

"Mama! Mama!"

Lexi huffed.

I laughed. "I wonder what Emilia wants now."

"I have no idea, but I know what her mama wants." Lexi pushed me back until I was sitting on the edge of the tub.

"Yeah?" I grabbed onto her hips. "And what's that?"

She only grinned and straddled my lap.

(Lexi)

I loved our daughters but when Luther and I had to sneak away into the bathroom after hardly seeing each other for a week, it got old. And fast. It didn't help that my brother instigated things. Between him and my nephew, I wasn't sure who was worse.

"Hey, Vanessa," I said, sitting down beside my sister-in-law and handing her a bottle of water. "How are you feeling?"

"Fat. And huge as a fucking whale." Although she was complaining, she placed her hands on her swollen stomach and stared down at her unborn baby with love. It would be her and my brother's third child.

Luther and I stopped having children after two. Especially when having Emilia almost killed me. And we were fine with that. As much as he wanted to have a house filled with children, having our two daughters was perfect. Although, his black hair had started sprouting some gray ever since Faith told him she liked a boy.

I looked around me.

Charlie was playing with his son, King. He bounced him on his lap which would result in an eruption of giggles from the two-year-old.

Vanessa would smile and also warn him every so often not to bounce their son too hard.

Emilia sat on the floor with her legs crossed beneath her, happy that she finally got to watch her cartoons.

Ricky poked her every so often. Being Charlie's and Vanessa's first born, I found that he was the most like my brother. And just as annoying.

Emilia slapped his hand away, giving him a glare but Ricky would keep poking her. He continued until she pushed him over.

"That's my girl," Luther said, his voice booming with pride.

I smiled, watching our family. I couldn't imagine a more perfect way to spend the weekend.

The cushion beside me lowered, a hot mouth kissing the back of my neck.

"I love you, pet."

I shivered. "I love you too." I glanced at Luther. "Sir."

He grinned, wrapping his arms around me and pulling me back against him. "I'm so damn happy, Lexi."

"Me too." I cupped his face. "I really am. And…" I glanced at Charlie. "Thank you for bringing him back to us."

Charlie's gaze flicked my way.

Even though it had been several years since it was revealed that Charlie's death had been fake, both Vanessa and I thanked Luther. Every damn day.

"I didn't do anything." Luther jutted his chin forward. "It was all him."

Vanessa sat forward. "You know, it's been a while but we still don't know everything that happened that night."

Luther stiffened beside me.

I gave my head a small shake.

Vanessa sighed. "Fine. I know you'll tell me eventually though."

Luther blew out a slow breath, muttering a *thank you*.

I only nodded.

It had taken me months to get out of him what happened and eventually I found out that he did in fact kill his best friend. I had a feeling all along that it went down that way, but it took a long while for him to outright say it.

While all of us sat in silence, watching our children, I couldn't help but wonder what life would have been like if I'd never met Luther.

But I didn't have to wonder for long because I knew that there was no place I'd rather be than right there in Luther's arms.

THE END

BONUS SCENE

Lexi

"I CAN'T DO THIS."

"Yes." Luther placed the end of the whip in my hand. "You can."

"No." I shook my head, shoving the whip against his chest. "This isn't right. Whip *me*. Take out your pain on me instead. But I can't…not to you."

"Pet." Luther grabbed my hand, placing the whip in my palm. "There's only ever been one woman who's whipped me. And I know, even though you won't admit it or haven't asked about it, you wonder where she is or what happened there."

I looked away, tightening my hold on the item in my hand. "I trust you."

"I know you do." He kissed my cheek. "And *I* trust you. I need you to make me feel better. To take me out of my head. To show me just how dominant you can be."

I looked up at him then. "But I'm not. I'm not dominant at all."

He gave me a small smile. "Yeah, you are. Maybe not with me. But I've seen you run your deli and bark orders at the staff. It makes me hard every single time."

I laughed lightly.

Looking down at the whip in my hand, I swung it back and forth. "I don't know what I'm doing."

"I'll teach you." Luther stepped away from me and began unbuttoning his shirt.

"But…" I swallowed hard. "What if I hurt you?"

He chuckled, turning away from me and slid the fabric off of his strong torso. He folded the shirt, placing it on a nearby chair. "That's the point, pet. I need you to hurt me. The pain is what I crave, and I know after the first couple of strikes, it'll turn you on, just as much as it'll turn me on."

"Did…" I hated to ask but I needed to know. "Did you fuck the woman who whipped you?"

Luther looked at me over his shoulder. "No, pet. I didn't."

I swung the whip, the sound of the end slapping against the floor ignited this newfound awareness inside of me. "Why not?"

"Because she was older for one. Much older." Luther stopped in front of the St. Andrew's Cross and turned toward me. "And it wasn't about sex."

"But it is now. Isn't it?" I took a step toward him, the heels of my shoes clicking against the tile floor.

"No, pet. It's not."

"What is it then?" I asked, closing the distance between us.

"It's more." He bent at the waist, placing a hard peck on my mouth. "Give me your wrath, pet. All of it. Every ounce of pain you have felt over the years. And take mine just the same. Please."

I looked away at the desperation dripping from his deep voice.

"Lexi." He pinched my chin, turning my head toward him. "Please. I mean it. If I didn't, I would be whipping you instead. But I'm not. I need this from you."

I searched his face, looking for something. Anything that meant he didn't actually want this. But when I couldn't find what I was hoping for, I stepped away from him. "Turn around," I whispered.

When he didn't move, I cleared my throat.

"Turn around," I repeated. "*Now.*"

A grin spread on his face and much to my surprise, he actually turned around.

My body buzzed, my heart jumping that he listened to me. *Oh, I could get used to this.*

Luther stepped up to the St. Andrew's Cross and reached his hands overhead. Wrapping his fingers around the leather cuffs, he waited.

"Should I cuff you?" I asked him.

"Do you want to?"

"N-Not really. No. I don't think I do." Restraining him would be something we could explore later.

"As you wish, pet."

I swallowed hard at the deep vibrato of his voice as it washed over me. It tickled my skin, sending courage coursing through me. Courage that I could do this. Courage that I wouldn't break the man I was destined to spend the rest of my life with. Courage that he wouldn't hate me for it in the end.

I stepped up behind him and ran my fingers gently down his spine.

He shivered, his head rolling back on his shoulders. He tightened his hold on the straps when a thought came to me.

"I think I want to restrain you," I murmured.

"Fuck," he breathed. "Go ahead, pet. Whatever you want."

I placed a soft peck on his back, running my fingers down his sides. "Are you sure? We can stop. We can do something else."

"No," he said, his voice rough. "Do it."

"Okay." I placed the whip on a table sitting by the wall and pulled the stool out from beneath it. Once I had it on the floor behind Luther, I stepped onto it and began shackling his wrists into the leather cuffs that hung from the ceiling.

"They're so high," I said, staring up at the cuffs hanging down toward me.

"They are but they're attached to a pully system, so I can make them lower. That way your toes aren't dragging on the floor." Luther kissed the side of my neck. "But if you're a bad girl, I'll hang you from the cuffs, so you can't touch the ground at all. Your shoulders would become sore and the only way out of it would be to use your safeword."

"Hmm…" I turned in his arms. "I like that idea."

It had felt like months ago that Luther first introduced me to the St. Andrew's Cross when in all reality, it hadn't been long at all. And now, there we were, standing in the basement of our home. He had the brand-new playroom designed and built just for us and this would be the first time that he was the one strapped to the cross instead of me.

"Does that hurt?" I asked him, remembering that he always asked me if I was in any pain.

"No." Luther tugged on the leather straps that I had shackled around his wrists. "I've never felt these before."

"Um…I mean…do we…do you need a safeword?"

"No, pet." His voice was raspy. "If I need you to stop, you'll know it."

"Okay. " I picked up the whip, slapping the tail against the ground. The sound shot through me. "Holy hell." I looked between the whip and his bare back. "I don't know if I can do this."

"You can, pet." Luther leaned his head back. "I promise that you can."

"Do you love me?" I asked him.

"Fuck yes. Please, Lexi." His muscles bunched beneath his skin, the tattoos on his body moving with every breath he took.

Before I could think twice about it, I drew my hand back and gave it a snap of the wrist. The end landed against Luther's back.

He jumped.

I gasped.

"More, Lexi. Whip me harder," he demanded.

"I…" My heart started racing. I had seen whipping enough in movies but never like this. I repeated the movement, faster and harder this time. The end left a red line across his back.

"Fuck," Luther groaned.

"Oh god, Sir." My chest ached.

"Don't stop, pet," he bit out. "Don't you dare fucking stop."

"But—"

"Lexi, come here."

I did as I was told and moved in front of him.

"I promise, baby. You can't do any damage. No more than has already been caused. Do you understand me?"

"But I—"

"I asked you a question." His dark eyes burned into me.

"Yes, I understand." But it didn't mean that I liked it.

"Good, now continue and keep going. Give me as many fucking lashes as you can."

"Okay." I went back around him and began pacing. I could do this. I promised him I would help him in any way that I could. Chewing my bottom lip, I braced myself and let the tail of the whip dance across his skin.

(Luther)

It had been a long time since I felt the sting of the whip slice across my back. The burn of the tip as it grazed over my skin. Or the heat of the leather as it pierced into my flesh.

My body shook, a sheen of sweat coating my skin.

Lexi repeated the movements. Over and over again. It was almost too much and then at the same time, it wasn't enough.

I pulled on the restraints wrapped tightly around my wrists.

With every whip, every smack of the leather against my skin, the love for this woman behind me, grew.

My soul called out to her. Begging. Pleading. Aching for that divine, delicious pain she so graciously gave me.

I was vaguely aware of the sounds leaving my mouth.

My body became hard. The hardest I had ever been.

The muscles beneath my skin twisted and bent as my body subconsciously tried to sway away from the sting when my mind was begging for more.

Yes, baby, just like that. A little more. Fuck, the pain is so damn good.

But as much as I enjoyed—no—*needed* the pain, my hands still gripped the chains in the ceiling. My arms still pulled. The sound of the drywall cracking still graced my ears.

A slow, wicked grin spread on my face.

My pet was enjoying this. Maybe more than I was. But little did she know that no matter how much I needed these sessions, I would always be her Master.

(Lexi)

I had whipped Luther ten times before I stopped. My chest heaved. Sweat dripped down the length of my spine.

"More," he said, his voice barely audible.

"Luther, your back is—" His back was torn up. All because of me. All because he begged me to whip him.

"More," he repeated, his voice firmer that time.

I did as I was told, letting the end of the whip slice into his skin.

"Stop!" A sound left him. It was unlike anything I had ever heard before. It was a cross between a sob and a groan.

But what surprised me most was when he pulled the cuffs from the ceiling and fell to his knees. Drywall fell down around him, hitting the floor in tiny clouds of dust.

I opened my mouth to say something, anything, but I couldn't.

Luther's chest rose and fell, blood dripped from the cuts in his back. He had brought me to watch a whipping scene at The Club a few weeks back but even that never ended up bloody.

His head turned, his dark eyes meeting mine as he looked at me over his shoulder.

My core clenched, the whip falling from my hand and landing on the ground with a thud. Taking a step back and then another, I turned to run because I wasn't sure what else to do, when I was tackled to the ground.

Luther tore at my clothes, bending over me and sunk his teeth into the back of my neck.

I cried out as the sharp delicious pain washed over my skin.

With rough hands, he had my dress to my hips and my panties shredded from my body in a matter of seconds.

He thrust inside of me, forcing a scream to fall from my lips.

He slapped a hand to the ground beside my head, keeping his mouth on the back of my neck. His hot breath scorched my skin.

I wrapped a hand around his forearm, the black leather cuff still wrapped around his wrist. "Luther."

His release spilled into me, his breathing ragged. "Fuck, I love you."

"Oh god." I rolled onto my back, staring up at him. "I thought you were mad at me."

"No, baby." His body shook, his eyes dark and glassy. "Never. I'm sorry that was quick, but I didn't want to cum in my pants."

"Oh." I chewed my bottom lip. "I'm sorry for—"

"Don't be." He leaned down, giving me a soft kiss.

I spent the rest of the night cleaning and dressing his wounds only for him to make love to me again. And again.

He whispered over and over how thankful he was for me. How much the therapy session helped and would continue to help.

When we were wrapped up in each other's arms later that night, I couldn't help but watch him sleep. His dark lashes fanned out of the top of his cheeks. His black bangs, he always had to push out of his eyes but refused to cut knowing I liked playing with them, were resting on his forehead.

I brushed my fingers over his cheek, placing a soft peck on his shoulder, careful not to touch his back.

"I love you, Luther," I whispered. "And I can't wait to make you a father."

His eyes popped open. "What the fuck did you just say?"

I laughed, a sly grin spreading on my face.

ABOUT J.M. WALKER

J.M. Walker is an Amazon bestselling author who also hit USA Today with Wanted: An Outlaw Anthology. She loves all things books, pigs and lip gloss. She is happily married to the man who inspires all of her Heroes and continues to make her weak in the knees every single day.

"Above all, be the HEROINE of your own life..." ~ Nora Ephron

Website: http://www.aboutjmwalker.com/
Facebook:
https://www.facebook.com/jm.walker.author
**Reader
Group:** https://www.facebook.com/groups/JMsJems/
Twitter: https://twitter.com/jmwlkr
Instagram: https://www.instagram.com/jmwlkr/
Goodreads: https://www.goodreads.com/author/show/5132169.J_M_Walker
BookBub: https://www.bookbub.com/authors/j-m-walker
Amazon: https://tinyurl.com/y7dpjkud
Newsletter: https://tinyurl.com/ya9hycak

WANT MORE?

Head on over to my website for my complete

backlist!

https://www.aboutjmwalker.com/books